LITTLE CHILD GONE

BOOKS BY STACY GREEN

LITTLE CHILD GONE

STACY GREEN

bookouture

Published by Bookouture in 2025

An imprint of Storyfire Ltd.
Carmelite House
50 Victoria Embankment
London EC4Y 0DZ

www.bookouture.com

The authorised representative in the EEA is Hachette Ireland
8 Castlecourt Centre
Dublin 15 D15 XTP3
Ireland
(email: info@hbgi.ie)

ISBN: 978-1-83618-610-6
eBook ISBN: 978-1-83618-611-3

Of all the escape mechanisms, death is by far the most efficient.

—H.L. Mencken

PROLOGUE

Rebecca closed her eyes and leaned back against the smooth leather, listening to the heavy rhythm of the drums. She ran her hands along the decadent leather of the red and black seat. Rebecca had never been in a car this expensive. She glanced at the guy in the driver's seat, trying to remember his name.

He turned up the volume as the next track started. The subwoofers made her ears itch. "What's this song called?"

"'Breaking Skin,'" her new friend answered. "It's about being miserable and trapped in it. You can't escape your thoughts, so you're constantly scratching at the itch. Like your body needs to purge the pain, but all you can do is scratch."

"I get that."

"Me too. I'm so sick of my parents making me feel shitty just because I don't know what I want to do with my life. I'm working at least. Who knows what they want at twenty?" He smacked the steering wheel. "It's not like it's inconveniencing them for me to still live at home. They can afford it."

Rebecca caught herself before she started laughing. He knew nothing of hardship, much less the real world. "What kind of car is this?"

He sat up straighter in his seat. "Nissan GT-R. Almost 600 horsepower. It's not just a generic coupe with a big engine either. It can compete with the Porsche 911, maybe even beat it. Spent over 100k on this baby."

Rebecca was glad he couldn't see the disgust on her face. Her family might have survived with that kind of money. Still, the car was beautiful, with leather black and red seats that were actually comfortable for bucket seats. Rebecca hadn't been in a car with a touchscreen that had so many options. "It's yours?"

"Yep."

She thought about asking how he afforded something that expensive, but he'd already told her his parents were wealthy.

"My parents have kept me down for so long," he droned on. "That's why I relate to the lyrics so much. I walk around anxious half the time because I know they're going to rag on me again."

She bit her lip against the tirade of emotions. This spoiled boy knew nothing of actual hardship, much less real life. But Rebecca did. She knew what it was like to have your entire world shattered over and over again until every last bit of hope had been extinguished. Some days she thought she'd rather die than continue carrying on like this. But she had people depending on her.

He switched lanes, barely making the exit for Stillwater. "Sure you don't want to come to mine for a while?"

Darkness prevented him from seeing her recoil. "Maybe another time. I have to get back before my mom figures out I'm gone."

"Don't worry about that," he said. "I can sneak you in."

Rebecca wasn't really worried about her mother. What could she do at this point? But the younger kids would be scared if she didn't get home until the crack of dawn.

"I'll take care of your mom if she finds out."

Rebecca nodded. "Just drop me off at the drive. I'll sneak into our apartment."

Rebecca sat up in bed, still in the shirt she'd worn out last night. She looked at the clock on her bedside table. How could it be this dark at nine a.m.? She peered out of the blinds. Storm clouds decorated the sky, lightning flashing through them. Her brother's bed was already made. He'd been asleep when she snuck back inside the dark house, just like everyone else.

She'd better get up so her mother didn't question why she'd slept in so late. Rebecca changed into a clean shirt and pajama pants and then wandered through the tiny apartment to the bathroom, where she washed her face and brushed her long, dark hair. Hopefully her mother didn't question the circles around her eyes. She grabbed a clothes basket and tossed last night's clothes in, along with several other dirty items.

The main house door was unlocked as usual. She balanced the basket on her hip and headed towards the door where her brother Jason now stood.

"Does she suspect that I was out last night?" Rebecca whispered.

"Don't think so." Jason squeezed by her. Her fifteen-year-old brother's peach fuzz needed a trim. "I'm going to take a shower."

Rebecca quietly closed the door behind her. Wind rattled the picture window in the living room, and she could see the dark clouds moving closer. She snuck past the master bedroom and then crept down the hall. Her mother and Bailey's room was right before the kitchen, and Rebecca could hear her mother talking to the toddler about making their bed. The room had no door, only heavy drapes that blocked the room from the hall. Rebecca tiptoed past the closed drapes, careful not to stumble on the two steps down into the kitchen.

She glanced to her right. The table and built-in booth had already been cleared from breakfast. Lightning flashed outside the large window behind the table, the oak tree's limbs straining under the force of the wind.

Rebecca snuck into the laundry room on the other side of the kitchen. It looked like a closed-in porch, and she loved how the scent of fabric softener seemed to make the whole house smell fresh. The washer was empty, so she jammed her dirty clothes inside. She dug through the pockets of last night's jeans in search of the ticket stub. It fluttered to the floor, but before Rebecca could grab it, her mother snatched the ticket.

"What the hell is this?" Bianca demanded.

"Exactly what it looks like." Rebecca shoved the jeans into the washer, turning her back to her mother. Bianca's rough hands closed around her arm, forcing her to turn around. Anger flashed in the sultry dark eyes Rebecca used to envy.

"You are not to go anywhere without my knowing."

"I went to a concert in Rochester," Rebecca snapped back. "No one there knew me, I promise." She yanked her arm out of her mother's grasp and headed back into the kitchen. The counter split the room, the refrigerator and stove across from each other in the narrow galley. She grabbed a bowl and spoon and then poured Cheerios into the bowl.

"You don't know that," Bianca hissed. She blocked Rebecca's path. "This isn't just about you, Rebecca. Other people could get hurt."

"You should have thought of that before." Rebecca stood toe-to-toe with her mother wondering why she'd once worshiped the ground she'd walked on. "All of this is your fault."

Her mother smacked her, her rough hands stinging Rebecca's cheek. Her fist clenched; she'd never hit her mother. She might not be able to stop if she did. Still, Rebecca couldn't help but get one last insult in. "Honestly, I didn't think you'd be sober enough to notice I was missing."

She waited for the battle, but her mother's face had turned white. Her shaking hand pointed past Rebecca. "Look."

At first, Rebecca saw only the storm outside the big kitchen window. It looked like nighttime, with rain hitting the window. Then the lightning flashed.

A piece of white material looked like it had been stuck into the tree with something. Bianca grabbed Rebecca's hand, and they crept toward the window.

Eternity passed as they waited for the next flash to light up the sky. It struck close, the thunder following quickly.

"It's my veil," Bianca whispered. "He's here."

Panic built in her chest until it reached Rebecca's throat. "Call the police."

Bianca picked up the phone and then set it back down on the receiver. "The landline isn't working."

Rebecca's knees weakened. She helped her mother pay the bills. The phone hadn't been shut off. "It could be the storm," she tried.

"It's not the storm." Her mother's brown eyes searched Rebecca's before pulling her daughter close. "It's going to be okay. We practiced this." She smoothed Rebecca's dark hair. "I need you to be strong, okay?"

"I'm not leaving you." Rebecca spoke into her mother's neck.

Her mother's nails dug into Rebecca's arms as she pushed her away. "Yes, you will. It's our only chance." She quickly took something from her pocket and pressed it into Rebecca's hands. "You remember where the gas station is?"

Lightning flashed again, and Rebecca thought she saw a shadow running across the yard. "Mom—"

"Go now! Get Bailey."

Rebecca raced into the guest room, where the three-year-old

slept. She gathered Bailey in her arms, ignoring the sleepy complaints. She raced across the house and breezeway, refusing to look outside. Once she'd reached the apartment, she locked the door and then set Bailey on the floor. Rebecca grabbed the bungee cords they'd kept near the door. She wrapped one end tightly around the doorknob and anchored the other to the cellar stairs.

Bailey seemed to understand something wasn't right and stayed quiet as Rebecca hurried them down the hall to the bathroom. She banged on the door. "Jason, get dressed. He's here."

Her brother opened the door, his wet hair plastered to his forehead, a towel around his waist. "What?" He looked terrified.

"Yes." She thrust Bailey into Jason's arms, smoothing the baby's soft hair. "I'll see you guys soon. You know what to do."

She hurried into the little kitchen while Jason and Bailey took refuge in the bedroom. Jason would secure the door the same way she'd secured the other one. Rebecca yanked open the drawer where they kept the burner phones. Both were gone.

She didn't have time to worry. Her running shoes were by the side door. She shoved her feet into them and reached for her sweatshirt. Her stomach bottomed out. The sweatshirt was in the bedroom, along with her wallet, just in case. She had no time.

Rebecca locked the porch door behind her, wishing she could do more to secure it. Cold rain lashed at her skin, and the sky seemed darker than ever. She reached for the cement block that hid the handgun her mother had purchased not long after they'd arrived.

But it wasn't there.

Instead of taking the stairs leading toward the main house, Rebecca slipped under the porch rail and shimmied down the wood, splinters embedding in her hands. Without looking back, she ran past the old machine shop, darting into the dead cornfield.

Heavy spring rains had turned the ground into mud, slowing Rebecca down. She kept running, knowing she would come out near the road, not far from the gas station.

Adrenaline carried her through the field, and she burst out of the stalks blinded by cold rain. She started for the road and slipped down the ditch.

She wasn't going to fail.

Rebecca crawled up the embankment, finally reaching the roadside. She didn't see a car in sight, so she started running toward the gas station, her lungs begging for air. Headlights emerged over the hill, and Rebecca ran into the other lane, waving her arms and jumping up and down.

The rain became a deluge, but surely he would see her in time. She had to get his attention.

As the white car bore down on her, Rebecca realized the driver was going too fast and the roads too wet. She ran to her right, and the driver must have seen her, because tires suddenly screamed, the car fishtailing. The back of the car collided against her spine, sending her into the air. A thousand memories flashed through her mind until her body hit the side of the road.

Blood gurgled from her throat. She didn't feel any pain, but she couldn't move. Black boots appeared next to her, and a familiar face suddenly loomed next to hers, screaming they hadn't seen her.

Rebecca pressed her most treasured possession that her mother had given her into his hands. "Save them."

ONE

Nikki checked to make sure she'd pressed "record" on her phone as Lacey tore into another birthday gift. Pink paper flew in every direction.

"The whole Harry Potter collection." Lacey ran over to Rory's brother and hugged him. "Thanks, Uncle Mark." She grinned, her smile a mix of baby and adult teeth. "Now I don't have to steal Mom's copies." Lacey carefully set the books next to the quilt Ruth had made out of her late father's shirts.

"They're as old as you," Nikki told her daughter. "I'd just started reading the series when I went on maternity leave. I was on *Order of the Phoenix* when I went into labor with you."

"Why didn't you name me Phoenix?" Lacey demanded. "That would have been so cool."

Nikki shrugged. "Whose present is next?"

"Mine." Courtney hefted a large box onto the table. Lacey immediately tore into it. "Oh wow, a microscope! And an entomology kit."

Courtney smiled, and Nikki was warmed by how much her and Lacey's bond had grown in the last few months. Courtney had always been a close friend, and Nikki had asked Courtney to leave Quantico with her when she'd started the unit in Minnesota. Courtney now ran the DNA labs and acted as head evidence technician for their FBI office. She had spent a lot of time with Lacey during her mandated time off from Nikki's team. She'd come close to losing her life in a terrifying case, but she had been feeling better by the day and had returned a few weeks ago. Nikki was relieved as Courtney was the best analyst she'd ever worked with. Lacey loved anything scientific, and Courtney had taught her all about DNA science and finger-printing, the latter resulting in throwing out Lacey's jeans. The entomology lab had been Lacey's favorite. She'd come into Nikki's office and announced she was going to be a bug investi-gator for the FBI when she grew up.

Courtney pushed her dark hair out of her eyes. She'd started growing it out, and now it had grown down to a shaggy bob. She'd also taken to wearing colored contacts, making her star-tling blue eyes a murky brown. "I'm glad you like it. It's a little advanced for your age, but so are you."

She helped Lacey take the microscope out of the box.

Lacey's birthday gifts took up much of the Todds' dining-room table. She stuffed the last of the wrapping paper into the trash bag Rory held. In addition to Courtney's gift, Rory's parents and Mark had gone overboard with the birthday gifts. Nikki wasn't about to complain; the Todds weren't blood rela-tives, but they had become the family Nikki longed for Lacey to have in her life. Lacey had bonded with Rory's parents and brother instantly, and they all doted on her, especially Mark.

Mark tapped Nikki's shoulder, a mischievous grin on his face. "Wait until you see this."

Rory sat the trash bag in the corner, and Mark jumped up, disappearing into the kitchen. Nikki heard the sliding-glass door leading to the patio open and close a few seconds later.

"Lace, you've got one more gift in here," Mark called from the kitchen.

She looked at Rory, who grinned back at her like a kid waiting for Christmas presents. Lacey raced into the kitchen, her screech filling the house.

"Did you get her a pony?" Nikki hissed at her husband as the rest of the group followed Lacey.

"Nope, even better."

"Mom, look, I got wheels!" Lacey perched on a blue and white ATV sitting in the middle of the kitchen.

"It's youth size," Rory jumped in before Nikki could say anything. "She loves riding with me, and she loves being outside. This is a great one to start with."

"Don't forget this." Mark slipped a hot-pink helmet on Lacey. "No helmet, no riding. Got it, squirt?"

"Got it." Lacey looked at Rory. "Can we take it for a ride?"

He grinned. "Yep. Mark and I can ride with you." Rory owned the house he'd grown up in, along with several acres of land for Lacey to ride on. He owned three full-sized ATVs, as well as a snowmobile. Lacey wanted to learn how to operate them all. Nikki had grown up just around the corner from Rory and Mark, and she remembered hearing their dirt bikes revving around the property. "But ask Mom first."

"It's fine, as long as you guys are with her and she wears the helmet." Nikki laughed as Lacey used her feet to push the four-wheeler toward the back door. Rory, Mark and their father hurried after her, grabbing coats and warm gloves.

While Lacey played with her new toy, Nikki, Ruth and Courtney cleaned up from the birthday party. Only a few pieces of Nikki's homemade lasagna remained.

"Did you hear from Liam?" Courtney started loading the dishwasher.

Nikki's longtime partner on the force had taken his girlfriend and her son on a holiday trip to Hawaii. "Plane is delayed in Denver because of weather."

Courtney rolled her eyes. "Why didn't they fly straight here from LAX?"

"Caitlin said the same thing," Nikki answered. "Liam tried to save some money on the trip home," Nikki said.

Courtney snickered. "I can't wait to see him at the office tomorrow."

"Yeah, a tired Liam is pretty cranky," Nikki said.

"Tired Liam is a bitch," Courtney clarified. "It's been nice not having him harass me for results."

Nikki put the extra pieces of lasagna into the refrigerator. Courtney and Liam complained about each other like siblings, but they both cared deeply for each other.

"You went back to work after Christmas, right?" Ruth's soft voice cut into the sarcasm. "How has that been?"

"It was a good decision," Courtney answered. "Less people in the lab, easier for me to get back into a groove."

"That's wonderful," Ruth said. "But how are you *doing*?"

Courtney's trauma had begun in October when she discovered a murdered co-worker in the lab. She'd been taken hostage from the lab and her hand signals had helped Nikki and the rest of the team find her in time. Despite her bravado, Courtney still had to face those memories. "I'm okay. My therapist and I prepared for a few weeks. Believe it or not, breathing really does help a lot of things. And Garcia has been really helpful, actually. He offered to clean out the storage room in the lab so I could have a new office. I couldn't put him through that, but he's the one who convinced the therapist that at this point, I need to be in the lab for my mental health."

"Garcia is the Special Agent in Charge, right?" Ruth asked.

"Yeah, he's our boss," Courtney replied. "I'm grateful he's been so understanding."

Lacey sped by the kitchen window on the quad, Rory and Mark right behind her. "They better not let her go too fast."

"It can't," Courtney answered. "The kid ones have a limit on them."

Nikki's phone vibrated in her back pocket, and as she looked at the phone, she was surprised by the name on the caller ID.

"This is Agent Hunt."

"Agent Hunt, this is Matt Kline."

Nikki balanced the phone against her shoulder. "How are you?" She slipped out of the kitchen to the hallway. Nikki had met Matt on a case last year, bonded over their similar tragic pasts. Nikki hadn't had the chance to spend much time with him lately. "I heard you bought the old Hendrickson place near Scandia." Like Matt's own ancestors, the Hendrickson family had been among the first Swedish settlers in the area. The Hendrickson place had sat empty for the last few years while the old man's children fought over the estate, the story making the news several times as the drama played out. "I saw a picture of the house on the news a few weeks ago. Looks like a lot of work to be done. Are you calling for Rory's advice on where to start?"

"I wish that was the reason." Matt's voice trailed off. "I bought the place to restore it. Luke wants to help me." Nikki remembered Luke well. He was Matt's stepbrother of sorts. "Anyway, Luke and I started tearing down drywall and found a hidden room." He paused and cleared his throat. "We found human bones."

"You're certain?" Nikki's head began to buzz the way it always did at the beginning of a rough case. She could practically predict them at this point.

"Yeah," Matt said. "Human skull stared up at me from the bottom of the closet. I don't know if an entire person is there, but something bad happened in that apartment."

"Apartment?" Nikki asked.

"Hendrickson's kids said he built this addition to the main

house. It looks like no one's been inside in years, so we started cleaning. Mattresses were blocking the bedroom door. We found the remains in the closet. I have no idea how long they've been there, but since the place has been closed up, I'm thinking a while. That's why I called you instead of the police."

Nikki understood Matt's distrust of the police. It had been Nikki who'd finally worked out what happened when his family were murdered, and given Matt, and Luke, the answers they'd needed.

"Sheriff Miller will have to be involved eventually."

"Yeah, I know," Matt answered. "I do trust him, but I'm near the county line. I'm not dealing with Chisago police."

The Chisago Police Department had played a big part in letting the man who killed Matt's family get away with it for decades. She couldn't blame him for not wanting to bring them in now.

"I know enough to realize we'll need a forensic anthropologist," Matt said. "This can't be a recent death. I hate to ask, but could you at least come out and look at things before we have to involve the police?"

Lacey's blue and white ATV flashed past the window again. She'd be out riding with Rory and Mark for a while.

"Text me the address," she told him.

Nikki went back into the kitchen where Ruth and Courtney had nearly finished. "Court, do you have any evidence collection kits in your car?"

Courtney looked insulted. "You know me better than that. I've got a basic collection kit, a box of gloves and paper booties."

"Is luminol in that kit?"

Ruth stopped putting the silverware away. Courtney had already tossed her drying towel on the table, eager to get back to what she loved. "Yep."

"Ruth, can you let Lacey know we had a work thing, but I won't be gone long," Nikki told her mother-in-law. "I promise."

TWO

Nikki flagged Rory down after Mark and Lacey had passed her. "Having fun?"

He smirked. "She loves it." Rory's gaze drifted to Courtney. "What's going on?"

Nikki told him about Matt Kline's call. "I understand why he wants me to look first. I just didn't feel like I could say no."

"Jesus. What do you want me to tell Lacey?"

"That I've got to help someone out and won't be gone long." She glanced at the swelled storm clouds. "Is it supposed to snow today?"

Rory nodded. "Please be careful. And don't slam the brakes for anything."

Nikki kissed her husband and hurried to join Courtney in the Jeep. She climbed into the driver's seat, tossing her bag in the middle row. Thanks to the automatic start, the inside of the Jeep was almost hot. Nikki shrugged out of her heavy coat.

"I hate winter." Courtney let loose a string of four-letter words about the weather.

"Well, it's January," Nikki said. "The worst will be over by March."

"Oh, shut up," Courtney replied. "You know damn good and well it could still be below zero in March."

Nikki snickered. Courtney hated the cold and would complain about it until every ounce of snow had melted. "Are you nervous about going into the field again?"

"A little bit," Courtney said, wriggling in her seat. "Even though this sounds like it will be some kind of cold case, right? It doesn't sound like it could be Eli Robertson."

Fourteen-year-old Eli had been missing for more than a month, with few leads. Stillwater police were in charge of the investigation, but Nikki had been keeping an eye on it just in case they needed her help. She and Sheriff Miller had both offered assistance on multiple occasions and had been turned down.

"Normally, I'd say we couldn't rule it out because there are ways to quickly decompose a body, even in this cold," Nikki replied. "But the Hendrickson place has sat empty for two years while the siblings squabbled over their father's estate."

"Well before Eli disappeared," Courtney said.

"Or Scott Williams." The fourteen-year-old had disappeared in the spring, his body washing up weeks later in the St. Croix River, several miles south of Washington County. She and Miller both believed his stepfather was responsible, but they hadn't found enough evidence to arrest him. Nikki had been told to leave the case alone. She'd still been spending her evenings searching through files, looking for something that could get the stepfather arrested.

Nikki remembered what Miller had last said. "We've been operating as though his stepfather killed him, but we don't have a lot of leads. It was dark and cloudy and all of the CCTV is lousy." Scott had left a friend's house late at night, claiming he had to get home. The walk was a little over a mile down a relatively busy road, but Scott had disappeared without a trace. Could she and Miller have been wrong about his stepfather?

"Eli disappeared near the ball fields southwest of downtown Stillwater," Nikki said. "Scott Williams lived on Interlochen Avenue, which is on the north side of the interstate. The ball fields are south of it. And this is far north Washington County. So, there are no connections yet. Hence why I haven't been called in. This is unlikely to be anything to do with either." Courtney nodded.

The Hendrickson homestead on the northeast corner of Washington County was one of the few remaining buildings built during the Swedish migration to Minnesota. "I read a lot about the Hendrickson place when it went up for sale," Nikki continued as she drove. "It was built in the 1890s. Karl Hendrickson's grandfather was first generation American, born on the homestead. The original house is gone, but the barn is still standing, and that qualified for the historic register." Nikki's interest had been piqued by the historical factor, but she'd followed the story for the drama.

"Karl Hendrickson died a couple of years ago," Nikki said. "There was something about a change to his will that caused the estate not to close and the house to sit empty, but I don't know the details." Nikki wondered how Matt Kline had come to purchase the place. His own ancestral home at Bone Lake had been the scene of grisly murders—twice—and Matt wanted nothing to do with it. "We go right by Bone Lake. I'm surprised Matt Kline bought this place."

"He still owns the Bone Lake house, right?"

"I don't know," Nikki admitted. "Caitlin encouraged him to sell it, but two murder sprees tend to bring down the value. From what I've heard, though, it makes the Airbnb even more popular." Nikki had wondered why Matt hadn't taken Caitlin's advice. Caitlin was a journalist, it was how she had met Liam, but she and Matt were old childhood friends. Nikki knew he trusted her more than anyone else.

"Why did Matt call you and not the sheriff?"

Nikki suspected Matt had more than one reason, but she explained his distrust of the Chisago police. "The Chisago County Police took charge of his family's murders since it was near the county line, and they got to the scene first. Egos botched that case from the beginning."

"Would Chisago respond?"

"I'm sure," Nikki said. "If I remember correctly, the Hendrickson place is only a few miles from the county line, too."

"Trauma sucks."

"It does."

Courtney adjusted her seat belt. "I hope you know how much spending time with Lacey helps me. She's so smart and advanced for her age. She reminds me of an inquisitive grad student who doesn't realize how tough the world is."

"I'm so glad," Nikki responded. "She certainly keeps your mind off things when she's around."

"She did. I'm glad she likes the microscope. Even if she shifts focus, I bet Lacey sticks with science. You should put her in STEM classes when the time comes."

"We probably will," Nikki said. "I don't want to think about her being in junior high yet. There's something I wanted to tell you, though." Nikki slowed down at the busier part of Manning Avenue north, houses and condos giving way to open tracts of land and blowing snow. "Lacey asked me how I felt about her calling Rory 'Dad.'"

Lacey's biological father had been murdered a few years ago, and Rory had stepped in to fill the role. They all made sure to keep Tyler in their lives. He had a Christmas ornament on the tree, and Rory had always been supportive of keeping Tyler's memory alive, including helping Lacey make an ornament for him this year.

"Oh my God, really?" Courtney put her hands over her heart. "That is so sweet."

Nikki nodded. "I told her that it was up to her. She thought about it for a minute and then said that Tyler would always be Daddy, but Rory had been Dad for a few years." Nikki could still remember Lacey's solemn expression when she'd asked if Tyler would be mad. "She worried it would hurt Tyler's memory, but I told her that he'd be relieved that she loved Rory so much. I think she's going to bring it up with him today."

"He's going to bawl like a baby," Courtney said.

"Probably." Nikki turned onto 240th Street, following it around the remaining cornfields. "Thirty years ago, the only things you saw out here were corn and farm equipment. Hendrickson owned a lot of land. Kids liked to race down the road at night because there was so little traffic."

Nikki's boyfriend at the time had owned a muscle car, and he frequently raced the Hendrickson drag strip, as everyone called it. Nikki had always refused to ride in the car with him, and he'd called her a coward. She should have dumped him then. "Damn. That gas station definitely wasn't there back then."

"Hendrickson must have been loaded, between selling the machinery business and so much land."

"I'm sure he was." Nikki turned right onto Olinda Trail. "One of our best K9 trainers lives around here." She gestured to the surrounding land. "I know progress happens, but I hate seeing houses gobbling all the farmland up."

"Is that a solar farm?" Courtney asked.

"Yeah, Matt said the driveway was just after the solar farm on the right." Nikki slowed down as they passed a grove of trees that blocked any line of sight from the road to the house. She'd never been to the Hendricksons' actual house, but she knew it was at the end of a long drive, trees surrounding the property and separating them from the cornfields. Nikki's tires handled the icy driveway with ease, following the drive to the house.

"That doesn't look like a historical house," Courtney said. "Looks like a seventies rambler."

"I think the original house burned down," Nikki said. "That's why Matt's house on Bone Lake is so important to the local history. It's original and in excellent condition, which is very rare."

Nikki and Courtney were still getting out of the Jeep as Matt Kline exited the front door and hurried toward them.

"He reminds me of Ryan Gosling, with shaggier hair," Courtney muttered. "Is he still single?"

"I have no idea." Nikki slung her work bag onto her shoulder. "Hey, Matt. Happy New Year."

"Yeah, Happy New Year." Matt wore only a black T-shirt covered with drywall dust and ratty, paint-stained jeans.

"You know it's, like, twenty degrees?"

"Yeah, let's hurry inside."

"Courtney was at my house when you called, so I brought her along."

Courtney held up her black bag that she lugged to every crime scene. "Head of FBI Evidence Response."

"Good. I think you'll have plenty to examine."

Nikki and Courtney struggled to keep up with Matt's long strides. "What made you choose this property to remodel?" Nikki asked.

"Couple of reasons," he said. "My parents were friendly with Karl. Members of the historical society and all of that. Even though the original house is gone, the property still means something. I also work with Spencer, Karl's grandson, at the fire department, so I knew I'd be able to get a good deal. My mom was really passionate about preserving Swedish history, and it just felt like the right thing to do. Luke really wants to help me restore it. He's excited to get started."

Cold wind made Nikki's eyes sting, despite the cover of the carport attached to the front of the house. They followed Matt through the carport, past his silver truck, into what amounted to a closed-in front porch, with green indoor-outdoor carpet. He gestured to the door directly across from the one they'd entered through. "Windows on both sides, plus the screen door. Designed for the wind to blow through."

"A breezeway." Nikki pushed back the pang of emotion welling up in her throat. Her parents had been thinking about adding a breezeway to their house the summer they were murdered. "Is this part of the original house?"

Matt led them through the front door, which opened up into a small living room. "No," he said. "The original place burned in the sixties or seventies. I believe Karl helped his father rebuild it. Started out as two rooms and they added on from there."

Matt gestured to the door to their right. "The addition is through there."

"A storm door?" Courtney said. "Weird choice."

"Hendrickson built the addition himself," Mark said. "Until today, my biggest worries were how many code violations it would have."

Nikki glanced at the door on the other side of the room. "Have you searched the main house?"

"I went through it with my lawyer before we closed the sale. It's pretty shabby, some stuff has been stripped. It's going to be a big remodel. But we looked at the closets and all of that. I really hadn't been concerned about the apartment, so we just checked to make sure the water was running and electricity connected. Luke and I got to talking about security out here over the holiday, and we decided it would be good for him to stay here. He wanted to live in the apartment, get his first real taste of freedom. So, we came over today to start cleaning. I never dreamed we'd find something like this." His worried eyes met Nikki's. She didn't know him well, but Matt Kline had experienced enough hell in his life that very little could shake him. His job as a firefighter had also led him into all sorts of scenes, including crime scenes.

A pit formed in the bottom of Nikki's stomach as she took a pair of booties from Courtney.

"We'll wear the booties. Even if they get dirty, it's much less interference with the scene than just walking on it."

Matt pulled the door open, and they followed him into a dimly lit, tight hallway, with wooden stairs leading to a dank cellar on their left, and a narrow water closet on their right. Nikki and Courtney followed Matt down the hallway.

"Who did Hendrickson build the addition for?" Courtney asked.

"Both of Karl's kids lived in it at one time or the other but obviously haven't been here for a long time." The hallway led to a small open area with a stone fireplace. Several layers of dust covered the sailfish mounted over the mantle.

"Is that why this place sat empty for so long?" Nikki asked. "Family issues?"

"Pretty much. Karl sold the family machine shop about a decade before his death, making him pretty wealthy." He glanced over his shoulder at her. "I guess he added some kind of addendum to his will. That's what took the estate so long to settle, and the structures paid for it."

"When did Karl pass?" Nikki asked.

"Four, five years ago," Matt said. "By then, a lot of the acreage had been sold off already. Karl had gone into the nursing home and had his attorney start liquidating things. He'd had some cows and horses, but they were sold with the other acres. I only have twenty acres." He pointed to a door at the left corner of the living area. "That's the bedroom." Matt led them to the open doorway.

Dust covered everything, including the wood floor.

"Did it look like something bad had happened in here?"

Courtney asked. "Like dark stains and stuff on the walls or wood?"

"No," Matt said.

Despite the dust, she didn't see any obvious signs of an attack, like bloodstains. She walked to the closet. "The flooring over here is crusted with black mold or something similar." She looked at Courtney and could tell her friend was thinking the same thing. Not black mold. Likely some kind of byproduct of a decomposed body based on what Matt had discovered.

"It's in the right corner," Matt said. "The remains, I mean."

Courtney reached the closet first. She shined her blue light on that side of the closet.

"I thought it looked like a full skeleton," Matt continued.

"I'd say so." Courtney stood at the open closet door. "Nikki, come look at this."

Dread washed through Nikki as she moved to stand next to Courtney. The closet was bigger than she expected. It wasn't very deep—two feet at most—but the closet was the same length as the wall. She didn't need Courtney's flashlight to see the skull on the right side of the closet.

The bones were easy to spot against the dark wood. "Yeah, it really does. Courtney, this is your area, so I'll follow you. I assume photos first. Do you have enough evidence collection bags for all of the bones?" She took a step closer to the bones.

"Probably, but I'm more concerned about that." Courtney pointed to the ancient steamer trunk in the opposite corner of the closet. Some of the slats had split with age, the old carpet caked black with something that had leaked out of the trunk.

THREE

"It could be something else that leaked." Nikki looked at Courtney. They'd both had the same thought about the leaking fluid. "I mean, doesn't have to be decomposition, right?"

Courtney rolled her eyes. "The decomposed body in the opposite corner would suggest this is likely another body. You know that."

"Do you have any kind of rapid field test that detects decomposition?" Matt asked from the doorway.

"Nothing that quick," Courtney said. "There should be lipids throughout the carpet. We may be able to narrow down time of death."

Lipids were one of the main byproducts of decomposition and could be detected in soil and textiles. "We can't see them with the naked eye, so we need to get a sample." Courtney pushed against the floorboard in front of the trunk. "This is half rotten, probably from decomposition."

Courtney slipped on latex gloves and reached for the padlock. "This is an old steamer trunk. The lock isn't nearly as old. We should remove the entire thing as one piece." She looked at Matt. "I hate to say this, but I'd like to remove these rotted floorboards. That's likely our best source for any biological material that isn't in the trunk."

Nikki looked at her. "Do you have a tarp in that bag?"

Courtney shook her head. "I didn't think to grab it."

"What do you need a tarp for?" Matt asked.

"To secure the trunk and anything inside of it," Courtney said.

"I might have one in the house," Matt said. "I know I have plastic sheeting."

"No, we can't risk contaminating the evidence." Courtney reached into her bag and dug around, retrieving her flashlight. She dropped to her elbows and shined her flashlight into the quarter-sized hole in the chest. "Pretty sure I see plastic."

Wrapping the body in plastic would help prevent air circulation and retain moisture, slowing decay, but insects would make their way through. And plastic alone wasn't enough to hide the smell. Nikki looked at Matt. "Did Spencer mention when this apartment was last used?"

"Years ago, is all he said. His grandpa had it boarded up. They were still there when I bought the place."

"Did he say why he boarded it up?" Nikki asked.

Matt shook his head. "He just said his grandpa went downhill after that."

Courtney shined her flashlight on the back of the closet wall. "See that white staining? I'll have to test to be sure, but that looks like lime."

"Does that really work?" Matt asked.

"It slows decomp and covers the smell, yes." Nikki looked at Courtney. "We need to call the medical examiner's office and get them out here. They'll be able to secure the trunk before they move it. We'll have to bring in a forensic anthropologist, too."

"Except it's a holiday weekend and they're short-staffed," Courtney reminded her. "You'd be better off calling Doctor Blanchard directly."

"I'll call her and Miller in a minute," Nikki said. "Where's the luminol? We don't know if this room is the crime scene or just where the victims were left. I'd like to have some idea before I talk to Sheriff Miller."

Courtney pulled a spray bottle out of her bag. "This stuff is supposed to be the holy grail."

"Lumiscene?" Nikki didn't recognize the name.

"It's the upgraded version of Luminol," Courtney answered. "Has less peroxide chemistry, which mean more protection from DNA degrading."

Courtney stood up and stepped away from the closet and told Nikki to do the same. She soaked the adjacent wall and the corner of the wall next to the closet.

A single spot of blood spatter stained the closet door, right where someone would have grabbed to open it. Courtney sprayed the rest of the floor and walls, but the chemical didn't react.

"So, they weren't killed here," Nikki said.

"I wouldn't think so," Courtney agreed. "They were left to decompose."

"Start taking photos while I make the calls."

"Wait," Matt said. "Could you please make sure Chisago County isn't involved? If this goes out on the radio, they'll show up."

Nikki understood his fear, but she couldn't bend the rules that far. "That's why I will call Miller and Blanchard directly. But I can't guarantee Chisago won't find out. That's the best I can do."

"Thank you," Matt said. "I just... I'm going to wait in the breezeway."

"I'll update you on Miller and Blanchard in a few minutes." Nikki rarely called the medical examiner at home. Luckily she picked up.

"Agent Hunt, I assume you're calling me at home because something terrible has happened." Blanchard rarely answered with "hello."

"You're nearly right." Nikki quickly told the medical examiner about their discovery. "We need to get this chest out of here without compromising evidence."

"How big is it?" Blanchard asked.

"Maybe 3x3 or a little bigger," Nikki said. "It's an old steamer trunk. We've got to be really careful with it to keep the bottom from falling out."

"I can handle that," Blanchard said. "I've got heavy-duty tarp and a furniture dolly. My Suburban is big enough to bring the chest in. We're going to need the forensic anthropologist, too. I'd like to see things for myself before I call her. Give me forty-five minutes or so."

After the call ended, Nikki turned to Courtney. "Blanchard has the equipment and transportation to collect the trunk. You still want to pull up the wood?"

Courtney held up the small crowbar from her bag. "I want the floorboards in front of the closet and all the gunk underneath them."

"I'll let Matt know."

She found him sitting on a folding chair in the breezeway. "Doctor Blanchard is coming with her personal vehicle. I've got to call the sheriff, too. Do you know anything else about the family?"

"Only what Spencer told me, which is what I already told you," Matt said. "My attorney worked with them on the sale."

"Can I have a copy of the sale sheet?" Nikki said. "As well as your attorney's phone number and Spencer's? Have you told him yet?"

"No," he said. "I waited for you. You want me to call him?"

"Not just yet. I'm going to call Miller now, but can we look at the rest of the property when I'm finished?"

Matt stood. "Sure, let me get an actual coat." He turned to go into the main house and then looked over his shoulder at Nikki. "You can come in here and look around. I ripped up all the carpet right after I closed, so watch out for nails."

She did as he asked, admiring the craftsmanship of the old place, despite its dilapidation. Swedish carpenters were among the best. While she waited for Matt, she called the sheriff.

"Miller."

"Hi, it's Nikki. Do you have a few minutes?"

"A few," he said.

"We have quite a find at the old Hendrickson place." Nikki quickly explained the situation. "Blanchard is coming to collect remains, and we have everything we need to collect evidence. But obviously we need to go through the rest of the house and property. I feel like you should be here for that, since it's your jurisdiction."

"Christ." Miller sighed. "The room has been closed up? So these have to be cold cases?"

"I don't see how they're not. No one had been in that room until Matt opened the door. We confirmed no signs of a break-in. Between that and the foot of dust, I think this is a cold case. I can't help but think of Eli Robertson, but if this place has been as secure as Matt's been told, the dots don't connect. At least not until we identify the remains."

"Right," Miller said. "You think that Blanchard and Courtney can handle things this afternoon, and then you and I can come back in the morning with additional technicians and hopefully a K9 to search for more remains?"

Nikki glanced at the ever-thickening snow falling. "We can do that. I've got to go to the office first tomorrow, so most likely mid-morning."

"Call me if you find anything else," Miller said. "I'll meet you tomorrow."

By the time she finished the call Matt had returned wearing a dark winter coat.

"Is Miller coming today? The roads are going to get nasty."

"In the morning," Nikki said. "He's going to try to bring a K9 to search. I assume that's okay?"

"Sure. Are you ready for the tour?"

Nikki put on her gloves and followed him outside. "I assume you guys haven't had time to explore the property much?"

"Not really," Matt answered. "I know that Karl's grandfather planted the maples. The white building next to the house is where the machinery business started, and that old barn over there is ready to fall." He pointed to the once grand Swedish barn south of the house.

"Did Spencer say why it had taken so long to settle the estate?"

Nikki pulled her hood up, buttoning it snugly beneath her chin as she and Matt walked across the driveway to the dilapidated machinery building. The snow continued to fall, the flakes getting heavier.

"He just said issues with the will because of the addendum. He said he thought his mom was going to have a stroke during the whole saga," Matt said. "His mom is a criminal defense attorney, used to snapping her fingers and getting her way, I guess."

"What's Spencer like?" Nikki asked.

Matt shrugged. "He's nice. He started at the fire department a couple of years before Karl died. He was in the nursing home then. But I know there were major issues between Spencer's mom, Stephanie, and Karl. I guess they never really got along."

"And Karl had a son, Spencer's uncle, right?"

"Patrick lives in Texas," Matt said. "He's a retired army major, I think. He was stationed at Fort Hood. I met him at the memorial service. Seemed a lot more down to earth than Spencer's mom." He glanced at Nikki.

"You really don't like her, do you?" Nikki said, smiling.

"My attorney said she's one of the worst people he's dealt with, and this was my parents' attorney. So, he's been around. Spencer even calls her a pain in the ass," Matt answered. "By the way, I have a shift tonight and I'll see Spencer. You want me to have him call you?"

Nikki debated keeping Spencer in the dark until she spoke to him but decided against it. He might be their only ally in the Hendrickson family, and right now they needed information. "Actually, why don't you see if he can meet us out here tomorrow so Miller can be part of the conversation? I'd like to talk to your attorney, too, since he handled the sale."

Matt took his phone out. "I'm texting you my attorney's number right now."

"Thanks." Nikki put her head down against the increasing wind. She walked over to the old, white building. It still had a faint outline of "Hendrickson Machinery, 1899" on the old cement. "So this is where the business started?"

"Yeah," Matt answered. "I think it operated out of here for a long time before getting the bigger building in Stillwater. And then they expanded into Minneapolis and St. Paul. Spencer said his grandpa didn't want this building torn down. It's a huge part of the county's history. It's got structural issues, but I think it can be saved. It's older than the barn and an important part of history. Karl's great-grandfather was the primary machinist in this area for a long time, so he did work for pretty much every farmer around. But it's not safe to go inside. The barn isn't either," Matt told her. "I took the drone through both of them when we first moved in."

"Send me the videos, please." Nikki peered through the

broken-glass window of the old Hendrickson Machinery shop. It was mostly empty save for a couple of large, rusted machines. The roof had fallen in near the back of the building.

A massive oak tree blocked most of their view of the barn. "That's an old Swedish barn, too. I bet it was in better shape when Karl was alive." Nikki hated seeing history tossed aside to rot.

"Probably. There are pictures of the original house and stuff inside. They were still hanging in the breezeway when we bought it. Guess the kids didn't want them." He stopped at the barn's entrance. "You can go in a little bit so you can actually see inside. Just don't go far. The wind could take this thing down."

Nikki stepped a couple of feet into the right side of the barn, her eyes adjusting to the light. The barn still smelled of old hay and very faint manure. Like the machine shop, little remained in the barn beyond the stalls and some junk. She debated going in further. "Did you get any actual footage in here?"

"Yeah, there's video, but it's dark. I flew lower so I wouldn't slam into anything," Matt answered. "I'm not sure how well you can see the floor."

"Send me what you have," Nikki said. "The sheriff's office can bring their drone as well, but I'm not sure how much more we'll be able to see." If there were other victims on the property, the K9 would have to find them.

"What's that?" Nikki pointed to the black-iron fence behind the barn. Dead weeds blew in the cold breeze.

"Family graveyard," Matt said. "It's morbidly cool. If you like history."

"I do." And a cemetery like this would be a fantastic place to leave additional victims. Nikki could see the headstones among the weeds.

"Three generations, including Karl." Matt wrestled with the gate for a few moments before finally pushing it open.

"Karl Hendrickson's in this cemetery?" Nikki counted more than a dozen stones, but they were all old.

Matt pointed to the maple tree in the corner of the family cemetery. "He wanted his ashes spread around that tree. Guess he and his mother planted it."

"Did his kids put up a marker of any kind?"

"Nope," Matt said. "Like I said, they weren't close, as far as I know."

Sadness swept through Nikki as she studied the graves of the Hendrickson family. Three generations, as Matt had said, each with at least one young child buried near the parents.

"People don't realize how lucky they are to have parents to fight with," Matt said.

"God, it took me so long to learn how to compartmentalize suspects who mistreated their parents, even if they were just talking badly. I wanted to shake every one of them."

"I don't know how you kept from it."

She blinked against the snow. "I had to, for my own sake. The anger is paralyzing." She debated asking if Matt had gone back to therapy, but it wasn't her business and Matt had to go on his own, not because people talked him into it. "No one's been in this place since they spread the ashes." Nikki crouched next to the stump. "Nothing looks disturbed."

"You sound disappointed."

"No." Nikki stood up. "I'm just used to finding something awful around the next corner. It's always a pleasant surprise when I don't."

Tires crunched on the driveway. "That's Blanchard." Nikki pointed to the black Suburban emerging through the blowing snow.

"You think you three can manage the trunk?" Matt flushed.

"I don't mean to sound sexist, but it's got to be heavy, and even if she backs up to the door, you've got a long way to carry it."

"Blanchard will figure it out," Nikki said. "You learn a lot of tricks when you've been in the business as long as her." Nikki shivered as an ice-cold gust of north wind blasted her, the heavy storm clouds getting darker. She glanced back at the old, white rambler. What had happened in that house?

FOUR

Nikki helped Blanchard unload her equipment, including the rolled blue tarp. "You brought the furniture dolly, right? I don't want to ask Matt Kline to help. That's one more person to account for in the chain of custody."

"I've got it," Blanchard said.

Matt Kline approached and introduced himself. "Thank you for coming on your day off. I really appreciate it."

"No problem," Blanchard said. "I have to admit, my morbid curiosity is pretty strong right now."

"It's morbid all right." Matt looked at Nikki. "Come in when you're done." He turned to leave.

"Wait," Nikki said. "We can't avoid stairs. Do you have anything we could use as a ramp?"

"Will drywall work?" Matt asked. "I've got plenty of that."

"It should," Blanchard answered. "I've got plenty of straps, so hopefully we can guide it down without having to step on the drywall."

"I've got it in the old laundry room. I'll set it up while you guys are doing your thing." Matt ducked under the carport.

"We go in the same way, but the apartment is to the right." Nikki tucked the blue tarp under her arm.

Blanchard followed. "Walk me through this again."

Nikki quickly explained everything they'd discovered. "Pretty clear it's a homicide since people don't usually end up in trunks on their own."

"How bad are those remains?"

"Messy."

They found Courtney on her hands and knees in front of the closet, booties and gloves still on. "Don't worry," she said before Blanchard could chastise her. "I haven't touched any remains. I've been looking at the floor under the carpet. It's old wood, lots of cracks."

"Find anything?"

Courtney held up two evidence bags, each containing a small object. "A Lego figure and some kind of little toy car."

"A child." Nikki felt half-sick. "The victim in the corner is at least a teenager. You can tell by the bones. Did this belong to them, or do we have another missing kid?"

"I don't know," Courtney said. "I agree about the remains, and we don't know if this belonged to the victim. It could have been here before them. It sounds like this apartment was used a fair amount before Karl boarded it up. Doctor Blanchard, what do you think?"

Blanchard leaned over Courtney to look at the skeleton sitting in the corner, its skull atop the rest of its body. "Agreed. Femur looks long enough to be at least pubescent. But boys keep those little cars a long time, too. It still could have been his."

"It's a male?" Nikki asked.

"You can tell by the pelvic bones," Blanchard said. "I'm confident about that, but I can't tell you age at death or how long it's been here, of course. I did arrange for the forensic anthropologist to come to my office tomorrow to look at these."

Dr. Willard was one of a handful of forensic anthropologists in the state and worked for the University of Minnesota. Because she was in such high demand, Willard usually had to focus on current cases and therefore older remains, like the ones in the closet, were often back burned until she had a free moment.

"She owes me a favor," Blanchard said. "And she's as curious as I am."

They spent the next hour meticulously collecting evidence from the flooring and other places in the room. Several hairs were found amid the cracks in the floor.

Blanchard laid out the large blue tarp next to the chest. It took a few minutes to get the chest onto the tarp without causing more damage, but they managed to get the tarp secured around the chest with bungee cords.

It took all three of them to get the trunk on the furniture dolly. Blanchard secured the chest to it with another long strap. She hooked two more bungee cords to the front of the dolly so they could pull it down the hall, the wheels rubbing against the cheap paneling.

Matt had set a big piece of drywall against the steps, with a cement block anchoring the lower part to the ground. The three of them shimmied the trunk out, putting it carefully on the drywall.

"Worked like a charm," Courtney said after they hefted the trunk into Blanchard's SUV. "I'll go back and get the carpet if you'll let Matt know we're done."

Nikki thanked Blanchard again before heading back into the main house. Matt opened the leaded-glass door before Nikki knocked.

"Are you guys done?"

"Yep," she said. "The drywall worked well. Blanchard will take the remains so she and the forensic anthropologist can do the autopsies. Courtney's finishing up right now."

"What about the flooring?" Matt asked. "I know blood can soak into wood."

"Right now, she's planning to use the light and swab it, but we might have to come back and pull some up," Nikki said. "You know better, but make Luke realize he should stay out of the house until we can come back and go through and clear it. Courtney will either come back or send Arim. He's the only other person she'd trust, and he'll keep quiet about it."

"Thank you." Matt leaned against the doorjamb. "I'll get all of the paperwork I have so you at least have all the information I do about the Hendricksons."

Heavy sleet battered the window, making them both jump. "It was snowing just a few minutes ago."

"I'm glad you have that big Jeep. Just be careful."

Nikki gripped the wheel as sleet pelted the windshield. Taking Manning Trail to the McKusick south was the fastest route home, but Nikki was starting to think the interstate might have been the better way to go, even if it did add on a lot of time.

She glanced at Courtney white-knuckling her seat belt. "Don't worry. This new Jeep can handle anything."

Nikki's Christmas present to herself for the next five years had been trading in her Jeep for the Jeep Trailhawk 4xe. Getting used to the electric model had taken a little bit of time, mostly because the acceleration was so much faster, and Nikki had a lead foot.

"This is a cold case, right?" Courtney asked. "I still don't see this being connected to Eli or Scott, do you?"

"As of now, no," Nikki said. "It was pretty obvious no one had been in that room in a long time. We profiled Eli's killer as someone close to him or the family, because he'd last been with his younger cousin and friends playing baseball. Miller managed to find out the immediate family's alibis were confirmed, but we don't know much more."

"What about Scott Williams?" Courtney asked. "I know he disappeared walking home at night, but his body was recovered. Was Blanchard able to figure anything out from his remains?"

"Too decomposed," Nikki said. "She didn't find any bullet fragments. There was a trace of water in his lungs, so we think he was at least breathing before he went into the water."

"And the river is nowhere near the route Scott walked home?" Courtney asked.

"No." Nikki turned her windshield wipers on high as the snow came down faster. "As soon as Miller heard about Eli, he checked up on Scott Williams' stepdad. The only connection between the boys is Stillwater High School, and Rodney Atwood—Scott's stepdad—was confirmed to be duck hunting in the north woods the day Eli disappeared. And I still haven't found anything to support Atwood's arrest."

"Do you know if Atwood has any connection to the Hendrickson property?" Courtney asked.

"Not that we've discovered. Atwood's a mechanic, and we were able to verify his work history. Nothing about the Hendricksons came up."

"Well, the remains may not be as old as we think," Courtney reminded her. "If they're only a year or so old, then maybe there is a connection to Eli. Maybe we have another serial on our hands."

The idea made Nikki's blood run cold. "The Hendrickson place has been closed up until Matt bought it," Nikki reminded her. "He said Spencer, the grandson, kept an eye on the place and would have noticed a break-in." She wasn't sure which was scarier—a serial child killer or multiple child killers operating on different levels. "And we don't know anything about the remains in the trunk."

Nikki flinched as a gust of wind rattled the windshield wipers, already working overtime against the sleet. The massive buck came out of nowhere, emerging from the ditch to Nikki's right, unconcerned with the weather or the headlights bearing down on him.

She knew better than to swerve not to hit an animal, especially in conditions like this. But she couldn't bear the thought of killing the deer—or worse, maiming it so it was in misery, and she'd have to put it down. "Hang on."

Nikki double tapped the brakes in an effort not to slam them down and slide on the slick road, pulling the wheel toward the empty left lane. The big Jeep had almost come to a stop, but her front tires connected with a patch of black ice. Nikki threw her arm out in front of Courtney, cursing as the vehicle nose-dived into the deep ditch. Somehow, Nikki managed to stop the slide before the new Jeep slammed into a snowbank.

Courtney clung to Nikki's arm for a few moments, both trying to catch their breath. The Jeep's headlights made the snowbank a few feet ahead of them glow. The massive buck meandered down the ditch, crossing in front of the Jeep without any clue he'd almost been hit.

She and Courtney looked at each other for a minute before breaking out in nervous, relieved laughter. Thankfully the engine was still running, and she had plenty of gas, so they didn't have to worry about freezing. "Do you know how many times Rory has reminded me to just hit the deer, never swerve?"

"I would have done the same thing. Killing it would have haunted me." Courtney smirked at her. "But do put the call on speaker."

Nikki rolled her eyes, Rory's cell already ringing. "Hey, babe. How close are you? The roads aren't getting any better."

"Um, I'm still on Manning Trail," Nikki said.

"What's wrong?"

"We're fine," Nikki said. "But we're in a ditch."

Rory sighed. "How did you end up in the ditch with that Trailhawk, honey?" Suspicion rose in Rory's voice. "I've seen you drive on solid ice and not slide."

Courtney snickered.

"You swerved to avoid a deer, didn't you?" Rory demanded.

"He was a beautiful, majestic buck who deserved to live," Nikki said defensively. "I don't think we've got much damage, but I have a feeling we're going to need to be pulled out of here."

He sighed. "Text me the location, dingus."

While they waited for him to arrive, Nikki and Courtney went over everything they'd learned today. "I need to talk to Stephanie and Patrick."

"Is Karl a suspect?"

"The bodies would have to be a few years old at least, I think," Nikki said. "Karl was ninety when he died. I have a hard time seeing a man in his eighties overpower two people. But who knows? It sounded like he bolted up the apartment at some point. Did he do something and try to hide it? The anthropologist might tell us the bodies are older than we think." Nikki loved working cold cases, even though she didn't get a chance to do so very often. "Hopefully Garcia is okay with my working this case, at least until something urgent emerges."

"He won't tell you no," Courtney said. "He rarely does."

Nikki had been at Quantico with their boss, Henry Garcia, and their interactions hadn't always been friendly. She'd been apprehensive when he was assigned to be their SAC, but he'd proven to be a good leader with an open mind.

"Liam's been gone for ten days, so I'm sure I'll be on my own," Nikki said. "He'll have reams of paperwork to catch up on."

Rory's F-250 arrived a few minutes later. Lacey jumped out

of the passenger seat in her bright-pink snowsuit and half-slid down the ditch, flashlight in hand. Nikki climbed out of the Jeep to hug her, snow stinging her eyes, but Lacey shook her head like a disappointed parent.

"Mom, you're supposed to hit the deer, not the ditch."

FIVE

2005

Rebecca shivered, clutching her brother's small hand in hers. Mama held Rebecca's other hand while she sobbed into Aunt Elena's shoulder. She watched the beautiful mahogany casket being prepared to be lowered into the ground and thought about a conversation she'd had with Daddy after church a few weeks ago.

She'd asked him if he really believed people went to heaven and, if so, did they recognize people they'd known in life? Daddy had smiled and pulled Rebecca onto his lap.

"Of course," Daddy answered. "Heaven is supposed to be peaceful and happy; I think we all have our own versions of heaven, with all the people we loved waiting for us."

"But how do they stand to wait so long?" Rebecca asked. "Don't they get bored?"

Daddy laughed his loud laugh, his dark eyes twinkling. "Time is different in heaven, I think. What seems like an eternity here is just moments in heaven. I think the ones who go before us are probably so peaceful they don't realize time is passing."

Her throat ached as Rebecca fought back the tears. Would Daddy be waiting for her when it was her turn? She was young, with so much time ahead of her. What if Daddy forgot about them while he was having fun in heaven?

Cold mist fell on her nose as a soft drizzle began to fall from the gray sky, creating delicate ripples on the sea of black umbrellas on the other side of the grave site. Daddy had been liked by so many people that his funeral had spilled out from the church into the parking lot, and now the cemetery seemed filled to the gills with living people.

Little Jason sniffled beside her. He still didn't understand why Daddy was never home. Rebecca didn't either. Why had the person who killed Daddy decided to drive drunk instead of getting a ride home? Why had Daddy gone to the store that night instead of just waiting until morning?

Over the last few days, Rebecca had heard the adults talking about accidents happening close to home and arguing about things like manslaughter and second-degree murder. She didn't understand any of it, but she knew it had something to do with punishing the man who'd killed her father.

The priest droned on, talking about how Daddy would be better off in heaven. Rebecca wanted to scream that it was a lie. How could Daddy be better off without them?

Rebecca couldn't stop staring at the casket, a simple but elegant piece of polished wood where Daddy would be locked away from them forever. The man who had been her hero, her protector, and her friend was now gone, and Rebecca didn't know what they were going to do without him. Memories of his warm smile, his hearty laugh, and the way he would lift her high into the air, making her feel like she could touch the clouds, flooded her mind. Maybe if she stared at the casket hard enough before it was all the way down, Daddy could still come back.

Rebecca was old enough to know better.

After a few years passed, little Jason would forget Daddy, too. He would never remember how much Daddy loved him, or

Daddy comforting them during a storm. One day, Daddy would be more of an idea than anything else.

Her mother's hand squeezed her shoulder. Rebecca looked up at Mama, the priest's words a distant murmur, lost in the patter of rain. Mama nodded at her. It was time.

Rebecca struggled not to tremble too much, because she didn't want to crumple the perfect red rose in her hand. She stepped forward, her boots sinking into the wet earth, pulling her little brother with her. Her small fingers traced the rose petals before she laid it gently on top of the casket.

"Goodbye, Daddy," she whispered, her voice barely audible over the rain. "I love you." She nudged her little brother, and he put his rose on top of the casket as well.

With one last look, she stood and returned to her mother's side. The world around her seemed a blur, but she felt her mother's arm around her shoulders, a comforting presence in the midst of her heartbreak. As they walked away clutching Mama's hand, Rebecca turned back for one final glance, etching the moment into her memory.

What would happen to them now?

SIX

Nikki's drive from Stillwater to the FBI office in Brooklyn Park took longer than usual. It seemed like everyone in the city was running late. She was ten minutes late by the time she rolled up to the newly installed security gates at the Bureau office, along with an additional security guard. After the building had been infiltrated a few months ago, the FBI's already tight security had become a noose. Nikki understood the incident had to be addressed, mostly because of the media scrutiny that had increased since the events last fall. Still, the situation had been one of a kind, the killer relying on the naivety of a young lab assistant to gain access. The poor girl had never seen it coming.

She parked in her usual spot and hurried into the building lobby, where she had to go through additional security checks. The ego in her wanted to pull rank, to remind the guards that was her commendation photo on the FBI wall of honor, but she complied like the rest of the employees. After the lobby check, she used her new ID badge to get onto the elevator. All elevators had to be accessed by key cards, along with each floor. After the tragedy in October, FBI security had issued new cards that allowed them to track an employee throughout the building instead of specific areas.

She'd debated calling Garcia while they were at Matt's yesterday, but it was Miller's jurisdiction and likely a cold case. Hopefully he didn't blow a gasket at her decision. Garcia had turned out to be a better supervisor than Nikki ever expected, but his ego still popped up every now and then.

Her phone chimed with a text. Courtney and Liam, Nikki's partner, were already in Garcia's office, but their boss hadn't shown up yet. Nikki hit the floor five button. Violent Crime had the entire floor, with Nikki's small, elite unit at the far end, near her boss's office and her own. She scanned her ID to enter the fifth-floor bullpen. Nikki always made it a point to say good morning with the other Violent Crime agents, because it was important they were all equals. Her team had profiling experience and the ability to travel out of state, but every agent on the fifth floor did solid work.

After last fall, security had wanted to put in an additional secured door between Violent Crime and Nikki's team. With Garcia on her side, she convinced them that wasn't necessary and wouldn't be good for day-to-day operations and morale.

She bypassed their bullpen and her office on the way to Garcia's corner office. Thankfully, he still hadn't arrived when she finally came through the door.

Courtney and Liam sat in two chairs in front of their boss's desk, and Nikki fell into the third. Courtney sipped her iced coffee and pointed to her left. "He came in, said hi, and went to sleep ten minutes ago."

Liam's fair skin had a pink hue, and white bits of peeling skin dotted his forehead. "I wonder how many times he forgot sunscreen," Nikki whispered.

"Dummy." Courtney rolled her eyes. "How does a freaking redhead forget to put on sunscreen."

"I didn't." Liam didn't open his eyes. "This is with the sunscreen."

Nikki looked at Courtney. "You didn't get a chance to tell him?"

"Tell me what?" Liam yawned and sat up straighter in the chair, his long legs crossed in front of him, his eyes finally opened.

"You'll just have to hear it when Garcia does," Nikki answered. "No point in repeating. How was the vacation?"

"Awesome. Exhausting. I need a recovery week."

"That's part of the reason I hate taking vacations," Nikki said. "It takes me months to feel caught up. Zach and Caitlin have fun?" Nikki wasn't sure if Courtney had known about Liam's plans to propose to Caitlin after nearly four years together.

A smile played at the corner of his mouth. "She said yes, and so did he."

"Congratulations," Nikki said.

Courtney punched his arm. "You're a lucky guy. I can't believe I'm saying that about Caitlin."

Nikki snickered. Caitlin had been her mortal enemy when she'd returned to Stillwater five years ago. Now she called her a friend, which still sounded odd.

Garcia finally arrived, coffee in hand. "I'm sorry." He dropped into the chair behind his desk. "Gil was supposed to take the dog to the groomer's, but he felt lousy this morning, so I did it."

Nikki tried to hide her smile. Garcia and his partner had a Scottish terrier named Daisy that ruled the house. "How did that go?"

"She hates it," Garcia said. "Complained all the way there. Then she walks into the groomer's like a queen. They all love her, and she never gets grumpy. She saves that for home."

"Sounds like a little kid." Lacey wanted a dog, but their

schedules were too hectic. It wouldn't be fair to the dog, no matter the breed. Courtney had suggested Rory's parents get one and keep at their house since Lacey spent so much time there, but Nikki didn't want to ask her in-laws. They adored Lacey and made Nikki's life easier, and she couldn't ask them to do any more.

"She is," Garcia assured her. "And Gil babies her so much, she knows she can get away with stuff when I'm not around." Garcia's partner had a regular nine to five job, so the dog had bonded to him. "Wilson, you awake?"

Liam jerked. "Sorry, boss. Flight was delayed and we didn't get home until after midnight."

"I understand," Garcia said. "I know you've got paperwork to catch up on, so I won't assign you any new cases until you're at least partially caught up." He opened the battered-leather portfolio he carried everywhere. "Nikki, were you able to get the trucker profile to the agents in Ohio?"

Nikki no longer worked at the BAU, the FBI's Behavioral Analysis Unit at Quantico, but law enforcement often called her for help because of her success rate. She attributed that to stubbornness and using the profile as a guide and nothing more. A profiler had to be willing to pivot whenever new information came in, and not all of them did. The Cleveland office had asked for a profile on a long-haul trucker, whom they suspected was responsible for at least four killings along Interstate 80. "I sent it a few days ago. I haven't heard anything more from the agents."

"Great. Has anyone from Stillwater PD asked for help with Eli Robertson yet?" Garcia asked.

"Nope," Nikki replied. "Chief Ryan is on family leave. Her mother is ill. Assistant Chief Palmer told me he'd work with the sheriff before dealing with the 'feds.' Apparently, he's had a couple of bad experiences with the FBI, so he is cutting us out."

"I don't care about his experience," Garcia fumed. "This is

about a missing child, and you'd think Stillwater PD would welcome all the help they could get. What does Miller think?"

The sheriff had been on leave to support his wife after her hysterectomy when Eli disappeared and had only been back at work for a couple of weeks. "Despite saying they'd be happy to speak to Sheriff Miller, they haven't actually called him." Garcia shook his head. "But Lieutenant Chen is under Assistant Chief Palmer. I'm going to call him and see what I can find out." Nikki had worked with Chen on previous cases and knew him to be a good cop with an open mind. "Which brings me to what Courtney and I found yesterday."

"Wake up and listen." Courtney nudged Liam's arm.

"We were called to the old Hendrickson property yesterday by its new owner, Matt Kline. He discovered two bodies in an apartment connected to the main house. One body in a closet, another stuffed into a trunk." The two men sat in silence while Nikki continued. "We already called Blanchard to the scene. She's worked the site and has the remains."

Liam sat up straighter, finally awake. "Caitlin knows that place. Matt talked to her about buying it before he did it. Matt called you personally?"

Nikki glanced at her boss. He hadn't said anything, but the vein in his forehead that always signaled irritation had begun to pulse. "Sir, I intended to call you, but Courtney, Blanchard and I agreed these had to be old remains. I called Miller and we came up with a plan for today. By the time that was done, I just decided to tell you everything in person since these are cold cases."

Garcia's shoulders inched down from his chin. "Fine. Blanchard called the forensic anthropologist? How long before she has time to look?"

Nikki nodded. "She's actually coming in today, but it's going to take a day or two for the autopsies, and unless there's something obvious in the skulls or other bones, we aren't going to know cause of death. I'm hoping to establish the time frame. It seems like this shouldn't be related to Eli or Scott's cases, but I can't rule it out yet. I've got contact information for Matt's attorney as well as both Hendrickson siblings, Patrick and Stephanie, and Stephanie's son Spencer."

Liam looked at her. "Stephanie? What's her last name?"

"Bancroft." Nikki's stomach dropped as soon as she said the name out loud. "Oh my God. I didn't even put it together until now, but Stephanie is a defense attorney. It has to be the same person."

Stephanie Bancroft was one of the most ruthless defense attorneys Nikki had ever encountered. She'd represented the man who'd murdered her parents when he'd finally been brought to justice a few years ago and done everything she could to make Nikki and her family sound like liars and all-around bad people. Her tactics had failed, thank God, but Nikki knew that had been luck. Stephanie's record spoke for itself.

"I can talk to her, if you'd like." Garcia knew the history, as did Liam and Courtney.

"No, I can handle it." Nikki appreciated the offer, but she wasn't the same raw live wire of emotions she'd been during that trial several years ago. Nikki definitely wanted to talk to Patrick and Spencer before dealing with Stephanie, or she'd be a step ahead of her the entire conversation.

"You said that you and Miller have a plan for today?" Garcia asked.

"I'm meeting him and a K9 deputy at ten a.m. at Matt's place. I know Matt had a shift at the fire station last night, so I left him a message. He's supposed to bring Spencer with him. We're going to search the entire property, and I hope to interview Spencer. I'm stopping by the neighbors' as well, assuming this is all fine with you."

"As long as you don't prioritize this over urgent cases,"

Garcia said. Nikki could tell he was still frustrated that they weren't working on Eli's case. "I know you've got some breathing room right now." He looked at Courtney. "What about the forensic evidence?"

"I came in early to test the swabs I took from the floor around the chest. It's clearly a body," she told them. "Matt let me take the floorboards, so we're going to try to get a full biological profile today to run through CODIS. I also collected hair from the flooring. Assuming it has epithelial cells, we can test for DNA."

He studied her intently. "And you're good?" Garcia had been adamant Courtney's mental health take priority after the events in the fall. He'd have no problem keeping her in the lab if she started struggling.

"I'm good."

"All right," Garcia said. "I understand you need to be in the field for your mental health. But you need to be honest if you have a setback. There's no shame in addressing your trauma, Courtney."

"I will, I promise."

Nikki headed for her office. The poinsettia on Nikki's desk had died during the holiday break. Nikki swept it off her desk into the trash.

She pulled the shades down a few inches to block out the glare of the morning sun off the snow outside and then sat down and turned on her office computer. Her wedding photo with Rory in his tux and Lacey in her pretty flower girl dress made her smile. Rory was still emotional about Lacey's request.

Even though she'd checked her messages during her week off, she still had several new ones, including profile requests for crimes in Wisconsin and Iowa.

Matt Kline had also emailed over all of his property paperwork. He and Spencer would meet them at the property at ten, as she'd requested.

Right now, they knew next to nothing about these two poor victims or the Hendricksons, but that was about to change. Her first call was to Matt's attorney, Brian Cass.

Nikki called the attorney, hoping she didn't get voicemail. A gravelly voice answered her call. "Brian Cass."

"Mr. Cass, this is Nikki Hunt. I'm calling at Matt Kline's request."

"Yes, Matt said you'd be contacting me," Cass said.

"You're not busy?" she clarified.

"Not at all," he answered. "I'm actually mostly retired. I've just retained a few clients. I was the Klines' estate and wealth management attorney. Matt doesn't trust many people, especially now."

"I can't blame him." Nikki flipped to a fresh sheet in her notebook. "Did he tell you what we found yesterday?"

"He did. Frankly, I'm still stunned. I debated contacting Stephanie, but I thought I'd speak with you first."

Nikki caught the edge in his voice. "I appreciate that. I've heard she's tough to deal with."

"You're familiar with her, then?" Cass asked.

"More than I'd like to be," Nikki said. "She's a great defense attorney."

Cass snorted. "Ruthless is the better term." He sighed. "I'm afraid she's been quite difficult to deal with. I'm certainly no criminal attorney, but knowing how Stephanie operates, I knew that you and I should speak first."

"How does she operate?" Nikki asked.

"It's her way or the highway," Cass said. "Fortunately, I didn't have to deal with her much during the purchase, since their family attorney handled things. She refused to compromise to sell the house. She would have been happy to let it rot. Her words, not mine."

"What did she want?" Nikki asked. "Twenty acres and a house in desperate need of a remodel seems pretty cut and dry."

"Her brother Patrick wanted to have the barn and house restored so they could donate the property to the historical society." He snickered. "Poor guy didn't have a chance in hell, even though he's a retired army major. Stephanie wanted to sell."

"Was she the sole executor of her father's will?"

"Fortunately, no. They were co-executors. Patrick had a copy of the will. I got the impression the amendment likely would have been buried if Stephanie had been sole executor."

"What was the amendment to Karl's will?" Nikki asked.

"I don't know," Cass said. "Whatever it was kept the estate from closing for several years." Cass cleared his throat. "My understanding is that it was only resolved late this summer."

"When did Matt approach you about buying the property?" Nikki asked.

"September," he said. "Matt works with Spencer, Karl's grandson, as you probably know. Matt wants to get into restoration, and this was the perfect place to start."

"Was it a cash sale?" Nikki clarified.

"It was, and I'm afraid we screwed up with the inspection. Matt knew the house still had a lot of furniture and other personal items that Karl's kids didn't want. Patrick did take a few things before he went back to Texas, and he took care of clearing the rest of the house out. We knew it needed major work, so Matt just had a structural inspection done to make sure the foundation didn't have any cracks."

"What about the apartment keys?" Nikki asked. "Did Stephanie or her brother have copies?"

"They both claimed they didn't," Cass answered. "Patrick—Major Hendrickson—did clean the house and searched for the keys. They were nowhere to be found, and the apartment had been boarded up. It was going to take some muscle to get inside. Matt just wanted the deal done."

"Did you have any interaction with Stephanie, or was it all through their attorney?"

"A couple of phone calls," Cass replied. "I tried to give her the benefit of the doubt, but she's just a cold person. I have no idea what her relationship with her father was like, but she certainly didn't appear to mourn him one single bit."

"Did you ever talk to her or Patrick about the amendment that caused the delay?"

"Stephanie refused to talk about it," he said. "Patrick said it had to do with the amount of inheritance money they'd each receive. He didn't seem interested in wealth. It's my understanding that when Karl's wife passed, the machinery business had been sold, and it was her wish the kids received a share of that after she passed away so that they could enjoy it before they got too old. Karl honored that, giving them each an undisclosed sum several years ago, making them both wealthy. Patrick didn't want any more money from the will and wanted to give his portion to charity. He just didn't want Stephanie to have it."

"Do she and Patrick get along at all?"

"I know they hadn't spoken in several years when their father passed." Cass coughed. "Pardon me. I'm fighting a cold. I suspect that if you met Stephanie Bancroft, you'd understand why."

Nikki confirmed both siblings' contact information. She thanked Cass for his time and discretion, reminding him they were trying to keep the media away from Matt and the others for as long as possible.

"Absolutely," Cass said.

After the call ended, Nikki opened a new browser window and started researching the Hendrickson family, but she couldn't find anything other than the siblings had spent two years disputing the will before finally putting the property up for sale. In Minnesota, a will-based estate plan required a probate filing, which made the details of the will public. She dug through the public records database in search of Karl

Hendrickson's final will and testament but found nothing. If he had it set up in trusts, those documents were confidential.

Nikki leaned back in her chair and sighed. They just didn't have enough information. Hopefully Spencer could shed some light on his family's lives. Stephanie had wanted to sell. Had she had any idea what might have been in the apartment?

She eyed the pile of mail and messages, wondering if she could spend a few minutes to straighten up her office before the onslaught of reports would arrive at her desk. Half an hour later, her blaring cell phone startled the hell out of her. Nikki scrambled to grab her phone before the call was sent to voice-mail. "Agent Hunt."

"It's Doctor Blanchard," she said. "The forensic anthropologist is on her way. I took samples from the trunk. I'm waiting for Doctor Willard before I clean the bones."

"What can you tell me?"

"The body in the trunk is an adult female. I believe the remains in the corner are a male that's at least reached puberty but not passed his early twenties. Doctor Willard will need to confirm."

So why had there been toys in the room? Nikki wondered. Of course, if the male was a teenager, still having his Matchbox cars wasn't out of the question. "I assume no cause of death?"

"No," Blanchard said. "The body in the trunk was wrapped in plastic, which slowed decomposition, but I didn't see anything obvious like a bullet fragment or ligature."

"How big do you think the female was?" Nikki couldn't imagine fitting a person into that trunk without breaking bones.

"Oh, they were forced into the trunk, if that's what you're thinking. Femurs and right arm are broken, postmortem. Again, I'd like for the forensic anthropologist to confirm all of this, but I'm confident she was petite. I can't tell you beyond that."

"Any sign of clothing or personal items?" Lack of clothing

could mean a sexual assault, but the remains were far too decomposed to tell.

"Not that I saw when I opened it, but I haven't taken anything out other than biological samples," Blanchard said. "But, of course, the forensic anthropologist will have the definitive answer. Doctor Willard will be working on reassembling both remains with her assistant while I catch up on autopsies and reports today, but she's due back in class tomorrow. If she doesn't finish, she'll have to come back in a few days."

Nikki understood they couldn't put cold cases in front of active ones.

"I'm working with Courtney on getting information into CODIS," Blanchard continued. "I've also contacted a friend of mine who happens to be the facial reconstruction artist for the state crime bureau. She's on standby until Willard has the skull completely assembled."

Nikki thanked the medical examiner for the update. She couldn't stop wondering who these two victims were, and if anyone had reported them missing. She hoped Blanchard would be able to find more defining details about them. If she didn't, how would they identify them?

Nikki needed to talk to Stephanie and Patrick, and she wanted to talk to Patrick before Stephanie to make sure she had as much information as possible before dealing with the defense attorney.

Before she left to meet Miller, she stopped to check in with Garcia. "I'll let you know what I find out, but I may not be back in the office today."

"That's fine," Garcia said. "Wilson stays here. He's helping Kendall on a case, and he's still catching up from being on vacation."

Nikki started to leave, but Garcia spoke before she reached the door. "How's Doctor Hart really doing after being back in the field? Coming face to face with death after what she faced can break even the strongest."

"She's okay," Nikki said. "I think the remains being older made it easier to compartmentalize, but I trust Courtney. If she says she's ready, then she is."

SEVEN

Miller exited his big Suburban as Nikki parked next to the second Washington County Sheriff vehicle emblazoned with "K9" on the side. She grabbed her bag and winter hat, pulling the warm wool down to her eyes. The trees surrounding the Hendrickson property provided a decent windbreak, but the gray sky blocked much of the sun's warmth.

"I sent the K9 officer to search around the perimeter of the property." Miller joined her. "Doesn't look like anyone is home. Do you have a key?"

"Matt texted he was on his way with Spencer," Nikki said.

Miller shoved his hands into his coat pockets. "Heard anything from Blanchard?"

"She and Courtney are still testing samples from the scene, and the forensic anthropologist is coming in. Blanchard is confident the body in the trunk is female and the bones on the other end of the closet male. The female is an adult, and the male is likely between thirteen and twenty-five, but the forensic anthropologist will be able to confirm." She shivered in the freezing wind. "I talked to Matt's attorney this morning. He spoke some more about how difficult Karl's daughter Stephanie can be, and how upset she was about the will."

"I remember Spencer coming into the station for something when I was still a deputy," Miller said. "This would have been around 2011. Drunk and disorderly perhaps? He threw a fit about things."

"He hasn't been arrested since then." Nikki had run a background check on Spencer Bancroft before leaving the office. "Matt seems to think pretty highly of him."

The K9 handler returned, his Belgian Malinois on a long lead. "He didn't pick anything up on the property beyond the family graveyard."

Miller pointed to the silver Chevy truck coming down the driveway. "Good timing. Matt's here."

Matt parked off to the side of the police vehicles. He jumped out of the truck, key in hand. "Sorry we are running a little late. We had a shift last night."

Spencer Bancroft exited the truck. He was a couple of inches shorter than Matt and stouter, with piercing blue eyes. He stared at the old house in silence for a moment before joining them.

"Spencer Bancroft." He shook hands with Nikki, Miller and Huse, the K9 handler. "I can't believe this is happening."

"Thank you for stopping by right after your shift." Miller looked at Matt. "Can we talk inside?"

Matt agreed and hurried them all into the house out of the bitter wind.

Despite not being heated, the breezeway was a nice reprieve from the wind. Matt explained the layout of the house to Miller as he set out the folding chairs from the corner.

"Take the dog through the main house first," Miller said. The handler and Malinois headed into the main house while Nikki and the others sat down to talk.

Spencer took off his Nike hat and perched it on his knee. "I just feel so bad for Matt. I pushed him to buy the place." He stared out of the window for a minute. "How long have they been there?"

"We don't know yet." Nikki kept Blanchard's information to herself. "Do you remember when your grandfather put the apartment in?"

Spencer thought about it for a few moments. "The original house burned down in the early seventies. I don't remember the year, but Grandpa was still a bachelor then. He helped rebuild the house and during that time met my grandma." Spencer shook his head. "Grandpa built the addition around 1992, maybe. The apartment was a rumpus room for my mom and uncle, and I lived in it for a while right after I graduated high school."

Nikki looked up from her notes. Spencer was younger than Matt. "What year?"

"2014."

"How long did you live in the apartment?" Nikki asked.

"Just that summer." Spencer flushed. "I was young and stupid and thought I should be on my own. I still stopped by to check on Grandpa, since he was getting older." He gulped and glanced at Matt. "When Matt told me about the bodies, I immediately thought about the young woman and her children who came the next summer to help Grandpa out around the house."

Nikki's fingers froze around her pencil. Spencer should have started with that information. "You know who the victims are?"

"No, I thought of them, but they ran off, they weren't murdered."

"Tell us about this woman and her children," Miller said. "How did your grandpa meet her?"

"He put a want ad in the newspaper." Spencer smirked. "Didn't tell my mom, who thought she was in charge by then. God, she was pissed."

Stephanie Bancroft, the sibling who'd fought the will. "Why?"

"She said it was because this woman came out of nowhere, and Grandpa hired her without letting Mom do any kind of background check." He shifted in his chair. "He and Mom butted heads a lot. She likes to be boss. He didn't like to be bossed."

"Sounds like most men," Nikki said. "Did your grandpa have any sort of background check run on her?"

Spencer snickered. "He was very old school. He went by his guts. And he told Mom the idea that Ms. Smith could hurt him was just ignorant. They didn't speak that whole summer."

"Did she not have a first name?" Nikki asked.

"Not that I heard," Spencer replied.

"Did your mom ever meet Ms. Smith for herself?"

"Not that I know of," Spencer said. "I met her a few times. She seemed nice. Grandpa adored her kids. She had a toddler and a couple of older kids."

"How old were they?" Nikki asked, thinking about her conversation with Blanchard this morning.

"Teenagers," he said. "I think the boy was a freshman and the oldest girl was a senior. Her name was Rebecca. She told me they were homeschooled."

A boy in his freshman year of high school could easily be the male remains. Blanchard hadn't mentioned whether the adult female had given birth, so she could be Ms. Smith or her daughter Rebecca. If Spencer was right, where were the surviving family members? Where was the toddler?

"Did Ms. Smith tell your grandpa anything about her life before she came to work for him?" Nikki asked.

"Not that he told me," Spencer said. "She was an incredible cook and doted on Grandpa. He bragged about how well she kept the house. She practically cleaned before it was dirty. And Rebecca played the piano. Grandpa let her play on his piano.

That pissed my mom off. Me and my cousins could never touch the thing." Spencer shrugged.

"Do you remember when Ms. Smith started working for him? You said summer but can you narrow down the date any?" Nikki asked, wondering if the neighbors had seen this woman or her children on the property.

"I know it was spring, because my mom said the kids not being in school was weird. That's when Rebecca told me they were homeschooled."

"Did you spend much time with Rebecca?" Nikki asked, noticing a change in his tone of voice.

He grinned. "She was beautiful. Thick, dark hair and these eyes that seemed to swallow a person whole. I know that sounds stupid."

"No, it doesn't," Nikki said, realizing he had a crush on her. "So you liked her? Did you date her?"

Spencer blushed. "I wanted to date her. We actually went to a concert the weekend they disappeared. I never saw her after that night."

"Can you tell us about it?" Miller asked.

Spencer looked at the floor for a few moments, rubbing a ring on a chain around his neck. "I invited Rebecca to see a concert with me in Rochester." He looked at Matt. "I was driving that Nissan GT I told you about. That car floated. I miss that thing, but I'd probably be dead if I'd kept it. Too much power for me." He shifted in the chair. "Grandpa had gone fishing at Big Marine Lake for the weekend."

"What exactly were the living arrangements?" Miller asked.

"I believe she stayed in a bedroom down the hall from Grandpa with her youngest son, and Rebecca and her brother used the apartment. That's how Rebecca was able to sneak out with me that night. Ms. Smith didn't want her dating or leaving the property much."

"She wanted Rebecca specifically not to go anywhere?"

"All of them," Spencer said. "It was weird, but Ms. Smith took really good care of Grandpa and he was happy, so I didn't really think about it. But I was kind of surprised Rebecca agreed to defy her mom and sneak out with me to go to the concert."

"Do you remember what time you two got back here that night?" Nikki asked.

"God, after midnight, I'm sure. I know the show didn't end until eleven p.m. or so and the drive back is over an hour. It might have been closer to one a.m."

"Was your grandpa home at that time?"

Spencer nodded. "He never left for the lake until after sunrise. But he slept like the dead, so I wasn't worried about him catching Rebecca."

"How did you discover they'd gone?" Nikki asked.

"He called me on that Sunday night, upset. He couldn't find any sign of them." He looked at Matt. "Honest to God, I thought he'd had a stroke and didn't know what was going on. I fully expected to see Ms. Smith when I got here, because it made no sense."

Nikki leaned forward. "Did you search the house and apartment?"

"Yes," Spencer said. "I do remember smelling bleach here and there in the apartment, but Ms. Smith cleaned with it. I never even considered anything bad."

"How did the bedroom look?" Miller asked.

"Fine," Spencer said. "It was clean. She'd even set the two twin mattresses up against the closet and swept the floors. You don't think my grandpa could have done this, do you? He wasn't a violent man."

Nikki nodded. "How long after that did your grandpa go to the nursing home?"

"A few years," Spencer answered, seeming more panicked. "He was devastated. I tried to spend as much time with him as I could, but I'd started taking classes by then."

"You never noticed a smell coming from the apartment?" Matt said.

"Lime," Nikki reminded him. "Courtney said the carpet was covered with lime. It was inside the trunk, too. Did you ever go back into the apartment?"

"No," he said. "Grandpa boarded up both doors and wouldn't let anyone inside it."

"Why did you decide they'd left on their own?" Miller asked.

"All of their things were gone," he answered. "The cash he kept in his nightstand was gone, along with the Swedish silver tea set that my great-great-grandpa brought from Sweden. Grandpa was devastated. He locked the apartment that day. I don't think he was hiding anything, I just think he was heartbroken and could barely stand walking by it."

"Did he report the theft?" Miller asked.

"No, he was embarrassed. I didn't tell Mom until after he died because he made me promise not to. We just told her Ms. Smith moved on. I did check pawnshops for a while, but the tea set never came up. Thankfully my mom already had Grandma's jewels."

Nikki looked at Miller. "Tea set would be valuable but difficult."

"Needs the right buyer," he answered. "Were there any other valuables taken?"

"I never heard of any. I remember being surprised she didn't take my great-grandpa's Rolex or pocket watch. They were both insured for a high cash value. But the Rolex has a serial number, so we figured that's why she didn't take it."

"Ms. Smith knew about the Rolex?"

"I'm not sure," Spencer admitted. "Grandpa kept it and the pocket watch in the closet in his bathroom. It wasn't locked. I'd guess she did from cleaning."

Nikki knew Miller was thinking the same thing. She didn't

run away. She didn't steal anything. Either Ms. Smith or
Rebecca was likely the female in the trunk.

"Do you remember exactly what weekend this was?" Nikki
asked.

Spencer thought about it. "Not exactly, but I bet I can
search for the band's concert schedule." He pulled out his
phone. "There are archives online with all that stuff now." He
scrolled for a few moments. "The third weekend in August."

"Is there anything else you can think of that might help us
figure out what happened?" Nikki asked.

"No," Spencer said. "Although every time he talked about it
after, Grandpa would say he should have known, because Ms.
Smith never really unpacked, even though the bedroom had a
chest of drawers and closet."

"What did Ms. Smith look like?" Nikki asked, thinking of
Blanchard's information. "Tall? Short? Dark hair, light?"

"Small," Spencer said. "She and Rebecca looked a lot alike.
They both had dark hair and eyes, real curvy figures, but
Rebecca said she got her height from her dad." He grinned.
"Rebecca thought being a few inches taller than her mom made
her officially tall."

"Did your grandfather ever mention her after the first
couple of weeks?"

"No, he never mentioned them again. At least, not until he
added her to the will." Spencer smirked.

Nikki and Miller looked at each other in confusion. "Wait,"
Nikki said. "Was the amendment about Ms. Smith?"

Spencer nodded. "Instead of splitting the inheritance
between my mom and uncle, he changed his will to give Ms.
Smith twenty-five percent. The will stipulated that time and
effort had to be put into searching for her. If she wasn't found
within eighteen months, the will reverted back to its original
form." His eyes sparkled. "I was excited. I thought we'd find
Rebecca and her family. Grandpa knew my mom wouldn't

honor his wishes, so he made sure Uncle Patrick and his attorney had a copy of the will. But even though they followed all the guidelines, they never found her."

Nikki tried to catch up with the racing thoughts in her head. If the bodies were members of the Smith family, a motive had emerged. "Did your mom or uncle know about that before your grandpa died?"

"Uncle Patrick said he didn't open the will, which were Grandpa's instructions. I think he suspected Grandpa would throw a wrench into things, even if it was just to make Mom miserable."

"They really didn't get along?" Miller asked.

"I'm not sure my mom gets along with anyone, to be honest. But it definitely got worse after my grandma passed. I remember my dad talking about the money they got then, because Grandma wanted her kids to enjoy the money from selling the machinery businesses. She hoped that would help Mom and Grandpa get along better, but it didn't. My father always said they were too much alike, but Grandpa had a heart."

This was the first Nikki had heard about Spencer's father. "Are your parents still married?"

He burst out laughing. "God, no. They should have divorced a long time ago." He thought for a moment. "I think they divorced in 2014. All blurs together."

"Was there a prenup?" Miller asked.

"No, but Dad's an engineer and his aunt left him some money. He just wanted out at that point."

One thing bothered Nikki. "How do you know your grandpa was of sound mind when he changed the will? Given his age, I'd think someone as familiar with the law as your mother would have been able to successfully dispute it."

Spencer chewed the inside of his cheek. "Can this stay between us? I don't want my mother to hear it."

"We can try," Nikki said. "I can't make any promises, especially without knowing the information."

"Grandpa had me as a witness when his attorney came with the changes. I told the attorney Grandpa knew what he was doing, even if I didn't know his reasoning."

"That was my next question," Nikki said. "Why did he want to leave money to this woman who disappeared and hurt him so much?"

"I don't know," Spencer admitted. "He told me it was none of my business, so I didn't push."

"Then how were you able to say he was competent to make the decision?" Miller asked.

"Grandpa was like that about everything involving money, mostly because my mother always had her nose in his business." Moisture built in his eyes. "It has to be them. Why didn't I open that closet?"

"Come on, man," Matt said. "Most people would have done the same thing, especially if everything seemed normal."

Deputy Huse returned. "The dog didn't scent inside. How do you want me to handle the apartment? It looks awfully small, so he's likely to scent as soon as he enters."

"Just walk him through," Miller said. "We know he will scent in the bedroom and hall, but I want to make sure we've checked every possible inch of this place."

Deputy Huse headed into the apartment. Miller looked at Matt. "We'll need to go through what's left of the original shop, too. I assume you have a key?"

Matt nodded. "Since the dog didn't scent, can we start cleaning and remodeling?"

"In the main house," Miller said. "Apartment needs to stay sealed."

Matt's watch vibrated. "I have to be somewhere in an hour and I have to drop Spencer off first."

Nikki fished a business card out of her back pocket and gave it to Spencer. "If you think of anything else, however miniscule, call me. Matt, we can lock things up."

He and Spencer headed back out into the freezing wind.

As soon as they were out of earshot, Nikki leaned toward Miller. "Is Ms. Smith a fake name? Was she running from someone?"

"My guess is it's a fake name or they would have found her," Miller said. "But which two family members are our bodies? What happened to the toddler, did one of them escape with him? Didn't Blanchard say the male was adolescent but had hit puberty?"

Nikki knew what he was getting at. "You're thinking he could be the same age as Eli Robertson. Did the killer assume these bodies would be found when the house was sold? Did the purchase act as a catalyst in some way? It's a jump, Miller."

Nikki thought he was on the wrong track, but they should follow up. "Do you think the assistant chief would give you any more information since we've discovered these remains?"

"I doubt it," Miller said. "Didn't you say something about meeting up with Chen?"

"He's going to try to meet me at the diner later," Nikki said. "I'll see what I can find out. It really bugs me that we don't have enough bodies to account for the Smith family. If the youngest child was a toddler then, they would be at least twelve now, if not older. Where is he? If the body in the trunk is Ms. Smith's, then where is Rebecca? Didn't their father or other family members look for them?"

By her count, there were at least three missing children in Stillwater. What had happened to the little boy? Had they all just vanished into thin air?

EIGHT

The first neighbors on Nikki's short list of four lived less than a mile from the Hendricksons' property. According to public record, the Watson family had owned the house next door for a few years. She wanted to find out what they knew about Karl; despite his age, his odd behavior around the apartment was making him seem suspect. She wanted to speak to Stephanie and Patrick and had left messages for both. Nikki turned into their driveway, surprised at how different the property looked from the one a half mile down the road. Unlike the old Hendrickson homestead, the Watsons only had a handful of shade trees, making their cute bungalow visible from the road.

Lush garlands wrapped around the porch spindles, and the snow on the two pine trees on either side of the home glowed from the multicolored lights. In the dreary winter daylight, the lights made the little blue home look like an old-fashioned Christmas card.

A late-model SUV was parked in front of the single-car, detached garage, the reindeer antlers still fixed on the front of the vehicle.

Nikki parked behind it and checked her bag to make sure

she had everything she needed. She gasped at the bracing north wind as she exited the Jeep. Ice melt covered the stone path that led up to the front porch, the ice crunching beneath her boots.

Her knock set off a rapid-fire chain of barking from at least two dogs. They sounded big, and big dogs made her uneasy when she didn't know the owners. She'd been bitten early in her career by a Dobermann protecting their owners. Her husband, Tyler, wanted the dog put down, but Nikki had fought against it. It was never the dog's fault.

Movement from the window caught her eye, and Nikki had to laugh at the mastiff pressing his face against the glass.

"Hello." A petite woman with silver hair and a friendly smile had opened the door, the second mastiff at her side. The woman clutched his collar as though he wasn't the size of a small pony that could drag her down the porch any time he wanted. "Hush, Duke."

The dog grumbled but obeyed. "I'm sorry to bother you, but I'm with the FBI." She held out her badge. "Do you have a few minutes to talk?"

Her eyes widened, but she beckoned Nikki inside. The other mastiff barked from their spot on the couch. "Major is our oldest. He knows when it's worth his time and when it isn't." She stopped at the stairs. "Jeff, come down here." She patted Nikki's arm. "Bonnie Watson. My husband's Jeff." She called his name again.

"I'm comin', woman."

Bonnie rolled her eyes. "We've been married forty years. He thinks he's cute." She directed Nikki toward the nineties-style kitchen. "Can I get you anything? We still have peanut butter fudge."

"No, thank you," Nikki said.

Jeff appeared, his jeans and Grateful Dead shirt splattered with paint. He grinned at Nikki. "Duke and Major always make sure we know guests have arrived." He stuck out his hand. "Jeff

Watson. You caught me trying to finish up an oil painting I've been working on."

"I'm sorry, I won't take much of your time." Nikki introduced herself as they sat down at the oak pedestal table. "I'm following up on some reports we had about odd activities a couple of months ago at the old Hendrickson place." Nikki didn't like to give away any more information than she had to and just wanted a feel for how much notice they took of the property next door.

The Watsons looked surprised. "Didn't Matt Kline buy it?" Bonnie asked. She smiled at Nikki's surprise. "I work part-time at the local community center. He hasn't come around to introduce himself, so we assumed he wanted to be left alone."

"He took possession right before Christmas," Nikki answered. "These calls came in about a month or so before that. Have you noticed any unusual activity in the last few months?"

Both Watsons shook their heads. "To be honest, we don't pay much attention to the place," Jeff said. "Karl's gone and his kids... well, it's not my place to judge."

"Judge them for what?" Nikki asked.

"For contesting the will," Bonnie said. "But then, Karl was always a bit of a hermit. We moved here a few years before Karl died. He was struggling to take care of himself and the house then, but he wouldn't ask his kids for help. He wouldn't explain why. Jeff and I checked on him every once in a while, brought him a hot meal." Nikki did the math in her head; the Watsons weren't here when Ms. Smith was.

"Did he ever talk about his kids?" Nikki asked. "Or any part of his family and life?"

"He was a World War Two veteran," Jeff answered. "He didn't talk a lot about his personal life, but we knew his wife had passed from cancer several years before, and it was obvious he was lonely."

"His kids and grandson live in the area," Bonnie huffed. "But I don't think they visited much."

"Did you ever see anyone else at the property?" Nikki asked.

"We spoke to him about getting a home health aide in a couple of times, but he didn't want strangers in his house," Jeff said. "My own mother had passed the year before, and her home nurse was just amazing. I gave Karl her information, but I don't know if he ever made the effort or not." Nikki made a note. It wasn't that suspect that Karl didn't want anyone in his home after Ms. Smith disappeared. Did he know about the bodies; was he hiding them?

"We were on a three-week cruise when he passed," Bonnie said. "By the time we got back home, he'd already been buried. We missed the funeral." She made a face. "I heard Stephanie gave him a bottom-dollar funeral."

"It sounds like a very sad situation. Did the siblings come around much at all before or after he died?"

"I don't remember seeing either of them," Jeff said.

"I do," Bonnie cut in. "We'd just gotten home from the cruise and heard about his passing. Jeff had gone to the store, but I was in the yard and saw a vehicle at Karl's place. I decided to see if one of his children had stopped by. I wanted to pay my respects." Bonnie's eyes darkened. "His son was loading up the antiques in the house."

"Those were family heirlooms, hon," Jeff said. "I can't blame him for taking them when they couldn't watch the place constantly."

"He was rude," Bonnie argued. "I told him I was sorry for his loss, and he grunted. I thought at first he was holding back emotion, but he got a phone call. It took me a few seconds to figure out that he and his sister were arguing about the antiques. I left."

Nikki hadn't gotten that impression of Major Hendrickson

from Matt's attorney. Grief affected everyone differently. She'd reserve judgment until she spoke to him.

"What reports did you receive, exactly?" Bonnie asked.

"Unusual activity," Nikki said. "If not much of value remained, it was probably kids looking to do something they weren't supposed to be doing."

Curiosity burned in Bonnie's eyes. Nikki stood and thanked the Watsons for their time before Bonnie could ask any more questions. "Before I leave, could I get the home health aide's contact information? My colleague's elderly mother needs help, and it's so hard to find someone you can trust."

"Of course, let me run upstairs to my studio. My files and all of that are up there."

"Thanks." Nikki walked slowly to the door, wary of the two dogs sitting on the couch.

Bonnie followed closely behind. "What's really going on over there?"

"I'm sorry?"

"Why would the FBI be investigating alleged illegal activity at an empty house?" Bonnie asked. "Isn't that the sheriff's job?"

Nikki wasn't about to tell her the truth, but Bonnie already knew Matt Kline had bought the place and hadn't bothered him or mentioned it to the media. She leaned down closer to Bonnie. "Just between you and me?"

"Absolutely," Bonnie said.

"Matt had heard about the reports and wanted it checked out," Nikki said. "I'm kind of doing it as a favor to him. To ease his mind. He's been through a lot."

Bonnie's hand went to her chest. "Bless his heart. Is there anything he needs? I'd be happy to bring food or help clean."

"He's wealthy." Jeff had returned. "He can hire people." He handed Nikki a crumpled business card. "She may have retired or be doing something else. But if she's still taking care of elderly people, I'd highly recommend her."

Nikki thanked the Watsons again and headed back to the Jeep, business card in her hand. She moved on to the next neighbor. Property records showed Jimmy Regan had purchased the twenty acres just north of Karl Hendrickson's home a few years before Karl died, after the land had been rezoned to residential instead of farmland.

Regan's double-wide mobile home sat close enough to the road he might have had a view of the Hendricksons' comings and goings. Christmas decorations still decorated the white porch, a striking contrast to the dark-blue siding. The short driveway hadn't been plowed since last night's storm, Nikki's Jeep creating fresh tracks as she parked next to a snow-covered Toyota Highlander.

She couldn't say why, but something about the place's isolation made Nikki take her gun out of the locked case and stow it into the holster. Regan had no criminal record, but Nikki had learned to trust the hairs on the back of her neck.

Snow and ice packed the porch steps. Nikki gripped the railing to keep from falling on her face. The porch didn't appear to have been shoveled either. What was she about to find?

Nikki knocked on the door, her right hand resting on the hidden SIG Sauer. Several seconds passed in silence before she heard what sounded like a deadbolt unlocking from the inside.

A tall, dark-haired man wearing a headset opened the door a few inches. "Can I help you?"

Nikki held up her badge and introduced herself. "Are you Jimmy Regan?" The man nodded. "I'm helping Matt Kline with something, and I just had a few questions. Do you mind if I come in?"

Regan pulled the scraggly hair on his chin. "Who's Matt Kline?"

"I'm sorry, he purchased the Hendrickson property."

"That place has been empty since Karl died."

"Right." Nikki couldn't get a read on Regan yet. "Matt

wanted me to follow up on reports of someone being on the property not long before the closing."

"I haven't seen anything." Regan still hadn't opened the door more than three inches. "As you likely ascertained, I don't get out much. Especially in winter."

Cold started to seep through her heavy parka. "I just have a few questions. And it's really cold out here."

"Fine." Regan opened the door just enough for Nikki to squeeze inside the mobile home. She wiped her boots on the mat. When her eyes adjusted, Nikki scanned her surroundings. She hadn't been sure what to expect, but the modern, open-concept home smelled and looked clean, with pretty laminate flooring throughout the main areas.

A large computer desk and an impressive setup with three monitors took up a large amount of the main room. Nikki had already learned Regan worked in IT, but instead of hanging up software certificates, Regan had gone for an entirely different look.

Nikki stared at the familiar, awful face adorning the wall. An autographed drawing by Richard Ramirez had been framed next to a photo of the serial killer in his prison jumpsuit. Two clown paintings by John Wayne Gacy flanked it, and a wanted photo of Ted Bundy, along with an authenticated letter from Bundy, held a place of honor above Ramirez and Gacy.

She stared at Regan. "Are all of these real?"

He puffed out his scrawny chest. "Ramirez's, yes. The Gacy and Bundy ones are replicas, but I'm always on the lookout for authentic memorabilia."

"You're a serial killer fan?" An interest in true crime was one thing, but the serial killer collecting obsession made no sense to her. Lack of real-life experience was the only reason she could come up with for people like Regan romanticizing ice-cold killers.

"Oh yeah." He grinned, showing bright, straight teeth. "If I didn't have anxiety issues, I'd have gone into psychology just to interview them."

Nikki struggled not to roll her eyes. He was one of *those*. Thanks to television and pop culture, too many people thought a degree in psychology was all someone needed to go into forensic psychology. Television and movies seemed more intent on making her job sound thrilling than helping the public. Given his fervor for true crime, Nikki was surprised he didn't recognize her or Matt Kline's name. "You collect serial killer stuff and don't know about Matt Kline's family? The Bone Lake murders?"

Regan shrugged. "I know. But killing for selfish reasons like covering your own ass doesn't interest me. I'm into the psychology."

"I interviewed Richard Ramirez in grad school." She looked Regan in his dark eyes. "I can assure you, it wasn't a fun experience." Her mentor Elwood had taken Nikki with him to interview Ramirez during her final year in graduate school. It had been her first experience of San Quentin and wiped out whatever idealized version Nikki had of the world.

Regan's eyes bulged, and she knew he was about to ask her all about that hot, miserable day. She beat him to the punch. "You have the only view of the Hendricksons' old place. Did you ever notice anything unusual?"

"Since it's been empty?" Regan thought for a moment. "I don't think so. But I also stopped paying attention after Karl died."

"Did you know him well?"

He shrugged. "I wouldn't say well, but I had a soft spot for the old codger. He reminded me of my grandpa."

"Karl lived alone, right?" she asked. "Did he have any sort of home health aide?"

"No, he didn't, at least not that I knew of. That's why I tried to check in on him when I could after I bought the place."

"What did his children have to say about that?"

He made a face. "I tried to check on Karl to make sure he didn't need anything. Once a week for three years until he died, and I only saw his daughter once. He mentioned his son lived out of state and they spoke weekly, but I hated seeing how alone he was. Money doesn't buy everything. And that's all she cares about," Regan added. "I don't know the details, but I know she tried to block the sale to me. She wanted the entire acreage kept together to sell as one."

"His daughter's an attorney. She didn't handle the sale for him?"

"No, some guy out of Forest City." Why hadn't Karl had his daughter handle the sale? Was it simply because they didn't talk?

"What about his grandson?" The Watsons didn't appear to have a good opinion of Spencer Bancroft.

"Never really met him," Regan answered. "Only time I saw him, he was digging through the old shop for stuff to sell, so he said. That wasn't too long before his grandpa died."

"You're in IT, right?"

His eyes narrowed. "How do you know?"

"I'm FBI." She smiled. "And that's public information. I take it you work from home?"

"Software engineer," he said. "Healthcare IT."

"Which healthcare system?"

He shook his head. "I work for the medical software company. That's why I work from home. If I worked for the hospital system, I'd have to go into work a few times a week."

"You like your peace and quiet?" Nikki asked.

"I don't like other people," Regan clarified. "I don't want to worry about kids running across the street or homeowners' associations. Or neighbors at all."

"Don't you have any friends?"

"Of course I do," he snapped. "How is this relevant to whatever you're investigating?"

Nikki smiled. "It's not. I'm just nosy. I understand your desire for privacy, but you're the only neighbor who can see any of the property. You're certain you never noticed things happening on the property? Something that just struck you as weird, but you knew the property was empty, so you didn't pay as much attention to it?"

Regan thought about it for a few minutes. "No. I'm a night owl, I admit. I probably would have noticed if someone was poking around at night. But during the day I'm buried in work and barely look out the window."

NINE

The rich aroma of coffee greeted Nikki as she walked into the Daily Grind, a downtown coffee shop on Water Street, not far from the river. A large display case of sweets made her mouth water. She ordered a giant cinnamon roll and a coffee loaded with cream and sugar to cover the awful taste. She found a two-seater table in the corner, perfect for a private conversation.

Nikki checked her messages, hoping to have something more from Blanchard or Courtney about the remains, but they were both likely busy with current cases that had to come first over a cold one. Nothing yet from Stephanie or Patrick Hendrickson.

She took her work laptop out of her bag to run Spencer Bancroft's name. His only brush with the law came in 2013, right after he'd turned eighteen. He'd been arrested for trespassing at an ex-girlfriend's work. Stephanie had stepped in and asked the judge to release him into her custody, with the ankle bracelet, promising to make sure he came to all his probation meetings, would keep a job and stay away from his ex-girlfriend. He'd joined the fire department a few years later and hadn't been in trouble since.

Both interviews with the neighbors had helped Nikki get a better idea of the family dynamics. She wanted to talk to both Patrick and Stephanie; had one of them been involved in the deaths of these two people?

"Sorry if I kept you waiting." Chen slid into the booth across from her, coffee in hand. Gray had taken over the lieutenant's dark hair, but he seemed to be in better spirits than he had been the last time Nikki worked with him. He'd still been reeling from personal issues affecting a missing children's case, but now he seemed more focused, with less darkness in his eyes.

"I have to say, I'm really intrigued," Chen said. "I heard the sheriff was out at the old Hendrickson place this morning. Rumor is remains were found."

"Two sets, in the addition," Nikki said. "We brought in a K9 this morning and didn't find anything else on the property. Matt Kline bought the place because he works with Karl Hendrickson's grandson Spencer."

Chen made a face. "Stephanie's son. God, that woman is a menace."

"What do you mean?"

"She's a defense attorney who will stop at nothing to get her wealthy, white-collar clients off. Plus, I went to high school with her."

Chen was a few years younger than Nikki, but she knew he'd attended Stillwater High School. "Did you have a lot of interaction with her?"

He shrugged. "Some, but it was more my friend. He had a huge crush on her and she was popular and wealthy. Laughed in his face when he asked her out and then told her friends an embellished version of the story. She did stuff like that all the time."

That lined up with everything else she'd heard about Stephanie. "What about Patrick? He's a couple of years older than her, but I don't think he was there at the same time as me either." She sipped her coffee.

Chen drummed his fingers on the table. "Patrick Hendrickson. Pretty sure he was a big lacrosse star. I always heard that he and Stephanie didn't get along. They were never seen together at school. He wouldn't even give her a ride most of the time."

"Wow." Nikki nodded. "Blanchard and the forensic anthropologist are working to establish a time of death, but I'm fairly certain we know who our two victims are." She told Chen what Spencer Bancroft had shared earlier that morning. "Spencer said Ms. Smith and her family showed up the spring of 2015 and then disappeared shortly before school resumed. The family assumed she'd left and stolen some valuables."

"I bet Stephanie was livid," Chen said. "She's a control freak. Wasn't there some weird shit with Karl Hendrickson's estate, too?"

"He left part of it to Ms. Smith and her children. They had eighteen months to claim it and never came forward. The family attorney did their diligence and searched for her as well. They never found anyone," Nikki said. "I also spoke to Karl's old neighbors this morning. Everyone has described Stephanie the same way: extremely difficult in general, contesting the will, pushing for the sale of the property. It sounds like Patrick tried to protect his father's wishes and took some antiques but supported the search for Ms. Smith."

"Did Spencer say if this Ms. Smith got along with Stephanie?"

"Stephanie wasn't happy," Nikki said. "We don't know what the conversations were about with Ms. Smith, but Spencer said she hated her."

"Good luck investigating that branch of the family tree," Chen said. "I'm sure Stephanie was thrilled when her inheritance was threatened."

"According to Spencer, his mother didn't know about the

change to the will until after Karl passed. Spencer is the one who acted as witness to confirm his grandfather was of sound mind to make changes. He asked me not to tell her if I could manage it."

"Stephanie made it a point to know everything about anything she viewed as important," Chen said. "She may not have known for sure, but she could have suspected it."

"If she did do something, she surely had help," Nikki mused. "One woman against a teenage boy and his mom and sister would be a tough task."

Chen's eyes lit up. "Spencer said this all happened in 2015?"

Nikki nodded, confused as Chen unlocked his phone and typed. "Let me search public records to make sure I have the year right."

She finished her cinnamon roll and let Chen do his thing.

Chen sat his phone down on the table with a smirk. "Stephanie and Daniel Bancroft divorced in 2014. He filed. They had a knock-down-drag-out over assets in court. I don't know anything about the guy other than he was part of the family and stood to inherit from Karl as long as he stayed married to Stephanie. Guess he couldn't stick it out any longer."

Nikki wrote the name down in her notebook. "Daniel Bancroft. Do you know if he's still living around here?"

"Pretty sure he moved out of state. Spencer didn't mention him at all?"

"Just briefly," Nikki said. "I left him a message this morning. I want to talk to him before Stephanie."

Chen grinned. "Good strategy. Anyway, this is Miller's jurisdiction," Chen said. "Why are you talking to me? If you think my going to school with Stephanie will help, I assure you, it won't."

"Because of Eli Robertson," Nikki said. "And Scott Williams. Two teenaged boys that disappeared within a year of each other, and now we've found one deceased, who was likely around the same age as the other two when he died. If the toddler is still missing, he could be a victim, too." The limited information about Eli made it impossible to compare the cases.

Chen leaned back in the booth. "There's a ten-year gap between crimes."

"So it seems," Nikki said. "Liam's searching for additional missing boys that would fit the age. We may be completely off, but given we currently have two missing teenaged boys and one is confirmed dead, I think we have to at least look at the possibility. The sheriff's office is handling Scott Willams' murder, but Miller has been shut out of Eli's investigation. We've offered help but it's been refused by the assistant chief."

"I know." A muscle in Chen's jaw tightened. "He's a cool guy in some ways. Supported Chief Ryan becoming the first African American police chief here. But he hates interference from the FBI. He says we can handle the case."

"Are you?"

"We've had surveillance on a family friend for the last week," Chen said. "I can't give you details, but they live in Minneapolis. We have reason to believe Eli may still be alive."

"I assume this family friend is a sex offender?" Nikki asked.

"Two-timer," Chen said. "Out early on good behavior. Because pedophiles should get multiple chances."

Scott Williams' body had been found washed up in the St. Croix River a year ago, weeks after he'd disappeared. His remains had not been in good enough condition for Blanchard to rule out sexual assault. "Do you know if your suspect has any connections to Scott Williams? Could he have taken him as well?"

"Other than attending Stillwater High School, we haven't found any."

. . .

"Uncle Mark, you cheated!" Lacey's shrill voice made Nikki laugh. "Stacking draw-twos is against the rules."

"No, it isn't," he retorted. "That's how we've always played, isn't it, Rory?"

Lacey folded her arms and glared at Rory. "Don't lie, Dad."

Hearing Lacey use the word still sent a swell of mixed emotions through Nikki. She loved that Lacey had made the decision, but Nikki would never be able to completely shed the guilt about her ex-husband's death.

"I won't." Rory looked at his older brother. "It's true. The actual rules say you can't stack draw-twos, only draw-fours."

Lacey smirked at Mark. "That means you still have to draw two."

He rolled his eyes but drew the cards.

Lacey smiled sweetly at Rory. "Sorry." She dropped a draw-four on top of the pile.

"You put a draw-four on me last time," he griped.

"I'm trying to win. Suck it up, buttercup."

Nikki and Mark burst out laughing. She'd learned a long time ago not to go after Lacey in UNO. She had a knack for always getting a draw-four, especially when she shuffled the cards. That was a trick she'd learned from her ex's father. Tyler's parents remained in Lacey's life, and she usually spent a couple of weeks with them in the summer.

Before she could take her turn, Nikki's cell vibrated with a call from an Arizona area code. "I have to take this," she said. "I'll play next hand." She left the kitchen, answering the phone before it stopped ringing. "This is Agent Hunt." Nikki turned down the hall, headed for her office.

"Agent Hunt, this is Patrick Hendrickson returning your call."

"Thank you for calling back." Nikki closed her door and settled into her chair. "Let me just grab some paper and a pen." She rummaged through the stuff on her desk, snagging her legal pad. She checked to make sure the pen had ink before continuing. "All right. Before I say anything more, have you spoken to Spencer? He's fine," Nikki quickly added, realizing how he might have taken her words.

"He called me this afternoon. I'm still in shock."

Nikki quickly scanned her notes on Patrick: high school salutatorian before enlisting in the army. He spent sixteen years in the army before entering the private sector as a cyber security specialist. As far as Nikki could tell, Patrick hadn't lived at his Dad's home for any length of time since leaving high school.

"I know it's a lot to comprehend. Did you know the Smith family? Do you think it's possible the remains could be theirs?"

"Well, they must be," he said. "They disappeared and Dad had Spencer board up that room. He never went near the apartment again. I guess that's why no one smelled anything, plus Spencer mentioned lime."

"We confirmed lime had been poured all over the closet floor and lower walls," Nikki said. "Is that apartment heated?" The furnace was in the basement, according to Matt, but it dawned on Nikki that she'd only noticed heating vents on the house, not the apartment.

"No," Patrick answered. "We always used the fireplace and an electric heater. I'd actually been discussing putting heat in there for the winter for Ms. Smith's family because I didn't want to worry about them having a heater and starting a fire."

"When did you discuss this?" Nikki asked.

"A couple of weeks before they disappeared," Patrick said. "That's part of the reason Dad was so stunned and couldn't believe they'd just left. I'd told him we'd get the heat installed, but that he needed to make sure Ms. Smith intended to stay."

Nikki sat up straight. "Spencer didn't mention that."

"He probably didn't know," Patrick said. "My father didn't share a lot."

"But Spencer helped search the property for them," Nikki

said. "Surely Karl would have defended his reason for thinking they didn't just leave."

Patrick laughed. "Agent Hunt, you didn't know my father. He never defended his reasoning because he didn't have to, at least in his mind. If he wanted you to help with something, the why never mattered. Only the how."

"Do you remember the last conversation you had with your father about Ms. Smith? Do you remember the names of her children? Her first name?"

"She kept her cards pretty close to her chest. The last time I visited Karl he was in the nursing home." Emotion thickened his voice. "He hadn't talked about her in a long time. I know he never accepted that she would have just left. He said she had to have been taken. Maybe even murdered, even though that made no sense."

"Spencer said she and the kids arrived in the spring and disappeared in August," Nikki said. "Your father didn't know her very long, yet he seemed confident she wouldn't have disappeared."

"He was lonely," Patrick said. "He never dated after Mom died. I think Ms. Smith brought some happiness into his life."

"So, she was his caretaker and housekeeper," Nikki said. "Let's say they were close and she might have confided in him. I know it's a long shot, but do you remember him talking about why he was so sure she didn't leave? Did he know something about her that he didn't share with anyone else?"

"No," he said. "Only that he'd confirmed she'd intended to stay."

"Your father told you this, but did you hear anything from Ms. Smith directly?" Nikki asked. "Is it possible he lied because he wanted you to put heat in regardless?"

"I suppose so, although I don't know why he would," Patrick said. "But he'd convinced Ms. Smith to register her son at school instead of homeschooling."

"Did she register him?" School records like that would be accessible. That would change the entire investigation.

"No," he said. "Ms. Smith planned to do it the Monday after the fishing trip. She wanted Dad to go with them. My father's mind was sound then, and I believe him. My sister didn't."

Nikki didn't miss the way he spit out "sister." "Stephanie didn't like Ms. Smith?"

"Oh God, no. Didn't trust her, saw her as a threat. Stephanie hates other women in general, though, so we mostly ignored her. Dad was happy with Ms. Smith and the kids being there, and that's what mattered to me. After they disappeared, Stephanie refused to consider anything other than Ms. Smith being a scam artist. She told Dad to his face that he was lying or senile about Ms. Smith telling him she'd stay. He'd been conned."

"How did that go over?" Nikki asked.

"Dad threw her out," Patrick said. "As far as I know, he never let her back into the house after that. Dad's health was good then, but within a couple of years, he'd gone downhill and couldn't be on his own. He'd stopped being active and gave up."

"You said the last time you visited him in the nursing home he talked about Ms. Smith, and then we went off on another track," Nikki said. "What were you going to say?"

"I visited him about a month before he died—spent a little over a week here and saw him every day—and every day he talked about seeing her there, in his room. Then he said Mom had been there, and his parents." Patrick's voice sounded strained. "She was visiting him, he said. I asked if that meant she was dead, and he said yes. You know how they say people start seeing their loved ones who've passed on before them when they're close to dying?"

"I do."

"Dad died four days later." Patrick exhaled shakily. "So,

when the will was read and I realized he'd changed it to include Ms. Smith, I was confused at first. I thought maybe he'd done it around the time she disappeared, but then I found out he'd changed it not long before he went into the nursing home. I know at that time that he was certain she must be dead."

"Why did you think he changed it then?" Nikki asked.

"Honestly, I thought it was to stick it to my sister. When he sent me a copy, he told me not to open it, but that I would need it when the time came. I'm not one to go against Dad's wishes. Then I heard the lengths we had to go to in order to fulfill our obligation to look for her and realized he'd taken one last shot at someone finding out what happened to the Smiths."

"Didn't anyone else ask about them?" Nikki asked. "No one ever came looking for them, a family member or friend?"

"Not a soul, as far as I know," he answered. "I got the feeling from Dad that Ms. Smith didn't know anyone in the area and was afraid to be social."

"Afraid?" Nikki echoed. "That's the word he used?"

"Yes," Patrick said. "I should have pushed finding out more about her, but like I said, Dad was happy."

"I understand," Nikki said. "Is there anything else I should know before I speak with Stephanie?"

"You've tangled with her before, Agent," Patrick said. "You can handle her."

"Do you and Stephanie communicate anymore?" Nikki asked.

"Not since the funeral," he said. "I no longer had any obligation to entertain her bullshit. I let the attorney deal with her."

Nikki wondered if it were possible for Patrick to have an unbiased opinion about his sister. "How did Stephanie act after the Smiths disappeared?"

"Cocky," he said. "Lots of 'I told you so's,' that sort of thing. Dad tossed her out over it."

"How did she take that?" Nikki asked.

"I wasn't here to witness, but Dad said she got violent with him." Anger thickened his voice. "She denied it, but Dad did have bruises on his arms when I visited not long after." Patrick hesitated before taking a deep breath. "You're likely trying to figure out how to ask me if my sister is capable of killing someone over money. As much as I'd like to defend her, I can't."

TEN

It took Nikki a few moments to understand the song invading her dreams was actually Miller's ringtone. Rory groaned and rolled over, putting his pillow over his head while Nikki blindly grabbed for her phone. A 5:30 a.m. call from the sheriff was never good. "Miller, what's up?"

"Just got a call about another missing teenaged boy. A high school freshman left school in the afternoon to walk to his job at Menards. It's less than ten minutes from Stillwater High School. He never showed, wasn't there when the mom came to pick him up. I'm headed to talk to the family right now."

Another missing Stillwater freshman. Once the news got out, people were going to assume the worst. The media would start talking serial killer because they loved to talk about serial killers and speculate about the worst possible outcomes. "I can meet you at the station in twenty."

She got out of bed and quickly found jeans and a sweater.

"Case?" Rory grumbled from bed.

"Yes. I'm sorry. Can you get Lacey to school?" Nikki liked to drop Lacey off when she could, but that wasn't going to happen today.

"Yep. Be careful." He started snoring softly.

Nikki quickly brushed her teeth and hair, slathered her face with moisturizer and hurried into her office to gather her things. She peeked in on Lacey, who was still asleep, her right foot hanging off the bed. "See you later, Bug," Nikki whispered.

Twenty-three minutes later, Nikki arrived at the sheriff's office. She grabbed her work bag and SIG Sauer out of its locked box underneath her seat. She never took her weapon into the house. Lacey wasn't a kid that snooped or got into things she wasn't supposed to, but it wasn't worth the risk.

She deposited the bag and pistol on Miller's back seat and got in beside him. Nikki immediately asked the question that had been nagging her since he'd called. "The kid wasn't there after work, and you said the call just came in?"

"Yep. Dispatch didn't ask any more questions."

Nikki adjusted her seat belt. "Where do they live?"

"Near Lake McKusick by Oak Glen Golf Course."

"Pricey neighborhood," Nikki said.

"My wife's cousin lives out that way. Their house cost nearly 700,000."

"Dang," Nikki said. "Doctor?"

"Engineer. His wife is high up at US Bank." Miller changed lanes. "This kid goes to Stillwater High School, just like Eli Robertson. Around the same age, too. Were you able to find out anything about that investigation from Chen?"

"They think it's a family friend," Nikki said. "He's been under surveillance and there's no connection to Scott Williams. I left a message for him on the drive over. Hopefully he calls sooner rather than later."

"My deputies are working with Stillwater Police to go door to door in the area around Menards. I need a photo of the missing kid for them and the drone pilots."

"We'll need Menards' security videos as well as the CCTV in the area."

"Deputy Reynolds is on it."

Nikki saw the Oak Glen Golf Course out of the corner of her eye, looking more like a snow-covered lake than a golf course. Despite its cost, Oak Glen was a sought-after neighborhood. Its low crime rate enticed people from the Twin Cities, and the school district often reeled them in, their test scores and graduation rates among the highest in the area. But its biggest draw was its proximity to some of Washington County's best parks and trails. Many homes were within walking distance to Brown's Creek Trail or backed up to it.

Miller parked in front of a beautiful two-story home at the end of a cul-de-sac. A mix of brown brick and siding, with a three-car garage, the home resembled so many others in the area. Snow covered a large garden bordering the big house, a mature oak tree the centerpiece. "Someone has a green thumb."

"I'm sure it's beautiful in the summer." Nikki followed Miller past the impressive garages to the front door. Lush garlands decorated the front porch, two red bows at each end. The front door opened before they could knock. A blond man wearing blue scrubs answered the door.

"Sheriff, thank you for coming." His gaze fell on Nikki. "Is this another deputy? Shouldn't she be out searching with the others?"

"Agent Nikki Hunt, FBI." She extended her hand. "Sheriff Miller asked me to come along. I hope that's okay. I assume you're Jared."

"Jared Hall." He looked past them to the street, worry in his eyes. "I keep thinking he's going to show up any minute."

"I can't imagine what you're going through," Miller said. "Every available deputy is searching for your son as well as the Stillwater Police Department. We're also using drones to make sure to reach as wide of an area as possible. I do need a recent photo of your son for them to show people."

"Of course." Jared motioned for them to come inside. "You can leave your shoes inside the entry."

Nikki and Miller took off their shoes in the large foyer and lined them against the wall next to the family's shoes. Jared took his cell phone out of his pocket and asked for the sheriff's number. "I can text you a couple of pictures from the holiday."

They followed Jared through the large great room to the kitchen. Vacuum marks on the thick carpet stuck out to Nikki. Had someone really swept and cleaned before they arrived? A petite woman sat at one of the two marble counters, staring into space. She appeared to be dressed for the day in jeans and a white cable-knit sweater, which made her skin look nearly as pale as the white cabinets.

"Honey, the sheriff is here. And the FBI." Jared looked at the two of them. "This is my wife, Christy. She was supposed to pick Taylor up last night at Menards after his shift."

Christy's gaze dropped to her lap. "I waited for ten minutes. His cell phone was off."

"I'm not blaming you." Jared squeezed her shoulder. "But we have to give the police all of the facts. Sheriff, Agent, please take a seat."

Jared stood next to his wife, his arm around her narrow shoulders.

"I think better on my feet." Nikki turned her attention to Christy. "Christy, can you tell us what happened? Why did you wait until this morning to report your son missing?"

Christy pushed her long, straight hair out of her eyes. "Taylor's done this a couple of times before, after he and I bickered. I thought yesterday was more of the same."

"What did you bicker about?" Miller asked.

"He was supposed to take the trash out the night before," Christy answered. "But he didn't, and we have extra garbage from the holiday. It's just going to sit in the garage for another week."

"He was angry with you when he left the house?"

"He wasn't happy," Christy answered. "The last time he did this was right after Halloween. He'd arranged a ride home after his shift without telling me, just to make me worry."

Nikki looked at Jared. "You didn't think anything of it?"

"I was at work until about five a.m. this morning," he answered. "I'm the chief attending plastic surgeon at Hennepin County Medical Center. By the time I got home, Christy and the kids were just getting up. She told me that Taylor hadn't come home or called." He glanced down at his wife. "The last time he did this, Taylor had texted me to let me know where he was. I hadn't heard from him."

Christy stiffened. "He promised me he wouldn't do that again."

Jared rubbed her back. "I called Menards and found out he never showed up for work. We reached out to a couple of friends to make sure he hadn't gone over there and just not told me because he skipped work."

"Christy, did anyone from Menards call about Taylor not showing up for work?" Nikki asked.

"No," she said. "They should have called me. That's why I just assumed he was doing this to hurt me. I had no idea he never made it into work." Christy pressed her hand against her mouth, fighting emotions.

"Are those the only friends' homes he'd go to?" Miller asked.

Both Jared and Christy nodded. "His circle is small. His two best friends are in band with him. Neena and Logan haven't heard from him since before school ended yesterday."

Nikki noted the names. "What does he play?"

"He's a drummer," Christy answered. "He's the only freshman to make the drumline for quads. Neena plays bass drum."

"And Logan?"

"Trumpet," Jared answered. "Kid is crazy talented. So is Taylor, but I play the drums. The trumpet mystifies me."

Miller leaned against the counter. "You're a blended family, correct?"

Both Halls nodded. "Jared has a son, Caden, from a previous relationship, and I had my daughter Amelia and Taylor from mine. Jared's the only father Taylor's known," Christy said. "He started calling Jared 'Dad' right away."

"His biological father isn't in his life?"

Christy flushed and looked down at her lap.

"Taylor's father left just after she had Taylor," Jared said. "Amelia never knew hers either."

"What happened?" Nikki asked.

Christy looked up, glaring at Nikki. "What does that matter?"

"We have to understand everything about a child's life in these cases," Nikki softened her tone. "I'm not judging you at all. We just need to know every little detail. Sometimes the smallest ones give us the answers. Is there a chance he might have been in touch with his father?"

"I can't see that," Christy said. "He hates him." She looked up at her husband. "What do you think?"

"I tend to agree," Jared said. "Taylor has never given me the impression he'd be interested in that." He squeezed Christy's shoulders again. "Go ahead, honey. This isn't about your past, it's about finding Taylor."

Christy brushed the tears off her cheeks. "After Taylor's father, Steve, left, I had no one to turn to for help," Christy said. "I was a foster kid. They threw me out when I got pregnant. I was so young and stupid, thinking that Steve was going to save me. Taylor was five weeks old when Steve disappeared, leaving me with rent and other bills I couldn't pay because I hadn't gone back to work yet. I ended up working on the streets and got pregnant with Amelia. I knew I couldn't raise two kids living like I was, so I took a job at McDonald's and worked as many shifts as I could. By the time Amelia came, I'd moved into a tiny, two-bedroom apartment in a decent area of Indianapolis." Christy focused on her French manicure. "I worked two jobs for a long time, but the three of us were close. It was us against the world."

"How did the two of you meet?" Nikki asked.

"I was working at the 1933 Lounge in Indianapolis. It's an upscale cocktail bar with fantastic tippers." Christy leaned against Jared. "It was love at first sight for me."

"Me, too," Jared said. "Seven months later, we were married. Taylor and my son Caden were co-ushers and Amelia was the flower girl."

"How long have you two been married?"

"Almost eight years." Jared squeezed Christy's shoulders.

"The kids all get along?"

"Oh yeah, Caden is a gentle soul," Jared said. "His mother died from breast cancer when he was a year old. I was in residency and my hours were awful. He spent more time with sitters than me until he met Christy." He squeezed her. "I'm so lucky they bonded."

Christy wiped her tears. "I fell in love with him even faster. He's mine."

Their love for the kids warmed Nikki's heart. "Tell us more about Taylor?"

"He's smart," Jared said. "Quiet." He looked at Christy. "Introvert, don't you think?"

"He is," she agreed. "He learned Spanish really quickly after Jared offered to teach him. The move from Indianapolis was hardest on him."

"Greenwood," Jared corrected her. "It's a suburb of Indianapolis. I hated to move the kids from school, but HCMC offered me more money as an attending, and they allow me to have office hours to work on cosmetic procedures." He shrugged. "I love working in the ER. I deal with all sorts of facial injuries, flexor sheath injuries in the hand, skin grafts. You get the picture."

"But the cosmetic stuff pays better?" Nikki assumed.

"Just a little bit, and when you have four kids, every dollar matters."

"Four?" Nikki asked.

"Penny is three," Christy said. "For the first time in my life, I'm able to be a stay-at-home mom. She's with Amelia and Caden."

"You worked before she was born?" Nikki asked.

"I did, but not at the bar. Jared got me an administrative job at county. We were together all the time."

"How did the older kids feel about the move?" Miller asked.

"Caden was fine with it," Christy said. "He's that kind of kid. Amelia was sad, but she understood and was excited for a change of scenery. Taylor wasn't happy at first, but he's a Twins fan, so he came around by the time we moved."

"No resentment about it?" Miller asked.

"Not that he really showed," Jared answered. "The only issue we've had—other than his and Christy's battles—was a fight at school. Taylor stood up to some kid who'd been bullying his sister. I don't have a problem with that, even if he did get suspended for a week."

"I do." Christy flushed. "Violence isn't the answer."

"Of course it isn't." Jared gave Nikki and Miller a look that made it clear he was only humoring his wife.

"You mentioned battles between the two of you," Nikki addressed Christy. "I have to ask, did they ever turn physical?"

"I would never hurt my children. Taylor hasn't forgiven me for his early childhood being so chaotic."

"He's also at the age where he thinks he knows everything."

"He doesn't talk to you the same way?" Nikki asked Jared.

"I don't have the past with him that Christy does," Jared

said. "And I think it's easier to be mean to flesh and blood sometimes."

"What do you mean, past?" Miller asked.

"It was still rough after Amelia was born for a few years," Christy said. "I couldn't always afford a babysitter and relied on Taylor too much." She covered her face with her hands. "It's all my fault. I've failed him from the beginning. I should have gone into Menards and talked to the manager instead of leaving and going to bed."

Miller asked for a list of friends and contacts in Indianapolis Taylor may have reached out to. Jared handed him a folded paper he'd taken out of his pocket. "I went ahead and wrote that down for you. I've also put Neena and Logan's information. They'll be at band practice."

"Do you mind if I look at Taylor's room?" Nikki asked. "It helps me get a feel for someone."

"Of course," Jared said. "The kids are upstairs. Should we call them down so you can talk to them before you head upstairs?"

"Please do. Do all three know what's going on?"

Jared retrieved his iPhone from his scrub pocket again and started texting. "Penny just knows Taylor's not here, but we told her he had to go to school early. One of us will distract her while you talk to Caden and Amelia. He hasn't called either one of them," Jared added. "That's what scares the hell out of me. Even if he was so mad at his mom that he decided not to keep me in the loop, he wouldn't put his siblings through this. Kids are headed downstairs."

Amelia led the way, her dark curls framing her face. Her eyes were red-rimmed from crying. Caden followed, holding little Penny's hands. She was blond like her father, but Jared's son Caden looked a lot more like Amelia than his dad.

Penny ran to her father, and Jared scooped her up, snuggling her neck.

"Why are all these people here?" she asked him. "Where's Taylor?"

"He's not here right now, sweet pea." Jared motioned for the older kids to sit at the table across from the counter. "Amelia, Caden, this is Sheriff Miller and FBI Agent Nikki Hunt."

Amelia stared at Nikki. "They called in the FBI?"

Nikki smiled at the two older kids. "Sheriff Miller asked me to help."

"Who's the FBI?" Penny wiggled in her father's arms.

"Nothing you need to worry about," Jared said. "Chris, I'm going to get her dressed while you guys talk."

Christy had been sitting silently, staring into space. She nodded at her husband. Jared looked at the older kids sitting at the table. "We don't care if you're keeping secrets for your brother. Hell, we don't have to know what they are. Mom can leave the room if you need her to, but you need to tell these people if Taylor confided something in you, okay?"

Amelia and Caden nodded. Jared left the room with Penny chattering the entire time.

"Your father is right." Christy finally spoke to her older children. "No one is going to be in trouble."

Caden and Amelia looked at each other but didn't say anything. Nikki walked over to the table and sat down across from them. "Can you tell us when you last talked to your older brother?"

"Yesterday morning, before school." Caden's voice cracked. "He had to work last night."

Amelia picked at her fingernails. "He texted me at lunchtime yesterday."

"About anything specific?" Nikki asked.

"Just about how bad lunch was." Amelia fought fresh tears. "I don't understand why he hasn't called at least one of us or told Dad where he is."

"Did you know about the last time?" Christy demanded. "That he texted Jared he was okay and let me worry all night?"

Both kids looked at each other but said nothing. Christy stood, shoving the barstool beneath the bar, making sure the stool lined up with the others at the counter. "I need to get some fresh air. You have my permission to continue talking to the kids." She left the big kitchen, taking most of the air out of the room.

"Mom's just worried," Caden said. "I'm sure she feels guilty."

"Why?" Miller asked.

"She always feels guilty about something," he answered. "She just worries a lot about everything being just right and doing everything just right."

"For Penny," Amelia corrected him. "She's trying to make up for me and Taylor's childhoods, even though we know she did the best she could."

"She seems to think Taylor has some resentment."

"He does," Amelia answered. "About the whole situation. But not really at her. She just takes it that way." Her eyes met Nikki's, and she could tell the teenager had realized they weren't helping their mom look any better in this situation. "She's a good mom. She's just never forgiven herself for some things."

"Sometimes it's easier to forgive other people for their mistakes than yourself," Nikki said. "Were you two up when your mom came back without Taylor?"

Both nodded. "She came upstairs and told us he'd done it again and checked our phones to make sure he hadn't texted us."

Fresh tears spilled from Amelia's eyes. "I told her not to worry, that he was probably being a brat again and to go to sleep. She probably would have gone looking for him if I hadn't."

Nikki wanted to hug her. "Honey, I don't think you're being fair to yourself. Your mom followed her instincts, and that's okay. We're not judging her. I know it's hard raising teenagers."

"Do you remember when your dad got home this morning?" Miller asked.

"He was home just as we were getting up at five thirty," Amelia said. "Why?"

"We just need to make sure we have the timeline right," Nikki said. "Your parents said Taylor had gotten into a disagreement with another student because they'd said something to you. Can you tell us about that?"

Amelia's eyes widened. "Why?"

"Because when someone goes missing, we have to talk to every single person they ever had an issue with," Nikki said. "We can't figure out what happened until we rule them out."

Caden nudged her. "Go ahead. Lynch should have to talk to the cops anyway."

"Adrian Lynch is a popular kid. He's a sophomore." Amelia worried her lower lip. "Mom and Dad don't know exactly what he said. Just that he was mean to me about my being half-Black."

Nikki had noticed the difference in skin tones, but genetics always surprised her. Amelia was light-skinned enough that she could have been white and taken after the other side of the family and just had a darker complexion. "I'm sorry that happened. Kids are cruel." She waited for Amelia to continue. "Guys, if there's more to it, we won't say anything to your parents unless it becomes crucial to bring Taylor home, I promise."

Caden nudged his sister again.

"Adrian's sister is in my grade, and I'd been to her house a few times. He asked me out, but I'm only thirteen and I said I wasn't allowed to date until I was sixteen. Then he laughed and said it was a joke, I was too fat and Black for him. Then he started calling me a slut."

Nikki and Miller looked at each other, disgust on both of their faces. "First off, he shouldn't have said that. It's not true, and no one should be judged like that. I promise you that kids like him are secretly insecure as hell. And some boys can't handle rejection. Men, too."

"Did the fight happen on school property?" Miller asked.

"In the high school parking lot," Amelia said. "The next morning. I thought Taylor was going to be in big trouble for getting suspended, and Mom yelled, but Dad said he did the right thing by sticking up for his sister, even though he shouldn't have laid hands on Adrian."

"Are you close friends with Adrian's sister?" Miller asked.

Amelia shrugged. "I thought I was until then. I went to her house a couple of times. Adrian has a school permit and picks her up from school sometimes. That's when it happened."

"How's school been for Taylor since?" Nikki asked.

"Some people bully him now because he hit a popular kid," Caden said. "But Taylor's a band geek. He spends his free time down there."

"Tell us about Taylor's friends," Miller said. "They're all in marching band?"

"Taylor played the quad drums at football games on the main drumline," Caden said. "He's really good."

"Do you guys play anything?" Nikki asked.

"Violin." Amelia didn't sound very happy about it.

"Not me," Caden said.

"Me either," Nikki answered. "I learned piano for a while, but I never practiced, so my parents stopped paying for lessons. Who are his closest friends?" She wanted to see if the siblings mentioned anyone different than their parents had.

"Neena and Logan," they both answered. "He doesn't really hang out with anyone but them."

"Are they both in concert band with Taylor? What time is practice?" Stillwater High School's impressive music department had several different options for students.

"They all do concert and jazz band." Amelia glanced at the clock. "Concert band practice starts in half an hour. Maybe he'll show up at school."

"We're headed there next," Miller said.

"You're not going to search for him?" Amelia asked.

"I've got my deputies out right now, and the police department is searching as well. We'll find him." He walked over to the table, intimidating in his uniform. "Is there anything else we should know? Any other secrets?"

Both shook their heads.

"Is he seeing anyone?" Nikki didn't like to make assumptions about sexuality, especially around younger generations. "Girlfriend? Boyfriend?"

"He's not dating anyone," Amelia said.

"Do you guys think he might go back to Indianapolis to stay with a friend?" His parents had disagreed, but Taylor's siblings likely knew him best.

"No way," Caden said. "He'd never leave us. Or Penny. He'd never put her through that."

Amelia nodded in agreement. "He's never stayed away this long. I'm really scared."

"I know." Nikki gave each one of the kids her business card. "You can ask your parents to call me any time for an update, or if you remember something. It may be something little and insignificant to you, but we still need to know."

"We don't have secrets," Amelia said.

Christy returned carrying a large, pink Stanley cup. "I'm sorry for getting up like that." She sipped from her cup. "I just needed a minute. All of this is just too much."

"Don't worry about it," Nikki assured her. "There's no playbook on how to handle this. We need everyone's part of the story to make a complete picture."

"Did the kids tell you anything to help find Taylor?" Christy asked.

"Nothing you don't already know," Nikki answered. "They both agree he wouldn't leave them and talked about how he'd be headed to band practice right now. Do you usually drive him?"

"Some days," Christy answered. "Some days Jared takes him because it fits his schedule."

"He never rides with a friend?" Miller asked. "Does he have his school permit yet?" In Minnesota, kids had to be sixteen to drive on their own, even with a school permit.

"He's still fourteen," Christy said. "And I wouldn't let him ride with a friend who just had a permit. He takes the bus unless Jared is able to take him."

"What about band practice?" Nikki asked. "I think marching band practices in the morning and evening sometimes, right? Did he ever ride home with a friend?"

"Logan," Christy said. "His mom gave Taylor a ride home a few times. But I usually picked him up. Why?"

"We need to know anyone he may have trusted enough to get into a vehicle," Miller said. "They just need to be eliminated as suspects." He checked his watch. "School starts at 8:35 a.m. What time does band practice start?"

"7:15," Christy answered.

"Any chance we could come back and look at Taylor's room?" Miller asked. "It's important for us to understand his mindset but given the time constraint, I think band practice is our next stop, especially since his closest friends are in the band. If anyone will know something, it's going to be them."

"What about us?" Christy said. "Are we just supposed to wait by the phone?"

"I'll make sure to have a deputy come by and update you in the next couple of hours if we aren't back." Miller reminded Christy that every available resource was being used just as Jared returned with a dressed Penny, her tangled hair wet and combed, the sweet scent of Johnson & Johnson baby shampoo surrounding her.

"What's going on?" Jared asked.

"As I told your wife, we've got deputies searching along with Stillwater PD, and they will be knocking on doors in the area. I'd like to get to the high school with Agent Hunt before band practice ends so we can catch the kids at once," Miller said. "We'll also start calling people on the list you gave us, and a deputy will be here to check in."

"Most cases like this end up with the kid coming home, right?" Jared asked. "He's probably holed up somewhere, punishing us."

"Do you think he'd do that to both of you?" Nikki asked. "Since he called you when he did this before?"

Christy drank from her cup before answering. "He might."

"Did the two of you argue over something I don't know about?" Jared asked, concern lacing his tone.

Christy stared at her husband. "No. It was his usual smart mouth and not doing what I told him to, that's all. Words were not exchanged beyond that. Did you take my side before?"

"Excuse me?"

"When he told you and not me, did you tell him that wasn't right?"

"Of course, and I told him if it happened again and he texted, I was coming to get him." Jared looked sheepish. "You're right. He probably wouldn't text me this time." He took a deep breath. "That's all this is. He's okay."

Christy closed her eyes and took another drink. "From your lips to God's ears."

ELEVEN

Before they left for the high school, Miller asked Nikki if she could have someone on her team contact Taylor's Indianapolis friends as well as the surrounding airports and public transportation. She called Liam while Miller called his chief deputy for an update on the ground search for Taylor Hall.

"We're not sure what we're dealing with yet," Nikki told her partner as she paced around Miller's big vehicle. "The family's insistent he wouldn't run away."

"They're usually the last ones to know," Liam said.

"He's very close with his siblings," she told him. "They're adamant he wouldn't leave town. Did you get the picture I texted? It's his most recent school photo."

"Yeah, looking at it now. I'll call the public transit authority in Indianapolis," Liam said. "They should be able to check buses and the train. Pretty sure Amtrak goes through there a few times a week. Hopefully they'll also be able to get me to the right people at Indianapolis Airport Authority."

Miller had wrapped up his call. "Keep me posted," Nikki told Liam as she climbed into the big Suburban. "We're trying to get to the high school before band practice ends."

"Deputy Reynolds is going through the CCTV around the high school." Miller accelerated through traffic. "They've talked to houses closest to the school. No one recognized Taylor's photo, so they're expanding the door knock area." He glanced at Nikki. "What do you make of the mom?"

"I'm not sure yet," she admitted. "She certainly seems to be in shock. I think Amelia's comments about her mother having guilt are interesting. Taylor's the oldest, so he's going to remember the bad times the best."

"Menards responded quickly this morning," Miller said. "Deputy Reynolds was able to confirm Taylor didn't show up for his shift. They also have Christy's SUV parked near the back employee entrance. Her story checked out."

"We should look at the CCTV near here, too," Nikki said. "Confirm both parents got home when they said they did."

"Jared emailed time-stamped security footage before I left," Miller said. "It doesn't look like it's been altered, but I'll have our techs make sure."

"I doubt it has been if he gave it that willingly," Nikki said. "He seems genuinely distraught."

"What do you think Christy put in that big Stanley cup?" Miller asked. "I thought her eyes looked glazed when we left, but I didn't smell anything."

"You can't smell vodka," Nikki reminded him. "But it could have been coffee for all we know."

"I want to know what friends and teachers have to say about the family dynamic," Miller said. "Who are you calling?"

"Chen," Nikki answered. "Voicemail." She left Chen a message asking for an urgent callback involving a missing teenager and then called Garcia to let him know about Taylor Hall.

"Damn it," Garcia said when she'd finished. "Could we have a serial kidnapper on our hands?"

"I'm not sure," Nikki said. "Chen told me yesterday they believe a family friend took Eli. I've contacted him about Taylor, but from everything Miller and I have heard so far, it seems like a stretch."

"Where are you on the cold case?" Garcia asked. "I read your email last night with the updates. Patrick said their family attorney handled the search for Ms. Smith. Did he say what the attorney actually did to find her? Did Spencer or anyone else sit for a sketch of her?"

"I don't know. It's so odd that no one knows Ms. Smith's first name, or if Smith is even her real last name," Nikki admitted. "I'd like for Liam to follow up on the dates and information from Patrick and Spencer, to confirm things as best we can. I have the family attorney's number, but I'd like to talk to them myself."

Garcia sighed. "Stephanie Bancroft called the office this morning. My administrative assistant took a message. The gist is that Stephanie is pissed, and you'd better call her today *or else*."

"Damn. Did she actually say 'or else'?" Nikki asked.

"She did," Garcia said. "I'll return the call and deal with her today, but you need to talk to her tomorrow, regardless of the new case."

Nikki thanked her boss and promised to update him on Taylor Hall throughout the day. "I can't wait to deal with Stephanie Bancroft." She glanced at Miller. "Did you read the email I sent last night?" After her call with Patrick, she'd forgone the UNO game and instead emailed Garcia, Liam and Miller the information Patrick had shared.

"Yeah, I did," Miller said. "I did a little research of my own last night. Started going through the county's unsolved cases, missing persons, looking for anything that remotely matched what we've been told about the Smiths." He blew through a yellow light. "There was a hit-and-run less than a mile from the

Hendricksons' place the same Saturday the family disappeared. Victim was a Hispanic female who'd given birth. She's still unidentified."

"So Ms. Smith ran for some reason," Nikki said, crestfallen. "That means the body in the trunk is likely Rebecca's." She and Miller sat in silence for a moment.

"We could still find the toddler," Miller reminded her. "I don't see any real connection between this cold case and our current missing kids, but the age bugs me. It all just bugs me. Something is off." He turned into the high school's massive parking lot.

The Halls lived less than fifteen minutes from the high school. Nikki had visited a few times since she'd returned to Stillwater, but the sheer size of the campus always shocked her. The horseshoe-designed building had always been large because it was the only high school in Washington County. It reminded Nikki of the government buildings, with a light-brick exterior and paved circle showcasing the United States flag, as well as the state flag.

"I still can't believe how different it looks since we went to high school." Nikki and Miller had been classmates, although they hadn't known each other back then. Miller had been a star football player, and Nikki had been in marching band the first couple of years of high school.

"Still Pony red, though." Miller parked in front of the school's main entrance, ignoring the parking rules. "After we talk to the principal, let's split up to cover the faculty and students. You want to go down and talk to the band kids, and I'll take the staff?"

"Fine with me," Nikki answered. "Does the principal know we're coming?" She followed Miller to the locked doors.

"No." Miller pushed the security button and waved his badge in front of the camera next to it. The door buzzed open.

Miller led the way through the doors to the front office near the entrance where they were buzzed through a second secure door.

A bottle-red, middle-aged woman greeted the two of them from behind the desk. "Can I help you?"

"We need to speak with Principal Carlson about a missing student."

"I'm Principal Carlson." An older woman stepped out of her open office door. "Is this about Eli Robertson?" Her voice shook. "Please tell us it's good news."

"Taylor Hall didn't make it to his shift at Menards yesterday afternoon," Miller said. "We're trying to locate him."

Principal Carlson's skin turned almost as gray as her hair. "Taylor is missing now, too?"

Miller introduced himself and Nikki. "We're searching for him, yes. But please keep that confidential. Can we talk in your office?"

"Of course."

They followed her into a mid-sized office filled with organized clutter. Nikki was impressed by the number of books about reading and critical thinking that lined the shelves behind the principal's desk. She motioned for them to sit.

"Do you think this is related to Eli?" Her gaze shifted from Miller to Nikki, a knowing glint in her eye. "I've seen you on the news, Agent Hunt. You work really bad cases. If you're here—"

"Nikki's not swamped with cases right now, so I asked her to come along," Miller said. "Two heads are always better than one."

Nikki smiled at the principal, hoping she believed Miller. "Nothing we've learned so far links the cases. Or says that this one is particularly 'bad' as you've put it. I'm just here to help. We're here to talk with Taylor's friends and the teachers who know him well."

"To answer your question about Eli, we don't know yet.

Can you see if Eli and Taylor had any classes together?" Miller asked.

Carlson opened the laptop sitting on her desk and typed for several long seconds. "No, they don't. Taylor's in concert band and Eli does theatre, so they may have interacted there. But no classes together." She looked at Nikki. "It's hard to think that we have two different people taking boys the same age, for different reasons."

Nikki decided to break one of her usual rules about giving out information—whether it was true or not. Tension drenched the small office, genuine fear in the principal's eyes. They had to stop panic before it started. "We suspect Taylor's taking some time to himself, but we still need to make sure we've spoken to everyone in his life. I'd like to get started with the band and the director."

Carlson seemed to relax a little bit. "All right. Holly?"

The woman from the front desk appeared in the doorway. "I couldn't help overhearing. I pray this isn't happening again."

"This is one of our paraeducators, Holly Black," Carlson said. "Could you please escort Agent Hunt to the music department?" Carlson looked at Miller. "I assume you'd like me to call in his teachers?"

Nikki had learned through Lacey's parent–teacher conferences that paraeducators were basically the teachers' helpers or assistants, which was what they were called when Nikki attended high school. She followed Holly out of the office into the massive building, fighting memories.

In 1993, Nikki's freshman class had been among the first kids to attend the newly built high school. Since then, the school had continued to grow into the sprawling campus it was today. If she hadn't been with Holly, she probably would have gotten lost.

"Things change fast," Holly answered when Nikki told her she couldn't recognize a single part of the building. "I've been here six years, and I'm amazed at how much certain things change every year. Usually technology." She laughed. "It moves way too fast for me to keep up with."

"Me too."

As they walked Nikki asked about Eli Robertson. "As I told Principal Carlson, we haven't seen anything linking Taylor to Eli's disappearance. But I'm not involved in Eli's case, so I don't have many details to compare. Do you know Eli?" With a student body of more than two thousand, she likely didn't know half the students' names. But given their limited knowledge about Eli's case, Nikki felt it was worth asking the question.

"I do," Holly answered. "I volunteered to help with the fall play. It was *The Outsiders*, and Eli played Randy, one of the rich kids. He was so good. Our last show was four days before he disappeared."

"What can you tell me about him?"

"He seemed to be well-liked," Holly answered. "Seemed to be friends with everyone. Or at least friendly."

"Did he have issues with anyone at school?" Nikki asked.

"Not at all," Holly answered. "He's close with his family, and his parents are both high achievers."

"He was walking home from school?" Nikki wanted to see if the information matched what Chen had told her yesterday.

"No, he was at the Jaycee Ball Fields, from what I've heard. They found his phone, but no sign of him." She put her hand over her heart. "A parent's worst nightmare. I don't know how you recover from the death of a child. I know he might still be alive, but it's been weeks now. After Scott Williams, I'm just terrified it's going to happen again."

Scott had also been a freshman when he disappeared and should have been a sophomore this year. Nikki had spoken with a lot of school staff during the initial days after Scott's disappearance, but Holly hadn't been one of them. "Did you know Scott?"

"No, and I'm selfishly happy that I didn't." Holly scanned her ID card to access the music department. Nikki heard the horns as soon as the doors opened.

Both the band and choir had been excellent during Nikki's time, and their successes at the state and national level over the years had led to a much larger space.

Memories flooded back as she neared the band room. She'd played clarinet in high school until her parents' murders, and she'd dropped everything but school. She'd enjoyed band, but Nikki was never serious enough about it to practice at home very often, so the clarinet was always stored in the instrument rooms.

She still had nightmares about not being able to find her clarinet in the sea of black cases.

"Was Principal Carlson going to call down and let him know we're coming?"

"I doubt it," Holly said as they neared the band room, the rich sound filling the corridor. "The music secretary doesn't come in for another hour, and Mr. Cohen ignores the phone during practice."

Holly stopped at the band room entrance. Definitely a larger room than she remembered, with several rows of tiered risers. Holly knocked hard on the open door several times before the band director finally signaled to stop.

"Can I help you?" His slim hands froze in midair, the conductor's baton in his right hand.

"Could we speak to you privately, Mr. Cohen?"

He scowled. "We're still in the middle of practice." Cohen raised the baton again, but Nikki cleared her throat, holding up her badge. High schools were breeding grounds for rumors, and they had to talk to the students, so it was only a matter of time before they all knew about Taylor. "Mr. Cohen, it's urgent."

The entire band stared at Nikki for a moment before the whispering started. Cohen put the baton on the music stand

and stepped down from the podium. His baby-blue sweater looked itchy, and his fair skin had splotches of red. Sweat lined the brow of his sandy-blond hair.

"You're an FBI agent? What's this about? Eli Robertson was in theatre, not band."

"My name is Nikki Hunt. I'm sorry to interrupt practice, but Taylor Hall is missing. I need to talk to the band together, as well as privately with his closest friends." Nikki's announcement sucked the air out of the room. She scanned the sea of faces, searching for any unusual reaction to the news. As much as Nikki hated coming in like this, time was of the absolute essence in these cases. If Taylor hadn't gone off on his own, they needed to find him in the first twenty-four hours. Their chances of finding him alive dropped substantially after that.

"Missing?" Cohen pushed his floppy hair off his forehead. "How could he be missing? I assumed he was sick like Logan."

Nikki checked her mental notes from earlier. "He's one of Taylor's close friends?"

Cohen nodded. "He left a message saying he had the flu. Are you sure Taylor isn't with him?"

"His parents called there first," Nikki said. "We'll be heading to speak with Logan, but right now, I need to speak with anyone in Taylor's orbit. Would you mind telling the kids?"

"Aren't you going to do that?" Cohen asked.

"I can," Nikki answered. "But I thought you might want to make the initial announcement since they have a relationship with you. Ms. Black is here to act as guardian while I talk to the kids since they're all minors. We'll need somewhere more private."

Cohen's red cheeks paled. He turned on his heel, motioning for her to follow him to the podium. He stepped onto the podium, the baton visibly shaking. "I'm afraid I have some unfortunate news." His Adam's apple stuck out of his thin throat as he spoke. "As Agent Hunt said, Taylor Hall has disappeared." He paused as the entire band gasped. "He's probably fine, but of course law enforcement has to take his disappearance seriously. Agent Hunt is going to tell you more."

He stepped down and offered her the podium. Nikki felt foolish standing on it, but she wanted to see the back of the room, where the drumline stood in shock. "Thanks, Mr. Cohen." She looked out at the sea of eyes, holding her badge for everyone to see. "My name is Nikki Hunt, and I'm a Special Agent with the FBI. As Mr. Cohen said, Taylor Hall hasn't been heard from since he left school yesterday afternoon to walk to his job at Menards. He didn't show up to work and wasn't there when his mom came at the end of his shift." She scanned the shocked faces in front of her. "Right now, we still think it's possible Taylor went somewhere on his own. That's why we need to talk with his friends. No one is in trouble or being accused of anything. I'm just trying to piece together Taylor's day yesterday. Who's closest with Taylor?"

Half the drumline's hands raised. "Okay, I'd like to talk to each one of you privately. Mr. Cohen, is there somewhere quiet we could go?"

"The smaller practice rooms are just down the hall," he said. "They should be unlocked."

Nikki pointed to the dark-haired girl standing next to the bass drum—the only female bass drummer. "You're Neena, right?" She smiled, trying to set her at ease. "The Halls spoke highly of you." Nikki knew how quickly certain types of kids could turn Nikki's focus on Neena into a weapon. "Why don't we talk first?

"Ms. Black is sitting in because you're a minor," Nikki told Neena when they reached the practice room. "She understands that everything you tell me stays here since it's an active case." Nikki glanced at the paraeducator to make sure she got the message.

Holly smiled encouragingly at Neena. "Absolutely. I can leave if you prefer—"

"I'd like you to stay," Nikki said. "Interviewing minors without a parent or another adult isn't ethical. And it's scary, I'm sure." She smiled at Neena, who'd yet to speak a word.

Her dark eyes met Nikki's. "I've seen you on crime shows on ID. If you're here, he's not just missing. This is bad." Her lower lip quivered.

Nikki wanted to give her a hug. "How long have you known Taylor?"

"Since band camp last August."

"Tell me more about him," Nikki encouraged.

"He's a really good drummer," Neena said. "We both played quads for marching band and ended up next to each other. I don't know how familiar you are with school bands," Neena said. "But band camp is really intense. You learn the routine for the fall, and it's worse for freshmen."

"I actually played clarinet my first couple of years in high school," Nikki said. "Please tell me the band uniforms aren't wool anymore. My sophomore year, it was really hot for the first home football game. Something like ten degrees above average, even at night. My friend nearly passed out."

"They're still wool," Neena said. "Itchy and awful."

"Seriously?"

"You can get uniforms in Dac Wool, which is a blend of wool and polyester, or even a hundred percent polyester. Wool's the most expensive and the material breathes better." Neena shrugged. "If we were in the south, I'm sure we'd go polyester. But those October games can be frigid."

"Fair point," Nikki replied. "I love drumlines. How many quads do you have?"

"Six during marching band season," she answered. "Taylor and I had to try out, and the rest are older kids. I think that's part of the reason we bonded. Freshmen aren't usually good enough for marching band drumline."

"Did you and Taylor get flack for that?"

"Not really," she said. "The older kids have been pretty cool."

"His parents said he's been dealing with some bullying. Do you know anything about that?"

Neena made a face. "Adrian Lynch. He's a sophomore and a total douchebag. Sorry."

"Don't be, I've known plenty of them," Nikki said. "What exactly happened?"

Neena bit her lower lip. "Didn't his parents or sister tell you?"

"They did, but kids your age tend to tell their friends the more accurate version," Nikki said. "I'm not judging him if he kept the details from his parents, but I do need to know the truth."

"A couple of weeks before Halloween, Adrian Lynch asked Amelia out in front of a crowd of her friends. She's friends—or was—with Adrian's sister. She told him her parents wouldn't let her date until she was sixteen." Neena sipped from her water bottle. "He called her a fat slut, started making fun of her in front of half her class, because they were waiting on the bus. Other kids started chanting, too."

"Kids can be awful," Nikki said.

"Taylor and Logan came to my house after band practice. Amelia called crying and told him what happened. That's the first time I'd seen him angry. Logan and I had to keep him from leaving my house to find Adrian."

"So he confronted him the next morning?"

Neena nodded. "He walked up behind Adrian in the high school parking lot, grabbed his shoulder, turned him around and hit him right in the face before Adrian knew what happened."

"You saw this?" Nikki asked.

"Logan did," she answered. "They were walking from band practice to first period."

"What did Adrian do?"

"He jumped at Taylor, and they rolled around on the floor fighting until one of the assistant principals broke it up." Neena scowled. "Poor perfect specimen got popped in his smart mouth. Taylor was suspended for a week, and Adrian just three days."

"Perfect specimen?" Nikki asked.

"That's what he calls himself." She rolled her eyes. "Adrian, I mean. He told one of his friends, who was nice enough to tell someone else." Neena smirked.

"Tell me about Logan," Nikki said. "The Halls mentioned he was another close friend."

"Uh, not much to tell," she said. "Logan and I have been friends since fifth grade. We started in percussion together, but Logan switched to trumpet. Taylor just fit in with us." Her eyes widened. "I need to text him. He has some kind of stomach bug."

"Actually, would you mind letting me tell him?" Nikki had to consider all of Taylor's friends as suspects at this point. She didn't want Logan to have time to come up with a story, but she couldn't tell Neena. "Initial reactions usually contain the most details. You don't think Taylor could be hiding out there for some reason?"

"And not tell his siblings?" Neena shook her head. "He's had his issues with his mom, but he loves his brother and sisters. He wouldn't leave them there."

Nikki homed in on her admission. "You mean with their parents? Why not?"

"It's more their mom. Taylor doesn't talk much about his dad, at least he doesn't complain about him. But he and his mom fight a lot."

"What do they fight about?"

"Everything," Neena answered. "Stupid daily stuff. She tells him to do something, and he doesn't want to, that sort of thing."

"He's just that way with Christy?" Nikki clarified. "Did he ever say why?"

"Not really," she answered. "Just that she was a mess until she met Jared. I think he's got some bad memories from when he was little. He doesn't like to talk about it."

"Has he talked about running away? Maybe going back to Indianapolis to be with friends?"

"No," Neena said. "He likes this school and band, and like I said, he would never leave his siblings. He and Amelia are only eleven months apart, and Caden's not that much younger. And he adores little Penny."

"He and Jared seem close, though, right?" Nikki had to consider the Halls as suspects as well. Nine times out of ten, missing kids were taken by someone close to them.

"I didn't know Jared wasn't his real dad until he told me," Neena answered. "Jared bought his first set of drums. He plays, too."

"I'm sure it's noisy when they're together." Nikki smiled. "Have you spent much time at his house?"

"Yeah, me and Logan have been over there plenty of times. His mom always makes a fuss. She's nice."

Nikki caught the note in her voice. "But?"

"I don't know," Neena said. "She just tries so hard, you know? Like, she'll make cookies or cupcakes for us, but she doesn't let them get snacks out of the cupboard, and they have to drink water or milk. She's always cooking, the house is always perfect. It's like she's afraid we won't like her or something. I think she's trying to make up for the bad times. Amelia told me her mom can't forgive herself for stuff. Taylor never wanted to talk about that sort of thing, though."

Nikki asked her a few more questions about the rest of

Taylor's friends, making sure she had all their names. Neena backed up the family's claim that his circle was small and while he was friendly with other kids in the band, he only spent time outside of school with Neena and Logan. "Thanks for not texting Logan."

"Yeah, but I bet he knows by now. The drumline has a group text chat."

"That reminds me, Taylor's iPhone is older and doesn't have GPS capability if it's not on."

Neena snickered. "I know, we tease him all the time."

Nikki glanced at Holly, who'd been listening intently without interrupting. "Listen, Neena. I know every kid has secrets. I don't care if Taylor has things he hides from his parents. I'm not going to rat him out if he does, but is there any chance he could have another phone? Maybe one that he paid for himself that his parents don't know about?"

Neena seemed genuinely surprised at the question. "I've never seen him with any other one."

"What about social media?"

"His parents are kind of strict about that. They're allowed to have Instagram, but Taylor had to beg them for Snapchat."

Snapchat's biggest draw was that it never saved any photos. The user had to take a screenshot, and the app informed the other person when the shot was taken. Nikki assumed the initial goal had been an effort to protect the user's privacy, but it also created a swamp for predators. "How did he convince them?"

"That's where all of the band group chats are, because everyone else has Snapchat. Me and Logan showed Jared the group chats and explained, and he finally agreed. He already does random phone checks to make sure there's nothing shady. My mom does the same thing."

Snapchat would be useless in determining the phone's location. "I'm going to talk to Mr. Cohen and anyone else you think I should, and then I'll head to Logan's. Where does he live?"

"Over by Bayport nature preserve."

First period had started by the time Nikki wrapped up her interview with Neena, so Holly escorted her back to gather her things and fetch Mr. Cohen.

"Please come back for me after I've finished with Mr. Cohen," Nikki told Holly. "I'll need to talk to Adrian Lynch."

Holly nodded. "I assumed you would. I'll send Tom right down."

TWELVE

Mr. Cohen joined her in the practice room after Holly had returned Neena to class. He sat down across from Nikki, red splotches across his fair cheeks. A thin line of sweat beaded his forehead, his blond hair standing on end. He crossed his legs, tapping his penny loafers against the floor. He fanned the collar of his button-down shirt. "Why did I wear wool today?"

Nikki pointed to his sweaty forehead. "Is that all from conducting?"

"I'm very animated," Cohen said. "Keeps me skinny."

"Can you think of any other band kids I should talk to other than Neena and Logan?"

Cohen shook his head, his blond hair flopping in his face. "I've only ever seen him with those two." He leaned forward. "He's just run off, right? You don't think something bad has happened?"

"My job is to assume something bad has happened," Nikki said. "What makes you think he might run away?"

"He wouldn't," Cohen answered. "He's working on a solo for the state competitions, along with two different quartets. He's serious about his music."

"What about his family?" Nikki asked. "Do you think he'd leave them?"

"I have no idea," Cohen said. "I don't talk to students about their personal lives. We barely have enough time to practice as it is."

Normally, Nikki would press the issue, but Cohen's sincerity was impossible to ignore. "Isn't it unusual in such a big marching band to have two freshmen quads?"

Cohen sat up straighter. "Last year, I would have said yes. But Neena and Taylor are both exceptional. Their commitment level blew me away. And they knew the music and routine better than some of the other kids in the line. That's all I care about."

"Do you do individual lessons with every kid?"

"God, no. Individual lessons are reserved for kids competing in state competitions," Cohen answered. "In addition to regular band practice, I practice with each instrument group twice a week, after school."

"Taylor was preparing for a competition, right?"

"Yes," Cohen answered. "He practiced with me during the lunch hour. I play the drums as well. I don't know how familiar you are with high school band culture, but most percussionists don't do individual solos. I did when I was in school, so I was excited for Taylor."

"So even though you didn't talk about personal things, you spent frequent time with him during the school day?"

"I suppose so."

"Did you guys practice at lunch yesterday?"

Cohen's brow furrowed. "Not as long as usual. Taylor said he had a headache, so we just ran through a few things."

"Did you notice anything else other than him having a headache?"

"Honestly, I wasn't sure that he had a headache," Cohen

said. "He didn't seem to be suffering from the noise. He did seem like he had something on his mind."

"How so?"

"He was very quiet," Cohen said. "I assumed it was illness or whatever, but he just didn't have his usual energy or focus. When he didn't arrive this morning, along with Logan, I assumed they'd both gotten sick."

"How was he before the holiday break?"

"Normal. Excited for Christmas and time off school."

"Did you have any band practice that week?"

"No," Cohen said. "The obsessive director in me wants to have practice that week, but I remember how much that can mess up a break. That just turns kids off band."

"I know you don't talk about personal things with the kids because of time constraints—"

"Not just that," Cohen said. "I don't want to get involved in their personal lives. It's about music for me."

Nikki nodded. "Even so, would Taylor come to you if he were in danger or if something was wrong at school?"

"I doubt it," Cohen answered. "The only personal conversations I've had are about his prior music experience and whether his sister will play next year. I do know he's close with his dad. He plays drums, too."

"What about his mom, Christy?"

"I've only met her once, after the fall concert. She was nice but didn't talk a lot."

"She let Jared do all the talking?"

"I wouldn't say that," Cohen said. "Her pupils were dilated, and I couldn't understand her."

"She was under the influence?" Nikki clarified. "At his band concert?"

Cohen held up both hands in defense. "I can't say for sure. I don't want to make accusations. Everyone has their issues."

"But you thought so at the time?" Nikki pressed. "That was your gut reaction?"

"Yes," Cohen said.

Nikki handed him one of her cards with her work cell and personal cell numbers. "If you remember anything else, however minute, please call. You'd be surprised how many times a little bit of innocuous information blows a case wide open."

Cohen nodded and stood. He adjusted the belt holding up his baggy khakis and smoothed his hair. "Please let me know if there's anything else I can do."

"One last question," Nikki asked as Cohen reached for the doorknob. "Where were you after school yesterday?"

He turned around slowly, his blue eyes hard. "Excuse me?"

"I have to know in order to cross you off the suspect list," Nikki said. "We're asking everyone who had contact with Taylor."

Cohen sighed. "I left here around six thirty, after quartet practice. Stopped at the grocery and then went home."

"Do you have a receipt from the grocery?" Nikki asked. "We can ask for their CCTV, but if you can show me now, it would save time."

Cohen retrieved his wallet from his back pocket and rifled through the billfold. "Here. I don't need it." He handed her the crumpled paper.

Nikki looked the receipt over, confirming the time and took down his address. "Hopefully CCTV footage nearby picks up your car arriving and that'll be it." She studied the band director, trying to figure out if he was just the anxious sort or really had something to hide. "The other option would be looking at the geo-tracking on your phone. It would show your exact path." She smiled.

Cohen tucked his wallet back into his pocket. "I don't have

it on me. If you can't figure it out with the CCTV, let me know." He turned around and walked out, leaving the door open and Nikki still confused about where Taylor Hall had gone.

Holly Black walked Nikki from the music department to Adrian Lynch's calculus class on the other side of the building. The high school had been big when she attended, but it had grown so much Nikki wondered how often kids were late to class just because of the distance they had to cover.

Holly pointed to the closed door ahead of them. "Adrian Lynch's class. Let me speak to the teacher and bring Adrian out."

"Thank you," Nikki said. "The principal should have let the teacher know we were stopping by."

She waited in the hall while Holly spoke to the calculus teacher. She emerged a couple of minutes later with a tall woman with dark glasses and an even darker look on her face. A tall, blond boy followed her, hands in his pockets and eyes on the floor.

Holly introduced the math teacher and Adrian. "As the principal already told you, Taylor Hall is missing. Agent Hunt is leading the search for him." She looked directly at Adrian, who immediately looked away. "Ms. Farber, you and I are here to ensure Adrian's rights aren't violated. That sounds terrible, doesn't it? He's a minor and Agent Hunt wants to make sure he's protected."

Adrian's shoulders relaxed a bit, and he finally snuck a glance at Nikki. He was a nice-looking kid, blond hair and striking blue eyes. The smirk playing on his lips showed his true character. "I'm not friends with Taylor."

"Oh, I know." Nikki returned the condescending smile. "You and Taylor have had some issues, right?"

"So?" Ms. Farber cut in. "Plenty of kids have issues with each other. That doesn't mean he did something."

Nikki looked at the teacher in silence for a few seconds. "I just need Adrian to answer."

"I thought we were supposed to protect him?" Farber crossed her arms over her chest.

"From my putting words in his mouth, eliciting a false confession, pressuring him. That's what can't happen," Nikki said. "Honestly, it's as much for my protection as his. Adrian, can you tell me what happened between you and Taylor?"

"We don't like each other." Adrian shrugged.

Nikki changed tactics. "You understand that I already know what happened, right? I'd like to hear your version of events."

Adrian's eyes flashed, but before he could speak, Holly stepped in. "If you can't cooperate, we can go down to Principal Carlson's office."

He glared at her for a moment. "I asked his sister out. He didn't like it because she's younger."

Nikki waited, her eyes locked with Adrian's. His expression sank as he realized he wasn't in control right now. "Fine. I was shitty when she turned me down. She lied and said her parents wouldn't let her date, and that's bullshit. I know better."

"Really?" Nikki asked. "How would you know better?"

"She and my little sister have some classes together in middle school," Adrian said. "My sister said that Amelia left a pregnancy test in the bathroom trash."

Holly and Ms. Farber gasped. Nikki didn't flinch. "Did your sister see Amelia put the test in the trash?"

"No, but she'd been the only one in the bathroom and it was on the top."

"That your sister knew of," Nikki said. "I don't know off the top of my head how many girls attend her middle school, but that test could have belonged to anyone. Unless your sister's a hall monitor and kept track of everyone using the restroom?"

Adrian's cheeks turned red. "No. But when I confronted Amelia about it, I could tell it was true."

He might be telling the truth. Nikki needed to speak with Amelia in private. But Adrian didn't need to know any of that. Amelia had told him no, and that should have been the end of it. "You and Taylor still had issues even after the suspension, correct?"

"We stay away from each other."

Ms. Farber shifted on her feet, rubbing her temples. "I'm sorry, I have a migraine, and these hall lights make it worse. Can we wrap this up?"

Nikki almost told the teacher to go back in and do her job since Holly had stayed with them. "I'm almost done. Adrian, what time did you leave school yesterday?"

His jaw twitched. "Hockey practice is at three. It was done at five thirty. I was home before six p.m."

"What did you do between the time school let out and practice?"

"Went to Culver's with a couple of friends. Got some fries and a shake. You can check my receipts."

"I will." Nikki didn't know if this kid was involved, but she didn't like his attitude. "We'll check Culver's security cameras, too, and we're looking at all the CCTV around the school and surrounding area. Do you understand what I'm saying?"

"Yup." Adrian's hands were back in his pockets. "I'm telling the truth."

"We're done here." Ms. Farber took Adrian's elbow and guided him towards the math room. The door shut behind them.

"Is she a friend of the family?" Nikki asked.

"I have no idea," Holly said. "She's got a reputation for being difficult, though."

Nikki checked her messages during the walk back to the principal's office. Chen hadn't returned her call, but Liam had spoken to public transit and airport officials in Indianapolis, as well as requesting flight logs from all flights between

Minneapolis and Indianapolis since yesterday afternoon, just in case Taylor had paid cash for a ticket. So far, Liam hadn't found any evidence that Taylor had gone back to his hometown.

As they neared the front office, Miller's angry voice carried down the hall. He paced in front of the office, barking into the phone.

"What's going on?" Holly asked the principal.

Principal Carlson flushed. "Taylor's final period yesterday had a sub. We didn't realize he'd skipped until the teacher arrived this morning and looked at the sub's notes." She sighed in frustration. "First time we've had this sub. He's fresh out of school, and I had a bad feeling about his attitude."

"Not your fault." No point in berating the school staff, but that missing hour could change the course of the investigation. Nikki turned to Miller, who'd just ended his call. "I assume you're having more CCTV pulled?"

Miller nodded. "I've got Deputy Reynolds pulling footage an hour earlier and checking the routes. I'm also having them look at older videos to verify his usual path to work. Hopefully we'll have the information shortly."

Nikki liked Chief Deputy Reynolds. She had worked with him on a few cases and had been impressed by his calm demeanor and focus on detail. She motioned for Miller to follow her into the hall for privacy.

"What did the band people say?" he asked.

Nikki quickly went over what she'd learned. "Adrian, the kid Taylor fought with, claims his younger sister told him Amelia threw away a pregnancy test in the school bathroom."

"Did she see her toss it?"

"She found it in the trashcan after Amelia had left. It was" —Nikki checked her notes—"on top, so Amelia must have been the one to put it there."

Miller rolled his eyes. "Could have been anyone, including a teacher."

"I know," Nikki said. "Adrian says that's why Taylor attacked him. But it sounds like he's got a decent alibi."

"Except we know now that Taylor left an hour earlier than everyone thought," Miller reminded her. "Let's get Adrian's schedule and see if he had any free periods."

They went back into the office and asked for Adrian Lynch's schedule the day before. She was disappointed to see Adrian would have been in class during the final period, but that didn't necessarily mean he wasn't involved. "And I believe Logan is absent today," Nikki said to the principal.

"Yes." Principal Carlson shuffled through some papers on the counter. "His mother called him out for the stomach flu."

"What can you tell me about him?" Nikki asked.

"Logan? I haven't had much interaction with him, but that's a good thing. His attendance record is good. I can have his Pony Center counselor call you, though."

Nikki had learned about the Pony Center investigating Scott's disappearance. With such a massive student body, having personal contact with every single kid was a tough task. The school had split the student body into four alphabetical groups, with a counselor assigned to each group.

Principal Carlson typed something into the computer on the front counter. "Logan Thompson. That's the Black Pony Center." And that was the same for Scott Williams. The counselor hadn't been able to tell them much about Scott other than he was quiet, made decent grades and didn't share much about his life.

"Can you give me Taylor's, too, as well as his counselor's name?"

"Gray Pony Center," Carlson answered. "So that's Tara Fink."

"Remind me how to get to the Pony Center," Nikki said.

"It's right here, on the other side of the building." Carlson handed her a map. "But I'll have Holly escort you. I'll call and let them know you're coming. If you're also headed to Taylor's, I'll let the assistant principal in charge of the Gray Pony Center know you're on the way."

THIRTEEN

Miller and Nikki decided to talk to the counselors while they waited for Reynolds to send the updated CCTV footage. Nikki's phone vibrated with a text from Matt Kline, asking for an update. She quickly let him know they were searching for a missing teenager and would get back to him when she could.

"What did Taylor's teachers say about him?" Nikki asked Miller as they followed Holly through the school.

"Good student, pleasant to everyone but doesn't seem to be close to a lot of kids, just his band friends. Only issue he's had is with Adrian Lynch."

Holly led them to the north wing of the high school. First period was still in session, but students in the halls stopped and stared at the sight of Miller in his uniform and Nikki, her FBI badge attached to the Frank Costanza "Serenity Now" badge reel Courtney had given her for Christmas.

Holly used her own badge to open the door to the Pony Center area. "Technology makes things so much easier. Even the kids can access certain areas with their student IDs."

During Nikki's high school years, security had consisted of a couple of guards and front doors that were unlocked early for

before-school activities. They remained unlocked and the
school accessible until the custodians locked up for the night.
Everything had been different then; the Columbine massacre
hadn't happened yet, and school still felt like a relatively safe
haven. She couldn't imagine having to worry about getting shot
at school in addition to all the other anxiety that came with high
school.

A stocky man with salt-and-pepper hair and a small woman
with big glasses and a concerned expression greeted them.
Holly introduced Mrs. Fink and Assistant Principal Brad
Jameson to Nikki and Miller before heading back to the main
office.

"Thank you for your help this morning," Nikki told Holly
before she left. She handed Holly one of her business cards.
"Please call if you hear anything, however minimal."

Assistant Principal Jameson led them to a small conference
room and offered them something to drink.

"No, thank you," Miller answered as everyone sat down. "I
trust the principal told you why we're here?"

Both nodded. "I know you're labeling him as a missing
person," Mrs. Fink said, "but I bet he just went somewhere. Did
his family give you contact information for his friends in Indianapolis?"

"We have them," Nikki told her. "Do you think he'd take off
like that without telling his friends or siblings?"

Mrs. Fink shook her head. "I'm trying not to think the
worst. First Eli Robertson, now him."

"Do you think this is related to Eli's disappearance?"
Johnson asked.

"It's too early to tell," Miller said. "Did Eli and Taylor have
any classes or extracurriculars together?"

"No," Johnson said. "Eli loved theatre, and the orchestra
handles the music, not the band. I don't remember Eli ever

talking about Taylor. Or vice versa." He looked at Mrs. Fink. "Did Taylor ever mention Eli?"

"Not before he went missing," Fink answered. "Taylor brought me a Christmas gift the day we left for break. He mentioned how sad it was for Eli's family. That's the first time I'd heard him mention him."

"I didn't know kids gave gifts in high school like that," Nikki said.

"Most don't," Johnson said. "But his mom made goodie bags for each teacher. Best peanut butter fudge I've ever had."

Nikki wasn't surprised to hear Christy had made such an effort. It lined up with what she'd learned about her from Amelia and Neena.

"How did Taylor seem before break?" Nikki asked.

"Fine," Fink answered. "Excited for the time off like all of us. I didn't get a chance to see him yesterday."

"We know about the fight with Adrian Lynch," Miller asked. "Did Taylor tell you what it was about?"

"Taylor said that Adrian disrespected his sister," Fink said. "Taylor knew he'd get in trouble, but it was important for him to defend his sister."

"He ever show any sign of anger issues beyond that incident?" Miller asked. "Or give any hint about issues at home?"

"Taylor's not an angry kid." Fink looked at Johnson, who nodded. "He and his mother have certainly had their battles."

"Can you elaborate?" Nikki asked.

"A lot of it's normal teenaged stuff," Fink answered. "But Taylor carries some resentment for his mother, I think. He's mentioned their lives being bad before his dad came into the picture."

"Jared, you mean?"

Fink smiled. "Yes, and it just warms my heart. There are plenty of good stepparents out there, but their close relationship is something I don't see very often. Taylor glows whenever he talks about his dad."

"How often does he talk about his relationship with his mother?" Nikki asked.

"Not often," Fink said. "He never really came to me for a counseling session, per se. He was a happy kid. But it was obvious their relationship isn't the same as his and his dad's. He didn't have to tell me much about before Jared came into their lives for me to know he had issues with his mom. I noticed he seemed more tense when he talked about her."

"Did he give you the impression he was afraid of her?"

"No," Fink said. "It was more exasperation and bitterness," Fink continued. "She keeps a perfect house and stays home to take care of his youngest sister. I got the impression Christy tries very hard to make up for the past, but in all the wrong ways. Taylor did tell me she cares more about appearances than them sometimes. He walked that comment back, but I knew he meant it."

"Back to the fight with Adrian Lynch," Nikki asked. "How was Taylor when he came back from suspension?"

"The same, as far as I know," Fink said. "His grades are steady. He participates in class and hasn't had an issue with anyone else."

"Agreed," Johnson said. "I'm in charge of bringing kids back in after suspensions, making sure things go smoothly. I haven't been around him as much as Mrs. Fink, but he didn't seem any different to me."

"What about friends?" Miller asked.

"He only talked about Neena and Logan," Fink said. "I got the impression he was friendly with everyone but kept his circle very small. He didn't share a lot of personal information in class like some kids do."

"I know you can't tell us anything Logan or Neena have told you in confidence, but did Taylor ever mention being angry or fighting with one of them? Or where he might go if he did?" Miller asked.

"No," Fink answered. "He just didn't share that much about his life. I can say I never heard him say anything negative about them."

"And Logan has an exemplary record," Johnson said. "Neena, too."

"I've spoken to Neena already," Nikki said. "But Logan isn't at school today. His mother called him in sick."

"You think they could be together?" Johnson asked. "Logan's counselor is in a meeting, but I don't think Logan would defy his parents like that. And his mother called in. She's an accountant, works from home."

Neena had already given her Logan's address, but Nikki had been worried about Logan being a minor home alone when they showed up to talk to him.

Nikki and Miller both left their information with the counselor and Assistant Principal Jameson escorted them to the main entrance and promised to let them know if he learned anything more.

Northern wind made Nikki's face feel like an ice block. Miller checked his phone and cursed. "Reynolds is still working on getting CCTV."

"Let's head to Logan's then," Nikki said. "I'm sure Neena has told him. And it sounds like his mom should be there. Surely Reynolds will have the footage by then."

"Honestly, I'm not sure this kid didn't just disappear for a while," Miller said, starting his SUV. "Maybe he's trying to punish his mother for something."

"I don't know. It doesn't sound like he'd do that to his siblings," Nikki reminded him. "But everyone has secrets."

"The obvious suspect is Christy," Miller said. "Maybe she did pick him up and they argued, and something happened."

"Taylor's taller than his mom," Nikki said. "I don't think she could physically overpower him."

"But if she was driving, she could have had something in her hand and snapped," Miller said. "Hits him harder than intended."

Nikki couldn't dismiss it outright. "Then Christy manages to drag him out of the vehicle and leave him somewhere?" The idea didn't sit well with her. "At this point, I'd believe that Taylor ran off before Christy hurt him. And we don't have enough for a search warrant for her Tahoe."

"Yet," Miller answered. "Let's see what Logan knows. And we need to talk to Jared separately. Get him away from his wife and see if he shares anything else."

"I want to go back and look at Taylor's room after we talk to Logan and his mother," she reminded Miller. "Hopefully I can talk to Christy privately then." She unlocked her phone and quickly found Logan's social media profiles on Instagram and Snapchat and skimmed through the last couple of weeks. He posted a couple of times a day, usually about band or something after school.

Nikki logged into Facebook next. Logan didn't have an account, but his mother did. Like everyone else, her Facebook page showed only the good parts of their lives. They'd had a wonderful Christmas, attending Midnight Mass on New Year's Eve. Logan was an only child, so his mother's page mostly revolved around him. From all appearances, he did well in school and band and didn't get into trouble. She scrolled through the photos, noting one of a smiling Taylor, Logan and Neena in their marching band uniforms after a football game. The photo was several months old, but Taylor appeared as happy as his friends.

Miller took the exit for Bayport, a small township within Washington County, close to St. Croix Prep Academy and the St. Croix Savanna Scientific and Natural Area, a large swath of protected land monitored by the Department of Natural Resources. "His house borders all that protected land. Even though it's cold, that's a good place for a kid to hide to punish his parents. I'll have a deputy fly a drone over the area and see if anything pops out."

Nikki exited the vehicle while he sent a message to his deputy and admired the two-story modern Craftsman with white trim. Bayport was a growing area, with home prices increasing as new houses like this one popped up.

"Nice place." Miller joined her and they headed up the cleared sidewalk. "Small lots here, though."

"Limited space with the preserve," Nikki said. "They shouldn't have tried to cram so many homes around it."

Clear Christmas lights decorated the front of the house, and a beautiful wreath hung on the front door, which opened before they'd reached the porch.

A petite woman with a stylish bob and a worried look stepped onto the porch. She looked at Sheriff Miller. "Logan got a text from his friend saying that Taylor Hall is missing. I'm hoping you found him, but I assume that's not the case."

"Not yet." Miller introduced himself and Nikki. "Can we talk to Logan for a few minutes?"

"Of course." She shook their hands. "Renee."

Inside, the home still appeared new, with a cherry-wood floor leading from the living area to the kitchen. Windows lined the back of the house, a freestanding counter with a granite top separating the kitchen from the living area.

Logan sat in the recliner near the fireplace, looking pale and scared. His blond hair stood on end. He stared at Nikki and Miller. "You didn't find him yet?"

Renee encouraged them to sit on the couch.

"Not yet." Nikki sat down at the end of the couch closest to Logan. "I know you're sick, but do you feel like answering some questions?"

Logan nodded as Renee perched on the recliner's arm.

"When was the last time you heard from Taylor?" Nikki asked.

"Lunch yesterday," Logan answered. "My schedule is different than his, so lunch is the last time we see each other before school ends."

"How did he seem?" Miller asked.

Logan shrugged. "Normal, I guess."

"What did you two talk about?"

"Usual stuff," he said. "Band practice, mostly."

"Did he mention his work shift after school?" Miller asked.

"Yesterday? I don't think so, but I know he hated his mom picking him up after work. He's not old enough for to drive yet, and she won't let friends pick him up or drive him a few blocks to work," Logan said. "At least he can walk from school to Menards."

"It's not that easy for a parent," Renee said. "You might be the best driver in the world. It's everyone else you have to worry about. The only reason I let you ride with older friends is because of my work schedule." She looked at Nikki. "I'm an accountant and mostly work from home. Logan's dad lives out of state and my parents are two hours away. I trust his friends, but I still worry every single day."

"Me too," Miller said. "All three of mine are old enough to drive. Sometimes I lie awake at night, thinking about all of the senseless car accidents I've responded to."

"I can't imagine," Renee said. "Christy is protective, that's all."

Nikki could tell by Logan's expression he didn't quite agree. "What does Taylor say about the situation?"

"He says she likes drama." Logan looked sheepish. "That if she doesn't have any in her life, she'll create it."

"What sort of drama?" Nikki asked. "Things seem pretty normal at their place."

"He doesn't talk about being a little kid much," Logan answered. "I know before his dad came into the picture, Christy had lived in few different tiny apartments in downtown Indianapolis. She worked all the time and Taylor watched his sister. Jared changed their lives, but Taylor thinks she doesn't really appreciate it."

"Sounds like she and Taylor butt heads a lot," Nikki observed.

"He's at that age," Renee said. "Logan and I would certainly argue more if it weren't just the two of us."

"Do you know what caused the fight between Taylor and Adrian Lynch?"

Logan's face reddened. "Adrian's a dick. Sorry, Mom."

Renee sighed. "That's fine, but they need to know what Adrian actually did, honey."

"He asked Amelia out, and she said she wasn't allowed to date. He said his sister found a pregnancy test in the bathroom after Amelia left, like she was the only other girl in the school."

Renee's lips pinched together in anger. "That poor girl. She's so sweet and quiet."

"I'm glad to hear Logan's version lines up with what Adrian told me," Nikki said. "Taylor didn't get in trouble for the fight and suspension?"

"His mom was pretty upset and wanted to ground him, but his dad said no. He stood up for his sister. He shouldn't have hit Adrian, but the week suspension was enough. Taylor said his mom was pissed off at his dad for that."

"Taylor's close with him, isn't he?" Nikki asked.

"Yeah," Logan said. "He's Taylor's hero."

"A knight in shining armor." Renee locked eyes with Nikki.

"Mom."

"Don't 'Mom' me."

This was the first negative thing they'd heard about Jared from anyone. "Why don't you like Jared?"

"It's not that I don't like him," Renee said. "He just seems... controlling."

"That's because you are anti-men," Logan said.

She rolled her eyes. "That's not true. His father and I were young and didn't stay together. We get along just fine, always have. I'm just busy."

"Is there any particular reason you think Jared's controlling?" Miller asked.

Renee hesitated, running her hand through her short hair. "I don't want to make Christy look bad."

"We're not here to judge," Nikki assured her. "We just need the truth."

"At the final band competition in early November, I noticed Christy drinking. I didn't say anything to anyone because it's their business, but I watched them the next couple of hours. He just seemed... shitty to her."

"She was drinking at the competition, Mom," Logan said.

"And there's a reason why she drinks," Renee said. "We don't know what that is, and we aren't going to judge. I don't think her husband should either, much less grip her arm the way he did."

"So she wouldn't fall down."

Renee ignored her son. "The competition was at our stadium, so a lot of the parents volunteered for concessions and things like that. Jared and I worked concessions together in the morning. He made several comments about Christy not being able to work concessions because she stressed over counting money back and would get disoriented. He laughed when he said all of this, but I've only spoken to him a few times, and I didn't like hearing him disparage his wife like that. That's why I started paying more attention that day. I remember thinking I might drink too if I had to deal with him."

"Doctor Hall is really cool," Logan said. "Taylor says

Christy has mood swings. You just don't like the idea of answering to anyone."

Renee glared at her son. "That's not true. I answer to your father about your life all the time. He doesn't talk to me like I need to be in a remedial classroom, though."

"Logan, is there any chance Taylor could be hiding somewhere, maybe teaching his mom a lesson?"

"I don't know," Logan answered. "He talked about getting her back sometimes, but his life's pretty good in general."

"I think it's safe to say that Taylor still has a grudge against his mom," Miller said after they'd left.

"Agreed." Nikki scanned her messages from Liam. "Still no sign of Taylor in Indianapolis. Liam is in contact with public transportation officials and the TSA. They have a BOLO with Taylor's photo on it."

"What about his old friends or a teacher he might trust?" Miller asked.

"Kendall's going through the list. We aren't coming up with anything so far," Nikki said. "Adrian Lynch can prove he was at Culver's when Taylor actually left school because of the receipt."

"But we don't know how long he was there," Miller said. "I'll see about getting CCTV from them, too." He glanced at her. "I need to get K9s and searchers around the wildlife preserve near Logan's. You want to split up?"

"I was thinking the same thing," Nikki said. "I can go back to the Halls' house and look at Taylor's room, see if anything stands out. I'd also like to stop at Menards and talk to his manager, make sure we're not missing anything."

"We know he cut school early," Miller said. "He headed east, so he could have been taking a longer route to Menards, through the soccer fields and into those woods. It's been searched, but I'm going to have a K9 go through. Taylor could have been hanging out and ran into someone up to no good."

"It does sound like the Halls shelter the kids somewhat," Nikki said. "I guess it's possible he was gullible. But that's so rare."

Miller called Reynolds as they neared the sheriff's station and asked him about getting CCTV from Culver's. "You're kidding me. Yeah, we're splitting up. Nikki's heading over there." He ended the call. "Guess what?"

"Someone lied to us?"

He snorted. "Am I that obvious?"

"I know how to read people," she said. "But yes, that was pretty obvious. What's up?"

"Christy Hall lied. Stillwater PD pulled all the closed-circuit video in the neighborhood, including the one at the intersection a few blocks from the Halls' house. She came home ninety minutes later than she claimed."

FOURTEEN

JULY, 2015

Rebecca laid the sleeping toddler into the pack-and-play in her mother's bedroom, listening to the rising voices in the adjacent room.

"Dad, what is wrong with you?" Stephanie had barely even acknowledged her mother or Rebecca when she'd stormed into the house. She hadn't figured out the entire situation yet, but Rebecca was pretty sure that Mr. Karl, as her mother called him, had hired them without consulting Stephanie. From the way she shouted, consulting Stephanie must be a requirement before doing anything in the Hendrickson house.

Mr. Karl's response was too soft for Rebecca to hear. He seemed so gruff and quiet, and no-nonsense. How could he allow his daughter to yell at him like that? Didn't she realize how lucky she was to still have her father even though he was in his eighties?

Rebecca slipped out of the room and leaned against the wall by the kitchen. She couldn't see her mother or Karl sitting at the table, but Stephanie paced the kitchen like an angry cat.

"Did you even run a background check?" Stephanie demanded. "Does she speak English?"

The disdain in Stephanie's voice brought Rebecca out of the shadow. "Excuse me? She speaks Spanish, English and French. How many languages do you speak?"

Stephanie stopped pacing and glared up at Rebecca, who still stood on the top stair leading down into the kitchen. "What did you say to me, child?"

"I'm eighteen," Rebecca snapped back.

"Then you should get a job and stop sponging off my elderly father."

"We aren't sponging," Rebecca answered. "We're taking care of him and this house because you won't. All you care about is getting his money."

Stephanie was fast, but she hadn't spent the last few years ducking fists. Rebecca blocked the smack and caught Stephanie by the wrist. The woman stared in shock before yanking her hand away. "How dare you speak to me that way!"

"How dare you speak to my mother that way," Rebecca countered. "You don't know anything about us, I promise you."

Stephanie's painted red lips curled into a cruel smile. "I don't need to. I know moochers when I see them."

"That's enough." Mr. Karl finally spoke. He used his cane to push himself to his feet and then pointed the cane at Stephanie. "Leave now before I say something I will regret."

"Dad—" Stephanie started.

"No." Mr. Karl waggled the cane. "I'm done trying to keep the peace. I don't know where your mother and I went wrong, but this isn't the daughter we raised."

Stephanie's face turned red. "You didn't raise me, you lazy shit. You passed that off to Mom and the nanny."

"Get out." Mr. Karl's entire frame trembled. "Don't you dare set foot in this house again."

FIFTEEN

Nikki took a few moments to clear her head before going into Menards. Why had Christy lied to them? Nikki's gut told her that Christy hadn't done anything to her son, but this certainly wasn't going to help her case.

Inside Menards, she asked for Mr. Livingston, the afternoon shift manager that had hired Taylor. After a few minutes, Livingston arrived at the customer service counter, out of breath. He was shorter than Nikki's 5'7" and balding, his cheeks pink from exertion. "My apologies, Agent. I had trouble getting off the phone with a customer."

"No problem," Nikki said. "Is there somewhere we can talk privately?"

"Follow me to the manager's office." Livingston led her past the customer service counter, through a narrow corridor to a large but cluttered office. "We all share this room, so I apologize for the mess."

Nikki took the seat across from the desk while Livingston sat behind it. He sank against the back of the chair and sighed. "My shift starts at ten a.m. By the time I got in, the sheriff's deputies had already received all the security videos." He shook his head. "At first, I thought the entire thing was ridiculous. I didn't realize he wasn't at home the entire time."

"I'm curious why you or another manager didn't call his parents when Taylor didn't show up for work?" Nikki asked.

Livingston's dark eyebrows knitted together. "I did. I spoke to a woman yesterday evening who said Taylor was sick. She called herself his mother."

Yet another lie Christy had told. "What's the number you have for Christy Hall?"

Livingston unlocked his phone and scrolled through his contacts. "Since we all share this office, I keep my employee contacts in my phone. Here it is."

Nikki scribbled the numbers he rattled off into her notes. That wasn't the same number Christy had given them for her contact information. Could it be a burner phone? Maybe Taylor had actually just gone to a friend's to lie low for whatever reason. Neena and Amelia had both seemed truthful about not having heard from Taylor, so who had pretended to be Christy?

Or had Christy just flat-out lied about all of it?

"Since Taylor is a minor, I know the hiring process is a little different. Have you met both his parents?"

"Just his dad. He's the one who brought him for the interview. Nice guy. Didn't hover, went and shopped during the interview."

"Taylor's last actual work day was last week, then," Nikki confirmed. "Did he seem any different that day? Worried? Nervous?"

"Not that I noticed, but he's a quiet kid. Great with customers, polite to co-workers, but not a big talker."

"Is there any co-worker he was friendly with?" Nikki asked.

Livingston shook his head. "I texted all of my employees that work with Taylor after I came in this morning. No one knows anything, and no one had noticed anything."

"Did he ever receive any visitors?" Nikki asked.

"I really couldn't tell you that," he said. "They come and go like customers. We don't really keep track as long as people do their jobs the right way."

"How long do you keep security videos?" Nikki hoped they hadn't already erased last week's. It was a long shot, but if Taylor kept secrets from his parents, especially a girlfriend or some other friend they wouldn't approve of, visiting at work was the best way to avoid getting caught by his parents.

"Thirty days," Livingston answered. "I thought you guys had everything you needed?"

"We likely do," Nikki admitted. "But I'd like to have my partner go through last week's videos and see if we can pick up anything unusual. He's really good at spotting little details like that."

Livingston rubbed his bald head, nodding. "It will be a few hours. Can I email it?"

"Yes, of course." Nikki gave him Liam's email address at the Bureau as well as her business card with all of her numbers. "Please call if you or anyone else remembers anything else."

She stood to leave. "One more thing. Do you know if Taylor changed his parents' contact information since he started?"

"That I can answer," Livingston said. "He gave me this number a couple of weeks ago, said his mom had a new one."

Once she was back in her warm Jeep, Nikki called the number Taylor had given his manager. An automated voice said the number didn't accept unknown callers. Nikki swore and called Liam.

"Wilson, buried under paperwork."

"Listen, I need you to run a number for me and see if it's a VoIP number." In other words, an internet phone number. VoIP was the acronym for the official name. "I don't have my laptop." She gave him the number. The FBI had software to trace internet numbers, but a savvy user also knew how to use encryption to protect themselves.

"It is, routed through the UK, which means nothing. Why?"

Nikki told him about Taylor changing his mother's contact information at work.

"That sounds like something was planned," Liam said. "I'll call public transport in Indianapolis back and ask them to keep checking, but Taylor hasn't shown up at the airport, train station or bus."

"A woman answered the phone yesterday and told Livingston that Taylor was out sick," Nikki reminded him. "Either Christy is lying, or the situation isn't at all what we think."

"You should ask for all of Menards' security videos from last week," Liam said. "If he is with this mysterious woman—assuming she exists—maybe she came in and talked to him, especially if they were planning to run."

"I'm glad you said that, because Livingston will be emailing you those very videos this afternoon." She maneuvered her way through Menards' parking lot. "I'm heading back to the Halls' house. Update Garcia for me, please."

Thanks to the mid-day lunch rush, it took Nikki nearly twenty minutes to get to the Halls' house. She pulled into the driveway, surprised to see one of the garage doors open and a stall empty. A steel-colored Chevy Suburban remained in the other stall. According to the background check Liam had run, Jared drove a black Tahoe. Perhaps he'd decided to drive around and look for Taylor. Hopefully Christy hadn't gone with him.

Christy answered the door, eyes glassier than when Nikki and Miller had left earlier. She'd clearly been crying—her eyes were rimmed red, and her face bright pink. "Did you find him?"

"No, not yet," Nikki said. "I did have some follow-up questions, and I'd like to look at Taylor's room, like we discussed."

"Why?" Christy asked.

"It really helps me understand the missing person better, especially teenagers. Kind of helps me step in their shoes a little bit."

Christy opened the door and motioned for Nikki to come in.

"Did Jared decide to look for Taylor?"

"He was called into an emergency surgery," Christy said. "He's the attending on call, and the other surgeon is on vacation."

"I'm sure that's rough," Nikki said. "Hopefully he will be home before long."

"He left about forty-five minutes ago," Christy said. "The surgery is four to five hours, so he said not to expect him until later tonight." She set her phone on the counter, messing with the buttons on the side. "I'm paranoid I will have the ringer off and Taylor will call."

"Are Amelia and Caden here with you and Penny?"

Christy nodded. "They're keeping her occupied." She stood in front of the refrigerator. "Would you like something to drink?"

"No thanks." While Christy's back was turned, Nikki texted Liam and asked him to call the number Livingston had given them. If Christy had procured the internet number, her phone should notify her of the call depending on its setting.

Nikki sat down at the counter they'd occupied earlier, watching Christy intently. "I do have some follow-up questions after talking to people at school."

Christy nodded. "I assumed you would."

"Really?" Nikki quickly read Liam's text. The call had gone to the same message about unknown callers, and Christy's phone hadn't made any noise.

Christy leaned against the marble. "Look, I made a lot of mistakes before Jared. Taylor holds things against me, even though it has been just over eight years since I met Jared. We got married soon after we met."

"What sort of things?"

"I wasn't abusive," Christy said. "But I worked multiple jobs and made bad choices. Taylor and Amelia spent a lot of time by themselves when they were little." Her lower lip trembled. "I've spent the last eight years trying to make up for it."

"I'm not judging you by any means," Nikki assured her. "I just need to know the truth."

"We've told you that," Christy said. "I don't understand what you're asking."

Menards had confirmed that Christy's Suburban was parked near the front of the store last night for about twenty minutes, which matched what she'd told them. Taylor hadn't appeared on the footage. "Christy, I know you didn't come home when you said last night. Traffic cameras showed you coming home over an hour later than you told us."

"I drove around looking for him," Christy said. "And then I decided if he wanted to pull this stunt again, he could text Jared like he did before."

"Before?" Nikki asked. "This was after an argument the two of you had?"

"It was a few months ago," Christy said. "I'd spent all day asking Taylor to do his damned chores while Jared was at work. He just kept ignoring me, so I told him he was going to be grounded if he didn't do his chores. He got mad and we argued. I told him not to leave the house, but he did it anyway. I spent hours worried sick, walking around the neighborhood, looking for Taylor. Finally, Jared called and said he'd texted that he was staying the night at Logan's. Taylor didn't give a damn about my worrying."

"I understand why you'd be upset," Nikki said. "Teenagers are tough."

"I was certain he did the same thing yesterday," she said. "If I'd called the police, he might be here right now."

"Is there anyone else you can think he might turn to?"

"I gave you everyone's name I could think of," Christy answered. "And I just don't believe he'd put his siblings through it this long."

Nikki hesitated before asking her next question. "Is it possible Amelia or Caden would keep it from you if Taylor checked in?"

"I... I don't think so," Christy said. "Why would they?"

"You're probably right," Nikki said. "But siblings have a unique bond. It's possible Taylor got into some kind of trouble and one of the kids knows or has heard from him. I know it's hard for you to fathom, and you know your kids better than anyone. But we need to cover all our bases searching for Taylor." She let the words sink in for a few moments. "Would you mind if I spoke to them when I go upstairs to look at Taylor's room?"

Emotion flashed through Christy's eyes, but Nikki couldn't figure out if she was angry or fearful or something else. "Jared might not think it's the best idea. You aren't supposed to speak to minors without their parents."

"How about this." Nikki smiled at her. She didn't like playing with the kids' trust like this, but she doubted Christy would allow her to talk to the kids if she didn't. "You come up with me and stay within earshot in the hall, just out of sight."

Christy was silent for a few moments before nodding her head. "Penny is napping, so please keep your voice down." They climbed the stairs in silence, Christy clutching her phone. Nikki followed Christy into Taylor's bedroom.

"Is her room near this one?" Nikki asked.

"Opposite end of the hall, why?"

"Why don't you bring Amelia and Caden into Taylor's room so we won't wake Penny. I know how bad it is when a toddler doesn't get a nap."

Christy shrugged and left to get the older kids. Nikki scanned the room, surprised at how neat and tidy it was for a fourteen-year-old boy. He didn't have a computer, because all of the kids shared a desktop computer. Band ribbons, drumsticks, but no drums. Taylor likely wasn't allowed to practice at home because of his little sister. Nikki sniffed the air; it smelled unusually fresh for a teenaged boy's room. His drawers were organized, with his socks and underwear fitting neatly into a fabric organizer.

Nikki slid the closet door open. The clothes were hung by color, just like the Halls' master closet that Nikki had peeked in earlier.

"Agent Hunt." Christy had returned with Caden and Amelia, who looked nervous as a scared cat.

"Mom said you haven't found him," Amelia said. "You talked to Neena? And Logan?"

Nikki nodded. "We're not going to stop looking, I promise. Can you think of anyone else we should interview?"

Christy's phone rang, making them all jump. "It's the sheriff."

"He told me he was going to call you with a detailed update on the door-to-door search." Nikki felt bad for putting Christy through an unnecessary call, but she couldn't figure out any other way to speak to the others alone. "You go ahead, we'll talk."

Christy hesitated and then hurried into the hall, closing the bedroom door behind her.

"Okay, guys, now is the time." Nikki looked at both of them. "And we probably don't have a lot of it. If there is anything else you aren't telling me, it's now or never."

They both shook their heads, Amelia's gaze flashing behind Nikki to the closet.

"Taylor never mentioned a new female friend?" Nikki asked.

More head shaking.

"What about this number, does it sound familiar?"

Both answered no, but Amelia remained fixated on the closet.

Nikki moved directly in front of Amelia, gently touching her shoulder. "What is it?"

"Mom will be mad," Amelia whispered. "Taylor isn't supposed to wear those shoes, only for special occasions."

Nikki looked back at the closet, searching for whatever Amelia was talking about. She looked at the floor where Taylor's shoes were in a meticulous line. An empty spot in the middle suggested a pair was missing. "What shoes?"

"His new Curry shoes. Mom said he had to only wear them in nice weather. She didn't want them to get dirty," Caden said. "He had on his boots yesterday when he left."

"Is there any reason he'd take these shoes?" Nikki recognized Stephen Curry's name and knew the shoes were pricey, but Taylor wasn't going to get much in a resale or pawnshop if that's what he was thinking. "Amelia, what do you want to tell me?"

"He kept money in there. All the cash he earned from doing anything. He had over seven hundred dollars in there."

Christy's footsteps made Amelia go silent. Once she'd returned, Nikki reiterated her questions about another friend and brought up the mysterious phone number again, her eyes on Christy.

"Whose number is that?" Christy demanded.

Nikki debated not telling her, but it wasn't right to keep it out of the investigation. "This is the number Taylor gave his manager a week ago. He told Mr. Livingston it was yours. Mr.

Livingston called last night when Taylor didn't show and spoke
to a woman who said she was Taylor's mother and he wouldn't
be coming in because he was sick."

Christy sat down on the edge of the bed, staring at Nikki in
shock. Nikki watched the two siblings' reactions, but they'd
seemed as shocked as their mother.

"You're sure there's no other family he'd go to?" Nikki
asked. "Maybe a friend in Indianapolis? Someone you've
forgotten?"

Christy insisted they'd given all the information they had.
"Talk to Jared, he will tell you. He'll set you straight."

"I'm headed there next." Nikki looked at each person in the
room. "Please call if you think of anything else or hear from
Taylor."

Nikki called Miller as soon as she left the Halls' home. "Thanks
for distracting her."

"No problem, but fill me in, please."

Nikki explained that Taylor had changed his mother's
contact information at work and that his boss spoke to a woman
claiming to be Taylor's mother on that number yesterday. "If
he's close to his siblings, they're our best shot at information.
But they seemed just as shocked as Christy, and I don't think
Amelia could have hidden her emotions well enough to be
acting." She told Miller about the missing basketball shoes.
"Taylor kept his cash in there."

"So he changed his mom's contact information to an
internet number, an unknown woman vouches for him yesterday, and he took his favorite shoes and all his cash. That sounds
more like a runaway."

"Liam is communicating with Indianapolis public transportation. He hasn't been spotted. But maybe we're looking too
far away."

"What do you mean?"

"Well, Taylor's a band kid, right?" Nikki said. "Granted, I only played two years, but I remember going to competitions all over Minnesota and Wisconsin and meeting new people. We didn't really stay in touch, but technology has changed all that."

"That's true," Miller said. "First thing my daughters do when they meet someone is create a contact in their phone."

"Exactly," Nikki said. "Taylor may not be allowed on social media, but he could get away with it at school. He could have been communicating with someone he met a while ago and decided to meet her somewhere."

"State troopers are looking within a fifty-mile radius of the county," Miller said. "I'll call the Wisconsin State Police since Hudson's across the river. I'd forgotten until you mentioned it, but I'm pretty sure my daughter had a band competition there at some point."

"We always did," Nikki said. "It's worth a shot." She merged into busy interstate traffic and silently counted to ten. "I'm headed to the hospital to talk to Jared when he's out of surgery. I'll let you know how it goes." She started to say more, but Blanchard's number flashed on the screen. "I'll let you know what she says," she told Miller before switching calls.

"Hi, Doctor Blanchard."

"Doctor Willard confirmed the skeleton in the corner of the closet is a male between twelve and twenty-five." Blanchard never bothered with niceties. "They're cleaning the bones of the victim in the trunk, so it will be at least a day before Doctor Willard can confirm sex. We were able to completely reassemble the male skeleton, and there are no obvious marks on the bones that would suggest cause of death. He might have been killed elsewhere, but he was left to decompose right there."

"What about CODIS?" The DNA database contained

profiles taken from violent crime scenes throughout the country.

"We're getting the male profile into the database now," Blanchard said. "I'll let you know if we get any sort of hit. Doctor Willard is going to bring me a DNA sample from the other set of remains later today. I'm going to upload them to NamUs as well."

The National Missing and Unidentified Persons System that had started as a passion project for an amateur sleuth had grown into the country's database for missing and unidentified people. Initially, the information had been limited to whatever the pathologist could glean from the victim's body, but now they were able to work with the DOJ for DNA collection.

"ViCAP too," Nikki reminded her. The database for violent crime was a long shot, but if the victims turned out to be related to a felon, they'd at least have a starting point. With so little information, identification through one of the DNA databases was their best chance at narrowing things down. "Did Miller mention an August 2015 hit-and-run to you?"

"He sent me an email, but I haven't got to it yet," Blanchard said. "You think that victim could be related to the ones from the house?"

"I do, and I haven't had a chance to talk to Courtney about any of this. Could you pull that 2015 record and send it to her for DNA comparison? Apparently, she was Hispanic."

"I'm about to go into the autopsy suite," Blanchard said. "I can do it after that."

"Thanks. I haven't had a moment to think about the cold case today. We've got another missing fourteen-year-old boy."

SIXTEEN

Hennepin County Medical Center occupied several blocks in downtown Minneapolis. Nikki parked in the garage with the easiest access to plastics on the fifth floor. She showed her credentials to the security guards checking people into the hospital and signed in. A volunteer offered to let the fifth-floor charge nurse know Nikki was on the way, but she declined. Hearing the FBI wanted to talk to a person tended to color their testimony. The massive hospital had multiple surgical suites, and Jared could be in a different department since he'd been called into emergency surgery, which gave Nikki the opportunity to talk to the nurses without risking Jared overhearing.

Nikki squeezed through the crowd on the elevator, grateful to be out of the box. Each department had security doors to enter the floor. Nikki waited a couple of minutes before someone returned to the main desk inside the department to buzz her in.

"Hi." She showed her badge to the student volunteer. "Is Doctor Hall still in surgery?"

"I'm not sure." He logged into his computer. "Yes, the surgical suite is still occupied. What's this about?"

"I'm not at liberty to say," she answered. "Is the charge nurse or another RN familiar with Doctor Hall available?"

"Not sure about that either." He motioned for Nikki to follow him and led her into the waiting area. "Let me see who I can find."

While she waited, Nikki checked her messages. Chen hadn't called, but she had several emails about other cases, including requests for profiles.

"Agent Hunt?" A sandy-haired woman about Nikki's age entered the waiting room. "I'm Melinda, the charge nurse tonight. Doctor Hall's in surgery, but he told me we might hear from the police or FBI. Is there any news on Taylor?"

So much for the element of surprise. "Not yet. I just had some follow-up questions for Doctor Hall, but while we're waiting, how long have you worked with him?"

"I've been here since I started nursing," Melinda answered. "I'd already come to the plastics floor before Doctor Hall arrived."

"I take it you think highly of him?" Nikki asked.

"Oh yes," Melinda replied. "Surgeons tend to be... confident, but Doctor Hall treats everyone like we know as much as he does. It feels more like a team than any other unit I've worked in."

"I'm sure that makes your job easier."

"It does," Melinda answered. "When the attending supports the nurses, the rest of the doctors on the floor tend to follow their lead."

"Have you ever met Christy or any other family members?"

"Of course," Melinda said. "Doctor Hall had a get-to-know-you party at his place the first few months he started. She's very nice. Very much the homemaker."

"Their home is beautiful," Nikki said. "This might sound strange, but does Doctor Hall share anything personal with you? Issues the kids might be having at school, the usual things co-workers talk about?"

"He talked about Taylor and marching band," Melinda said. "Going to football games and competition. Stuff they wanted for Christmas, that sort of thing." She worried her lower lip. "I really hope Taylor's okay. Do you think he was kidnapped?"

"I can't really share details," Nikki said. "We're doing everything we can to find him."

Melinda's pager beeped. "I'm sorry, I've got to check on this patient. I've already called the OR to let Doctor Hall know you are here. He was finishing up, so he should be with you shortly."

Nikki handed her a business card. "If you think of anything else."

Melinda tucked the card into her pocket and rushed out of sight. Nikki wished she hadn't checked in with the operating room, but she understood Melinda was just trying to help.

She went back to her email, eager to read the one that had just come in from Liam. She skimmed the short message and clicked on the attachment.

"Shit." Nikki read the Marion County, Indiana, arrest report. Taylor had been a witness to the violence and testified that he'd seen his mother throw a beer bottle at Jared.

She heard Jared's scrubs before he entered the room. "Agent Hunt, did you find Taylor?" He towered over her, Snoopy scrub hat still on, circles under his eyes.

"Not yet." Nikki grabbed her bag and stood. "We need to talk about Indianapolis."

Jared sank into the chair next to her. It was clear he knew exactly what Nikki was referring to.

"It was nothing, really." He pulled his scrub cap off, running his hands through his thick hair. "Christy's had it rough most of her life. She was a foster kid. They kicked her out when she got pregnant with Taylor, and she had to learn to survive on her own. That sort of thing takes its toll on a person. She fell into certain bad habits, which affected the kids."

"But the arrest happened less than two years ago," Nikki reminded him. "You two had been married for several years, you'd adopted the kids and given her a good life. And Penny had come along. Things weren't better for her?"

"Oh, of course they were," he answered. "But she's had a hard time forgiving herself for those early years. She stopped drinking when she was pregnant with Penny, but she fell off the wagon from time to time. That was one of those times. I should have known better."

"What happened?"

"I'd come home from a long shift. Penny had a cold and was being a little bear. Amelia had taken her upstairs, and the boys were playing video games loudly," Jared said. "I asked Christy what was going on, why she was so upset. It just went downhill from there. I tried to calm her down and she threw her beer bottle at me." He touched the scar on his right cheek. "One of those perfect throws you'd never be able to repeat. I wouldn't have called the police, but Taylor saw it happen. He called 9-1-1. I told the police it was an accident, begged them not to take her to jail. But they had to, and it was pretty obvious who was the aggressor."

"The arrest report says she pleaded guilty and had to go through anger management and alcohol abuse classes," Nikki said. "How did that affect her relationship with the older kids?"

"Taylor has never really seen her the same way after that night." Jared sighed. "He and I have always been close. He feels like she doesn't appreciate me and what I did for them. I thought things were getting better after we moved, and they seemed to for a while. But the first big argument they got into, he decided not to come home to freak her out. He texted me, but I was in surgery."

He wiped his teary eyes. "I love her so much. She's a great mom. It's just her demons."

"Do you think something could have happened between Christy and Taylor?" Nikki said. "We know she drove around longer than she admitted to last night."

Jared stared at her. "She did?"

Nikki nodded. "She left Menards like she said, but she drove around for an hour before she came home. Christy told me she was looking for him."

"I was on call," Jared said. "Amelia and Caden both said she was livid when she got home, yelling about Taylor making her wait and how that was the last time."

"You didn't mention that this morning."

He stared at her. "I didn't think it was relevant. Where are you going with this?"

"We have to consider she and Taylor could have had an argument that went badly."

"No, no, no," Jared said. "Christy would never hurt the kids, no matter how much she'd had to drink."

"Has she ever gotten physical with any of the kids?" Nikki asked.

"No." Jared's eyes shined with intensity. "Agent Hunt, I promise you my wife would never hurt her kids. Even Taylor."

Nikki told him about the mysterious female caller yesterday but omitted the information about the money in the shoes, for now.

"You're kidding me," Jared said. "That's... Taylor would never run away. He knows Amelia would be devastated. There's got to be more to this situation, Agent, I promise."

SEVENTEEN

After talking to Jared, Nikki drove back to Washington County to meet up with Miller and go over things. Inside the government center, she followed the smell of pepperoni to the big conference room. "Thank God. I'm starving."

Two large pizzas sat on the table, one of them half eaten. Miller motioned for her to sit, quickly washing down a bite. Nikki grabbed two pieces before calling Liam on FaceTime. She balanced the phone against her bag so that he and Miller could see each other.

"Wisconsin troopers are going through CCTV near the bridge that goes into Hudson," Miller said. "So far they haven't seen anything, but it's hard to spot a passenger in a car on CCTV sometimes. They've checked the bus station and train station, too. No sign of him."

"No sign in Indiana, either," Liam said. "And I was able to track that internet phone number to a server at a coffee shop near the University of Minneapolis. It's very popular with students because of the free Wi-Fi. That's available to everyone, too."

"We'll never be able to get a warrant for their CCTV yesterday with just that," Nikki said.

"Nope," Liam said.

"I'm not ruling out a kidnapping because we're talking about a minor, but right now it looks like Taylor left on his own," Miller said while Nikki ate her second slice. "Or he was at least manipulated into doing so. My deputies looked at the CCTV on the route Taylor takes to Menards and went to each business to ask to look at their security footage. I'm confident Taylor never went in that direction because we've got a traffic camera at the intersection. If Taylor had planned on going to work, he would have reached that intersection and turned left. He never showed up. Between leaving school an hour earlier than he was supposed to and everything else we've learned today, I don't think he was kidnapped. There's nothing related to Eli Robertson either."

"Jared and Christy both insist that Taylor wouldn't put his siblings through this," Nikki said. "I wanted to ask Amelia more, but I didn't have the chance. I did notice that Taylor's closet was arranged by color just like Christy's master closet. The kids say she has OCD and seemed fearful of her finding out about the shoes. But Christy seemed genuinely shocked when I told her about the woman pretending to be her yesterday."

"Is that why you had me call the internet number earlier?" Liam asked.

Nikki nodded. "She'd made sure her phone was turned up and said something about being afraid the ringer would be off. It's not a guarantee, but if she had notifications set up from that internet number, her phone would have made some sort of noise. It didn't."

"It sounds like Christy and Taylor don't get along," Liam said. "Maybe he just needed a break from her and didn't tell his siblings so they wouldn't have to keep his secret."

"That's what I'm wondering," Miller said. "Nikki, do you think Amelia knows anything else?"

"She might, but like I said, I don't think she's capable of pretending to be surprised given her emotional state. I don't think either one of those kids know where their brother is."

A familiar number flashed in front of Liam's face. "Daniel Bancroft is calling me back; I have to take this. FaceTime Miller, Liam. I'll be back as soon as I can." Nikki excused herself to take the call. "This is Agent Hunt."

"Hi, Agent, this is Daniel Bancroft returning your call." His deep voice seemed loud on her cell phone. "Spencer called me, too. I cannot believe this has happened."

"I appreciate your calling back." Nikki wished Spencer hadn't said anything, but she'd expected him to fill his parents in. "How much did Spencer tell you?"

"That human remains were found in the apartment's closet, and it's likely Karl's former housekeeper." He cleared his throat. "Spencer's mom and I were separated, and I hadn't moved to Wisconsin yet, so I'd check in on Karl now and then. I remember specifically seeing him just a couple of weeks after Ms. Smith and her kids disappeared. I was in that apartment, Agent. Granted, I didn't scour the place, but—and I know this sounds crude—I should have smelled something. I didn't."

Nikki was surprised at how forthcoming he was being after everything she'd heard about Stephanie. "It's nice that you checked up on him even after the divorce."

"I'd known Karl since I was eighteen," Bancroft said. "He and I always got along well. He was devastated about Ms. Smith. Karl kept insisting she wouldn't have left without telling him, regardless of missing items. I'd already planned on seeing Spencer that trip and I visited Karl. He and Spencer were both devastated. He liked the daughter."

"You said you went into that apartment," Nikki said. "Why didn't you move the mattresses from in front of the closet door?"

"These were old, heavy mattresses and box springs," Bancroft answered. "At the time, I was dealing with a herniated disc in my back. We just assumed she and the kids put them back where they found them when they moved in."

Nikki hadn't heard that detail. "Really? Why were they standing up?"

"If I remember correctly, Karl had the apartment's carpet cleaned before Ms. Smith and her kids moved in. It was thick with dust. I'm pretty certain that's how the carpet guys left the beds."

But who outside of Karl and his immediate family would have known that? "Do you remember who cleaned the carpet?"

"I'm sure it was Spencer or his uncle Pat, although I don't know if Patrick was even visiting then," Bancroft answered. "You'd have to ask him."

"What about Stephanie? Portable carpet cleaners aren't that heavy."

Bancroft laughed. "No. She never did any sort of manual labor, and she hated that her father refused to pay for services like that. He lived pretty lean despite the money in the bank. Stephanie is the opposite."

"I know you were living in Wisconsin, but do you have any idea what she thought about Ms. Smith?"

"Hated her. She saw her and her kids as a rival for her inheritance. Guess she was right." Bancroft snickered. "I would have loved to see the look on her face when the will was first read."

"Did she think Ms. Smith was trying to charm her dad into marrying her?" Nikki asked.

"Who knows?" Bancroft said. "Stephanie's got a temper and when she lands on an opinion, it's really hard to change it. To be honest, I assumed that's why the Smiths left."

"You think Stephanie threatened them?" Nikki asked.

"I know she did at least once," Bancroft said. "When

Stephanie drinks, she gets aggressive and brings up everyone she thinks has wronged her. She called me one night drunk and accusing me of cheating, even though she and that damn Atwood were running around behind my back for months. Anyway, she told me that she'd talked to Rebecca, the oldest daughter, and told her that if she didn't get her family out by the end of August, Stephanie would do it for her. At the time, I assumed that's why they left."

"Spencer didn't mention that."

"He doesn't know unless his mother or Rebecca told him, and I think he would have said something to me about it if she did. He really liked that girl."

Nikki thanked him for the information and promised to let him know if they were able to identify the bodies as the Smiths. "Did she mention anything about her past to you?"

"I only met her once," Bancroft said. "She was very nice, well spoken. She asked about my work and seemed knowledge-able about engineering in general. I thought she was likely educated, but Stephanie had a more derogatory opinion, given Ms. Smith's heritage."

"She was an immigrant?" Nikki asked.

"No, I don't think so, but she was a Latina without a doubt. I don't remember Rebecca or her younger brother having an accent either. Whether or not she was born here wouldn't have mattered to Stephanie, I assure you."

Nikki jotted down the note about her being Latina. "How old do you think she was? At least, a ballpark figure?"

"She had teenagers, so I would say forty, give or take a few years. But she looked youthful." Bancroft snickered again. "I remember Stephanie complaining about Ms. Smith not having any wrinkles. She insisted the woman had Botox done, but I don't think she did. She just took care of her skin and had good genes."

Something he'd said a few minutes ago nagged at her. "You

mentioned her cheating with someone named Atwood. Do you know his first name?"

"Rodney Atwood," Bancroft said. "By that summer, she'd moved on to a younger guy named Brandon Kelly. I'd hear stories about them bar hopping and her telling lies about me. That's a big part of the reason I accepted the job here. I just needed to get away from her."

Nikki barely heard the last few words.

Rodney Atwood was Scott Williams' stepfather and the main suspect in his death.

EIGHTEEN

Nikki's alarm yanked her out of an uneasy sleep. She'd spent the night at the station going over the same information with Miller until they were both nearly in a stupor. Nikki turned off the alarm and sat up, rolling her neck muscles. Why did she always end up sleeping on the same couch in the break room? It gave her a neckache every time. She'd have been better off sleeping in the Jeep.

"Nikki." Miller poked his head in the break room. "Making sure you're up. Hendrickson's attorney is going to be here in twenty minutes."

Nikki gave him a thumbs up and reached for the overnight bag she kept in the Jeep for cases like this one. She normally wouldn't take time on a cold case like this, especially with a missing teenager, but the new connection between Scott Williams and Stephanie Hendrickson changed everything. Were all these missing kids, these cases, connected? Was there a serial killer on the loose? Nikki shuddered as she checked her messages, hoping for an update about Eli Robertson from Lieutenant Chen, who'd promised to let her know when they planned to raid the suspect's apartment in the city, but she'd yet to hear anything.

She went to the women's locker room and splashed ice-cold water on her face until she didn't feel like her eyes were going to glue themselves shut any second. She changed clothes, brushed her teeth and freshened up with seven minutes to spare.

"God!" Nikki almost ran into Miller in the hallway outside the locker room.

"Sorry. The lawyer's here. I put her in the small interview room with a window."

Nikki grabbed her work bag and hurried across the sheriff's office to the conference room reserved for victims' family members. She paused at the open door to collect her breath.

"Thanks for meeting with me on short notice." Nikki put her things on the table. "Especially on your way to the airport for a transatlantic flight."

"I'm glad to help." Deandra Price had been the Hendrickson family attorney until Karl's death. Her fantastic white hair was cut into a stylish bob, her jewelry understated and her perfume the familiar Chanel No. 5. "Karl was a friend."

Nikki shuffled through her things until she found her pencil and notepad. "How long did you work for him?"

"Nearly twenty years," Deandra answered. "But I've known him much longer. I was the senior partner at Price and Lawry by then. My father had been the Hendrickson family attorney since Karl's parents were young. I believe the Hendricksons were some of the firm's first clients by then. Point being, I've known Karl since I graduated law school and joined my father's firm. Nepotism I know, but I assure you I was qualified."

Nikki smiled. "I have no doubt." Nikki had done her research before meeting with Deandra. Until her retirement three years ago, she'd been among the top estate and tax attorneys in Minnesota. Her clients were all among the wealthiest in the area.

"Well, when my father retired, I took over the Hendrickson account," Deandra continued. "Karl and his wife were well off then, but they'd been entertaining the idea of selling the machinery business to a national chain. At the time, they were past traditional retirement age. Both of their children had graduated from college and moved on. They wanted to travel."

Nikki caught the wistful tone in her voice. "What happened?"

"A few weeks before the sale closed, Mrs. Hendrickson was diagnosed with stage 4 breast cancer. Karl was devastated. She was gone within six months."

Nikki couldn't imagine being diagnosed with cancer, or, God forbid, Lacey or Rory. The idea of spending your life with someone to have them ripped away like that terrified her. It could happen to anyone at any time. "That's awful."

"It was," Deandra agreed. "I thank God every day I still have my husband."

"I know Karl and Stephanie had a strained relationship, but he seemed to get along with his son."

"Patrick is a nice man." Deandra's lip curled in disgust. "Stephanie is... Stephanie. I'm no psychologist, but if she's not a sociopath, I'd be shocked. I've never met a colder person."

"That's what makes her such a good defense attorney," Nikki said.

"I suppose." Deandra shifted in her chair. "I assume what you really want to know is about the amendment for Ms. Smith."

"Yes, please. Did you ever meet her?"

"No, and I could kick myself. I took the summer off that year. My husband did, too. He was a corporate accountant. We both just needed to get away."

"So, you don't think Ms. Smith was trustworthy?" Nikki clarified.

"That's not it at all," Deandra said. "I just wish I'd met her.

Maybe I could have found her if I'd known something about her. Do you know we didn't even have any photos? I don't even have a first name. Karl called her Ms. Smith. He didn't know much beyond that. I tried to convince him I would never have a chance to find them without at least one name. He refused. Part of me wondered if he even knew himself."

"But you were certain that he was of sound mind?" Nikki asked.

"Yes," Deandra said firmly. "We talked at length about current and past events, including various professional sports and politics. Karl kept up with everything."

"This was before he went into the nursing home?" Nikki clarified.

Deandra nodded. "It was really astounding how fast he went downhill after we finished up the will. It was like he'd used up his last bit of strength figuring how to make one last-ditch effort to find her." She worried her bottom lip. "I don't know if either of Karl's children or Spencer knows about this, but Karl first talked to me about putting Ms. Smith in his will that July before she left."

"No, I didn't. After only knowing her a few months?"

"He said she was the daughter he wished he'd had," Deandra answered. "I told him never to say that near Stephanie or it would not end well. And then I encouraged him to think about the change."

"He was receptive to that?" Nikki asked.

"He was, because Ms. Smith had finally agreed to stay through the fall and winter. She'd initially told him they would only be able to work that summer and would have to move on. I suggested revisiting after Ms. Smith had been with him for a year. He agreed."

Nikki took a few seconds to digest what she'd just learned. "Did he ask her why they would only be there for the summer?"

"He said she preferred not to say." Deandra shrugged. "I

confess, we both assumed she was afraid of someone. I even suggested that Karl get a security camera in case someone did come after her, for his own safety. But he was too set in his ways."

"Did he ever say anything about telling Stephanie or Patrick?" Nikki asked.

"He wanted to tell Patrick but didn't want to put him in that position. I said someone from the family needed to confirm his competence in addition to me, and he brought in Spencer. Kid knows his mother—he's the one who thought Patrick should have a copy of the change, because his mother would do everything possible to hide it. Patrick really never looked at it until the will was read."

Nikki tried to pluck one of the questions from the dozens currently racing in her mind. "So between the time the family disappeared and Karl's death, how often did Karl bring up putting Ms. Smith in the will?"

"Several times," she said. "He wanted to believe that she was alive, or at least one of the kids was out there somewhere, but deep down Karl believed they were dead. He refused to believe that Ms. Smith would just vanish like that without saying goodbye. She'd talked about getting the kids enrolled in school and staying the winter."

"Did he have any theories?" Nikki asked. "From everything we've learned, there weren't any signs of violence when Karl returned from his trip."

"Karl believed she was running from an abusive partner," Deandra said. "She had a couple of scars in her eyebrow and on the side of the neck. When Karl asked about it, she'd only say it was from an accident. And she was very skittish about her or any of the kids leaving the property. It took him all summer to convince her to enroll the middle one in school."

"Going back to the amendment in the will, what did you have to do in order to find her?"

"Everything in my power." She sighed. "Karl believed the Smith family came from Pennsylvania, near Amish country, because she talked about driving on the roads with the Amish, starting with Iowa. I told him there were Amish in several states, and he said that Ms. Smith said they came from 'back east.' The middle child was a fan of all the Pennsylvania sports teams." Deandra held up her hands in frustration. "Everything in my power wasn't a lot. I looked through missing persons reports, called police departments all over Pennsylvania, and then Ohio. I just didn't have enough information."

"It was an impossible task," Nikki said gently. "I would have been in the same boat."

Deandra pulled a tissue from her bag and dabbed her eyes. "I'm just sorry that I couldn't truly honor his last wish."

"You are," Nikki reminded her. "We're going to find out who she was and what happened." Nikki gave her a few moments. "One last question: what was Stephanie's reaction when the will was read?"

"Utter shock." Deandra grinned. "I'm familiar with the will because I wrote it, so I was able to look at Stephanie's face when I read the amendment out loud. She had no clue. Her father got the best of her, somehow."

Nikki parked in front of the historic building at 109 Myrtle Street, an 1880s Victorian at the top of the hill, overlooking the river and bluffs. Packed snow and ice still covered the street. Nikki checked to make sure the parking brake was on before exiting. Ice melt covered the sidewalk, but she still grasped the old iron railing. The building had been turned into private offices run by an investment group. Stephanie had the largest office on the second floor.

She and Miller had spent most of last night going through Rodney Atwood's file in search of anything they might have missed that could link him to Ms. Smith or Taylor Hall. Nothing linked Atwood to Taylor.

Atwood being Stephanie's lover before the Smiths disappeared was an easier one to theorize. By all accounts, Stephanie wasn't one to get her hands dirty. Nikki believed Atwood was capable of murdering his stepson. Killing the Smith family for Stephanie wasn't that big of a stretch.

Garcia had warned her that Stephanie was already threatening lawsuits for slandering her family name, claiming any theory her family was involved was nothing but heresy, especially with Karl gone. But Stephanie couldn't know that Nikki knew about her relationship with Atwood, unless her ex had spoken to her in the last twelve hours. Given his obvious vitriol toward her, Nikki was confident he hadn't given Stephanie any sort of heads-up. She wanted to find out if Stephanie was the woman Taylor was talking to. Was she the link between all three cases? Her two missing boys, and poor Scott's murder?

Nikki wiped her boots on the entry mat and checked the bulletin board to make sure she went to the right office. Stephanie's law firm had offices in both Minneapolis and St. Paul, but, apparently, this was Stephanie's personal office.

Nikki climbed the wood stairs, admiring the quality of the craftsmanship. Like most houses its age, the narrow stairs were barely large enough for her foot, cherry-wood panels lining the wall.

A slim woman a couple of inches taller than Nikki greeted her. Her Chanel earrings and necklace were no doubt real, along with the cashmere sweater that perfectly fit her willowy figure. "Good morning, Agent Hunt. You're looking... healthy."

Nikki rolled her eyes at the veiled insult. She was fine with being a size eight and didn't give a damn what this woman thought about it. "You look tired." Nikki smiled sweetly. "Having trouble sleeping?"

Stephanie turned on her stiletto and directed Nikki to

follow her into the corner office overlooking the lift bridge and the river. Unlike the rest of the building, the eggshell white on the walls made her brightly colored contemporary furniture stand out.

Stephanie sat down behind her dark-wood desk, the windows behind her overlooking the frozen St. Croix River. She gestured for Nikki to sit down in the uncomfortable-looking chair and waited.

"Well?" Stephanie demanded. "Aren't you here to question me?"

"I'm here because you threw a fit and demanded to talk to me."

"Because you are spreading lies about my family."

"I'm trying to find out who murdered those people in your family's apartment. You didn't trust Ms. Smith at all, did you?"

"Why would I?" Stephanie snapped. "This woman shows up out of the blue, answering my father's ad, with her damn kids. Instead of at least doing a background check, he moves her in!"

"I do see how that would be upsetting," Nikki agreed.

"Do you?" Stephanie shot back. "You don't have aging parents to worry about."

Tension clogged the air, Stephanie's smirk making it clear she thought she'd scored a point.

"That's true." Nikki summoned every ounce of self-control and smiled. "But a background check just seems like common sense to me. Did she have references?"

"Dad said she did, but he refused to show them to me. I think he was infatuated with her. He always had a thing for Mexican women."

"Was she a Latina, though?" Nikki asked.

"I don't know," Stephanie admitted. "She looked Mexican, so that's what I called her."

"How much interaction did you have with her?" Nikki

could see how much Stephanie wanted to badmouth the woman. She would keep talking with the right push. "I assume you or someone in the family kept an eye out after this strange woman arrived."

"I could hardly be in the same room with her," Stephanie said. "She was just so phony, it was obvious. But Dad, Patrick, Spencer and my own husband were mesmerized by her beauty. She was exotic, but how pathetic can you be?"

"Well, you know how men can be when it comes to a gorgeous woman. They get stupid. You've experienced that before, I'm sure."

Stephanie fluffed her hair like a vain teenager. "Yeah, over me."

"Did your father ever give you any idea why he trusted this woman so much?"

"No," Stephanie said. "But my father and I always had a bit of a contentious relationship. We're a lot alike. When I found out he'd hired help, and that she had children with her, I told him they were going to screw him over and steal from us. He hung up on me." Her eyes darkened. "We've argued my entire life, but that was the first time he hung up on me, over that woman and her scrubby kids."

"When was the last time you saw her?"

"I only saw her once, not long after they arrived. It was obvious to me that she was buttering up my father. I told him I expected them to be 'in love by the end of the summer,' or she would have robbed him blind. We didn't speak much after that."

"When you found out they disappeared, you didn't think that was weird?"

"I didn't think about it at all," Stephanie said. "I said good riddance when Spencer told me they'd left. I thought Dad would get over it eventually, but he just didn't care about anything after she abandoned him."

"How often did you see him?"

"When I could," she snapped back. "What does that have to do with anything?"

The sheer disgust on her face made Nikki want to shake the woman. She'd had her father until aged ninety. Couldn't she see how precious that was, especially given her mother had died early of cancer? "I just wondered if you two reconnected."

"He was too stubborn and proud for that."

"Do you remember that weekend?" Nikki asked. "I know your father was out of town. Did anyone check on the house?"

"I'm sure I didn't," she said. "I didn't speak to Dad after he hung up on me. Spencer checked up on things, so whatever he told you is accurate."

"Any idea what you did that weekend?"

Stephanie narrowed her eyes. "Why?"

Nikki couldn't hide her quizzical look—Stephanie wasn't stupid; she knew Nikki suspected her.

"That was years ago. I have no idea what the hell I did that weekend." Stephanie's dark eyes flashed. "Agent Hunt, I know you're well respected among your peers. But I assure you that I'm not intimidated by FBI posturing. You of all people should know that."

"Oh, I do." Nikki leaned forward, going in for the kill. "What about Rodney Atwood? Do you know where he was that weekend?"

Stephanie stilled in her effort not to react, but she couldn't hide the shock and fear in her eyes. "I guess you spoke to Daniel first and believed his lies."

"I'm just following up on information," Nikki said. "You do know Atwood is the number one suspect in the murder of his stepson?"

"Oh, I do." Stephanie folded her hands on her desk. "He came to me for legal advice. I told him that if he wasn't guilty, you wouldn't find any evidence to convict. I guess that turned out to be right, since he's still walking free."

"For now," Nikki said. "It's good to know you've stayed in touch with Atwood, though. You parted friends, then?"

Stephanie's jaw clenched. "Tread lightly, Agent. I will not stand for false accusations."

"I haven't made any accusations," Nikki said. "I've simply asked questions. Have you ever met a Taylor Hall?"

For a second, she thought Stephanie was going to jump across the desk and throttle her. "No. If you don't have any more questions for me, Agent, I'm very busy."

"That's all for now." Nikki needed to search for Taylor. She didn't have any more time to waste on Stephanie. "I have a missing child to find."

"Poor Eli Robertson. It's going on a month or more, isn't it?"

"Not my case. I'm working on something else."

"Good luck." Stephanie's cold voice almost make Nikki laugh. She'd finally gotten under the woman's skin.

"Thanks." Nikki walked toward the door. "Actually, I do have one more question. Did you have any idea about the amendment for Ms. Smith?"

Stephanie's jaw set. "No. No one did." She gestured to the door. "See yourself out, Agent Hunt."

Nikki smiled and turned to leave. "By the way, Stephanie, I assure you that I'm not intimidated by power and wealth," she said without turning around. "I will find out who killed those people." She shut the door before Stephanie could respond.

The meeting had gone as Nikki had expected given the woman's reputation, but she still couldn't believe the sheer callousness. She started the Jeep with the key fob as she shoved the door open. Her eyes stung in the cold wind. Thankfully she'd been able to park in front of the building, but the Jeep was still chilly inside. She tossed her bag into the passenger seat, digging for her phone.

Stephanie's fingers had trembled while they talked about Atwood. And she'd slipped up and admitted she'd had recent contact with him. That meant she'd be giving Atwood a heads-up, but Nikki didn't mind taking that risk. She would break Atwood when the right time came.

She played Miller's message through the speakers. "Culver's CCTV came in. Taylor Hall was there that day. He and Adrian got into an argument. Can you meet me at the high school?"

NINETEEN

Miller had already informed the principal as well as Adrian Lynch by the time Nikki arrived. Holly led her to the office. "Mrs. Farber is here as his guardian. She's his aunt. I didn't know that."

"It makes sense."

"They're in the big meeting room just down from the principal's office."

Principal Carlson and Sheriff Miller sat on one side of the table, with a sour-faced Mrs. Farber and Adrian sitting across from her.

Mrs. Farber looked like she smelled something bad when Nikki entered. Adrian Lynch smirked at her. Miller must not have shown the tape yet. She looked at the sheriff.

"I haven't shown the video yet," he told her. "I thought I'd wait for you."

She sat down next to him, directly across from Adrian. "I can't wait."

Miller unlocked his tablet, the video from Culver's cued. They watched in silence as Adrian Lynch emerged from Culver's to stop Taylor Hall from coming inside. The boys stood nose to nose, insulting each other. Adrian shoved his index finger in Taylor's chest, the same smirk on his face. Taylor turned and walked away, out of frame. It looked as though Adrian might go after him, but someone inside grabbed his arm and led him back into the restaurant.

"You told me you hadn't seen Taylor," Nikki reminded a now white-faced Adrian. "But this video tells a different story. It also makes me wonder if you didn't follow him."

"I didn't, I swear."

"Don't act like a criminal." Mrs. Farber patted his arm and glared at Nikki. "Just because he didn't tell you about an altercation doesn't mean he's involved. I won't have you railroading my nephew."

Nikki had had her fill of arrogant women today. "We're trying to find a missing kid that you've had in class. Do you have any empathy?"

The air seemed to have been sucked out of the room. Mrs. Farber didn't respond.

"Let's all take a breath," the principal cut in. "Adrian, explain yourself."

"He doesn't have to—"

"Yes, he does." The principal leveled an icy stare at the teacher. "I allowed you to sit in because you're family. Holly and I can act as guardian, and this is all being recorded. Please let Adrian do the talking."

Nikki ignored the glowering teacher, her eyes locked with Adrian's. No longer the cocky popular kid, his face had gone pale, fear in his eyes. "Look, Adrian. We know when you came back to campus. You didn't have time to follow him. You had practice after school. So unless you ran into him again, I don't think you're a suspect. But I do think you know more than what you've said." She paused for a beat. "What did Taylor say? Did you see where he went?"

"I'm not in trouble?" he asked.

"Not if you tell me the truth now," she promised.

Adrian took a deep breath. "He didn't say much. I called him names, tried get him to swing. He wasn't interested."

"Tell me exactly what he said."

"'I don't have time for your bullshit,'" Adrian said. "'I just want to get a shake before my ride gets here.'"

Mrs. Farber finally spoke again. "That's it? That's all? You should have told them yesterday, Adrian. This could change things for them."

"I thought you were on my side," he whined.

"I am," she said. "I'm here to make sure you aren't taken advantage of, and you certainly weren't. What if Taylor got in the car with a really bad person?"

"It's all right," Miller said. "He's telling us now. What else did he say?"

"Nothing," Adrian said. "Right after he turned around, a dark car stopped aways down the street. He ran toward it and got inside. They went east on Market. That's all I know, I swear to God."

"What kind of car?" Nikki asked.

"Chevy Malibu. Not brand new, not old. Darker color."

"Did you see the plate?"

"I wasn't looking, sorry."

Miller allowed Mrs. Farber to take Adrian back to class. "Principal Carlson, could we look in Taylor's locker?"

The principal hesitated. "Our privacy rules... we can search the lockers at any time, but searching personal possessions inside is another story. Parents can be really difficult."

"You have the right to look in his locker," Miller said. "We need to do it."

Carlson sighed and called Holly Black into the office. "Take them to the freshman corridor and Taylor Hall's locker." She fished a key out of her desk. "This key will unlock the school-issued padlock."

Nikki hung back to talk to Miller while they followed Holly down the hall. "Play the CCTV video again," she said.

This time, she focused on Taylor's shoes. "Those are the missing shoes from his closet, the ones he hid cash in. The Curry shoes."

Miller shook his head. "What is this kid playing at? I'll put out an APB for the vehicle with his photo, even though it's really common. What if the shoes and money are in his locker?"

"Then I'll rethink my theory," Nikki said.

"Wow." Nikki couldn't believe the state of Taylor's locker. Unlike his room, the locker was stuffed full of paper, books, and food. The size of the school meant students only had room for a half-sized locker, making the Curry shoes and Taylor's backpack impossible to hide and possibly unable to fit.

"Teenagers are messy."

"Not this kid." She reminded him about Taylor's meticulously organized room. "More proof of his mother's influence." She gestured to the open locker. "This represents the real Taylor." Nikki studied notes stuck to the inside of the locker door. Most were school related, but at the bottom of the whiteboard, Taylor had written the name "Bailey" along with the same August 2015 date the Smiths had disappeared, followed by a question mark.

"What the hell?" Nikki asked. "Why would Taylor know anything about the Smiths?" She didn't recognize Bailey, but they didn't know the male skeleton's name or what had happened to the youngest member of the Smith family. She looked at Miller.

"Maybe the date is a coincidence," Miller said. "We don't even know if Bailey was the youngest one's name. Still doesn't explain how Taylor would have found out about a family we can't find."

"He doesn't know anything about his father," Nikki reminded him. "What if he was searching for him and stumbled onto something really bad?" Her phone dinged with a text from Liam. "Brandon Kelly wants to talk now. He's willing to meet us at the station."

"Who is he again?" Miller asked.

"The guy Stephanie dated the fall the Smiths disappeared. Atwood was the affair that broke her marriage, but she dated Brandon publicly."

"Then let's go see what he has to say."

When they arrived at the sheriff's station, Nikki took time to drink a bottle of water and collect her thoughts. Brandon Kelly had been seeing Stephanie Bancroft when the Smiths had disappeared. If she had anything to do with what happened, she might have said something to him. Nikki had no idea if Brandon was going to be hostile or helpful, but he was likely their last chance at figuring out Stephanie's mindset when the Smith family disappeared.

She tossed the bottle into the recycling bin and headed to the interview room, where Miller waited with Brandon Kelly.

"Thanks for coming into the sheriff's station." Nikki smiled at the man across from her. Brandon Kelly shifted nervously in his chair, still in his mechanic overalls. A few strands of gray stuck out amid his dark hair. He was younger than Stephanie, but his smile lines made him look older.

"Yeah, I don't know what I can tell you," Brandon said. "Like I said to Agent Wilson when he called, my relationship with Stephanie was just sex."

"That's fine." Nikki turned to a fresh page in her notebook. "How did you get involved with her?"

Brandon sighed. "I had a DUI that year. She helped me out of it and said I didn't have to pay her in cash." His face reddened. "I'm not proud of it, but it was ten years ago. I was young and stupid."

"No judgment," Nikki said. "Did you two start dating that summer?"

"My DUI was in May, so that sounds right."

"How long did you guys see each other?" Miller asked.

"A year, maybe."

"This might be tough to remember, but did Stephanie ever confide anything to you that made you uncomfortable? Did she mention Ms. Smith or her children at all?"

"Yeah, she complained about her all the time. Called her racist names. I got sick of it and told her I didn't want to hear about it." He shifted in his chair. "I know that sounds mean, but talking is not what Stephanie and I got together for, you know?"

"Is there any one time that stands out?" Miller asked. "Was she different later in the fall? More relaxed?"

"God, I don't know, probably not. I don't think that woman knows how to relax. As for times that stood out, what do you mean?"

"Is there anything specific she said about Ms. Smith?" Miller clarified. "Did she make direct accusations about her?"

Brandon thought about it for a few moments. "Well, yeah, I guess there was one time that seemed especially off the wall, even for her." He rubbed his scruffy chin. "She showed up at my apartment one night in July, out of her mind. She'd been drinking, so I didn't pay a ton of attention to what she was saying. The gist of it was that her father had added Ms. Smith to the will without telling Stephanie."

Nikki and Miller looked at each other, and she knew they were both thinking the same thing: when had Stephanie found out and how? "Hold on," Nikki said. "You're certain that she talked about her father adding Ms. Smith to the will?"

Brandon nodded. "That's all she talked about. I'm sitting there playing video games in my apartment when she barges in smelling like gin and ranting about her father. I tried to tune her out at first, but when she's angry, her voice has this piercing pitch that makes you want to crawl out of your skin."

"Did she say anything about doing something to the Smiths?" Miller asked. "Even if you thought it sounded ridiculous at the time, we want to know."

"Honestly, no," Brandon admitted. "I asked her why she'd showed up so late just to complain about that, and she got really nasty. Took the PlayStation controller right out of my hand and threw it against the wall." The muscle in his jaw worked. "I had to go into my bedroom and lock the door to keep my cool. She pounded on the door for a while and screamed, but she finally left. That's actually the last time I spoke to her."

"We have to ask this," Miller said. "But where were you that weekend in August?"

Brandon looked between the two of them in confusion. "What?"

"We have to rule everyone out," Nikki said. "I know it's ten years ago—"

"No, it's fine," Brandon said. "Just surprised me is all. I was on a family vacation on Lake Superior, up by Duluth. My grandparents had a cabin, and we all went every year."

"That should be easy enough to confirm." At least one thing in this case would be easy.

"Yeah, my aunt owns the cabin now. She's the one who arranged all the reunions. I can give you her number if you want."

TWENTY
UNKNOWN

The streets blurred past as the teenaged girl sprinted down her street, her heart pounding in her chest like a drum. Panic surged through her veins, propelling her forward with a speed that astonished her. She barely registered the curious glances of passersby, her mind singularly focused on one thing: getting home.

It had been a week since her missed period, and the dread that had nestled in her stomach had grown into a suffocating fear. The girl had tried to ignore it, hoping that it was just a fluke, but the gnawing anxiety refused to be silenced. Her friends had noticed her distraction, but she had brushed off their concerns with forced smiles and hollow reassurances. Her brother was too busy with basketball season and her mother didn't seem to notice much of anything unless it was to freak out about how the canned vegetables weren't perfectly organized or to scream at her kids if they tried to get into one of the locked cabinets because the small portions of food they were allotted a day just weren't enough.

She'd told herself that her period would be starting any moment all week. Stress caused hormonal issues, especially in girls who didn't have a regular period. It wouldn't be the first time her period came at the wrong time, but by the seventh day, she couldn't ignore the nagging fear in the back of her head any longer. The weight of uncertainty was unbearable.

During lunch break, she had slipped away to the nearest pharmacy, her fingers trembling as she handed over the money for the pregnancy test. The small rectangular box now felt like it weighed a ton in her backpack, each step making it seem heavier.

As she neared her house, the girl's breath came in ragged gasps. Her neighborhood, usually a haven of comfort, now seemed alien and foreboding, even though she knew the house would be empty, at least for the next thirty minutes or so. She fumbled with her keys, her hands slick with sweat, and finally managed to unlock the door. The familiar creak of the hinges greeted her, but it did little to calm her racing heart.

She dashed up the stairs, taking them two at a time, and burst into the bathroom. Locking the door behind her, she leaned against it, trying to catch her breath. The silence of the room was deafening, broken only by the sound of her rapid breathing.

Her hands shook as she pulled the test out of her backpack, the plastic wrapper crinkling loudly in the quiet space. The instructions blurred with the tears already building in her eyes, but she forced herself to read them carefully, her mind racing with a thousand what-ifs.

As she waited for the results, the seconds stretched into an eternity. She stared at the tiled floor, her vision unfocused, and tried to steady her breathing. The test lay on the edge of the sink, its white plastic casing stark against the porcelain.

Her thoughts spiraled in a chaotic whirlpool of fear and hope. What would she do if it was positive? The future, once so bright and full of promise, now loomed before her like a dark, impenetrable fog.

Finally, the timer on her phone beeped, startling her out of her reverie. She took a deep breath and forced herself to look at the test. Two lines. Positive.

The world seemed to tilt on its axis, and she sank to the floor, her legs unable to support her. Tears welled up in her eyes, and she pressed a hand to her mouth to stifle the sobs that threatened to escape.

In that moment, the weight of the future pressed down on her shoulders, and she felt more alone than ever before. Her mother would never believe the truth.

TWENTY-ONE

After confirming Brandon Kelly's alibi, Nikki spent the rest of the day going over all of her notes on Taylor, the Smith family, and Rodney Atwood. Atwood murdered his stepson, Scott. Atwood had an affair with Stephanie, who really hated the Smiths. Stephanie had been in contact with Atwood since Scott's death. Taylor was the wild card. Where did he fit in? Nikki hadn't noticed anything strange about Stephanie's reaction to Taylor's name. She didn't think Stephanie was the woman who had pretended to be his mother.

Had Taylor been searching for his biological father? Nikki felt like she was going in circles right down the drain. None of it made sense.

That night at home, after she tucked Lacey into bed, Nikki went into her office to go over the last couple of days. So far, the circumstantial evidence supported Taylor being alive, but why would he disappear without telling his siblings? What was she missing?

Her vibrating work cell pulled Nikki out of her thoughts. She didn't recognize the number, but the caller ID read Indianapolis.

"This is Agent Hunt."

"Agent Hunt, I'm sorry to call so late," a female voice replied. "I called your office number, and your machine said to call this number in an emergency."

"Yes, this is my cell phone," Nikki replied. "You're calling from Indiana?"

The woman cleared her throat. "Yes. My name is Kelsey Richard. I'm a family law attorney in Indianapolis. The evening news ran a segment about Christy Hall's son Taylor. Is he still missing?"

Nikki entered the attorney's name into the search bar. Kelsey worked for a large firm in Indianapolis specializing in domestic cases. "Unfortunately. Do you know if he's turned up in the city?"

Liam had been tasked with staying in communication with public safety in the greater Indianapolis area. He'd enlisted an agent from the local bureau to make sure Taylor didn't slip through the bus or train station without being seen by the police or CCTV.

"Not that I know of, but I do think there are some things you need to know. You're aware Christy Hall was arrested for domestic battery a little over a year ago?"

"Yes," Nikki replied. "Jared confirmed she received probation with anger management."

"I'm sure he did." Kelsey's tone made Nikki sit up straighter. "How did they seem to you? Jared and Christy?"

"What exactly happened in Indianapolis?"

"Christy Hall met with me about a week after her arrest," Kelsey said. "She told me that Jared was the abusive one. He hurt himself during that fight. Taylor heard the glass shatter and saw Jared bleeding, but he didn't see who actually threw the glass."

According to her online bio, Kelsey had more than twenty

years' experience in family court. "Did she seem like a battered woman to you?"

"I believed her," Kelsey replied. "Jared controlled every aspect of their lives so well the kids weren't even aware of what he was doing. He monitored what Christy ate, drank, her entire routine. Their bedroom was soundproof. She hid the bruises."

Nikki thought about Christy letting Jared take control of all the conversations.

"She had to look presentable at all times," Kelsey continued. "No loungewear. Slacks, shirt, hair curled and makeup on. She'd been working in restaurants when they met. He swept her off her feet and said she would be able to stay home and take care of her kids. She was so excited, and they were married within a few months. Christy didn't have any family to tell her to stop and think things through."

A predator's favorite sort of victim, Nikki thought. "Did she have any medical record of the abuse? Or anyone to back her up?"

"No," Kelsey replied. "Jared had the kids on his side before they were married. Christy said they were happy and didn't carry a lot of resentment toward her until Jared showed up and started pointing out flaws. By the time they were married, Taylor had started talking about how hard things were when he was little, even though they had a lot of good memories."

"Christy gave us the same impression."

"She's probably been gaslit into believing it," Kelsey said. "Once they were married, everything changed. Sometimes the sex was so rough she couldn't walk the next day. Jared would tell the kids she had a bad hangover and needed to be in bed all day."

Disgust rolled through Nikki. "He broke her spirit."

"He really did," Kelsey agreed. "She told me more than one story like that. He made her look unstable in front of her kids every chance he got."

"Did she try to leave?"

"She had nowhere to go," Kelsey said. "He told her she could leave whenever she wanted. By then, Jared had adopted Taylor and Amelia. Six months before the arrest, Christy had gone to the store and wound up with a DUI. She was driving erratically and then became combative. She hadn't been drinking and swore she didn't do drugs, yet she tested positive."

"Jared's a surgeon," Nikki said. "He could probably get his hands on anything he wants."

"He's a bastard," Kelsey spat. "The only time she fought back caused the fight Taylor overheard. She'd caught Jared watching underaged porn. He said they just looked young, but this wasn't on Pornhub. She didn't recognize the site name, but Christy was positive that the address ended with a dot onion, not dot com."

"The dark web." Tor users weren't all criminals. Regular users did use the Tor network for anonymity. But porn with a dot onion almost always meant child pornography.

"Christy wasn't going to let him hurt Amelia or Penny. She told him they were leaving. He cut himself with his own knife, slammed the bottle to the floor to break it and screamed. Taylor ran in and believed Jared. That was supposed to be the last straw for her," Kelsey continued. "That's why she came to me. I think she was shocked that I believed her."

"Was that first appointment the only time you talked to her?" Nikki asked.

"She was supposed to come back three days later for a second appointment, but didn't show. I called her a few times and she didn't answer. I finally found out she'd gone with a public defender and taken the plea. I had no idea they'd moved until I saw the news tonight."

After ending the call with her, Nikki did a deep dive on Kelsey Richard to make sure she didn't have anything controversial in her past that would suggest she was making up the story.

For all Nikki knew, she could have been an old girlfriend of Jared Hall's looking for revenge.

Kelsey was in her mid-fifties with grown children, a lifetime public servant fighting for families and kids. She'd received several awards over her career and had worked with the state on several child safety initiatives. Nikki hadn't been able to find anything derogatory about her on any database or social media. Nikki had decided to go through social media in search of Christy's life in Indiana, but her only profile consisted of Facebook updates on her kids. And the account had been opened after she married Jared.

Nikki opened the copy of Christy's arrest report Liam had emailed her, hoping someone had written her maiden name down, but she didn't see it. She switched gears, logging onto Indiana's public database. It took a few moments to narrow down the long list of Jared Halls to the right marriage certificate, but Nikki finally located it.

"Christy Martin," Nikki said to the empty office. Within seconds, she had Christy's old Facebook profile pulled up on her laptop. The account was still technically active since Facebook couldn't be bothered to delete accounts, even when a deceased's relative requested it. Her old account was set to private, so only a handful of public posts from a few years ago were visible to Nikki. A healthier-looking Christy posed with two other individuals wearing the same black, button-down dress shirts. Nikki had confirmed the bar Christy had worked for in Indianapolis had permanently closed, but she didn't recognize any of the names tagged in the photo captioned "Besties forever." Every person from Indianapolis that Jared and Christy had told them to call appeared on her new Facebook profile, clearly friends of Jared. Nikki scrolled through every photo Christy had uploaded since starting the newer profile, checking for the young man and woman from the photo with a happier version of Christy.

They didn't appear in a single image, including the dozens from the large goodbye party Jared's hospital had thrown him before they moved.

Nikki debated messaging Christy's old friends, but decided an email from her official FBI address might get a faster response. She kept it brief, stating they were searching for Taylor Hall. Both work numbers were included in her email signature, and she added her personal cell, urging them to call her day or night.

Email sent, Nikki stared at her computer, the adrenaline from Kelsey's call dissipating. A yawn made her jaw pop.

She headed to bed, making sure her cell wasn't on silent.

TWENTY-TWO

Nikki left before Rory and Lacey woke up, leaving the house when it was still dark and cold. She'd only slept a few hours, her mind racing with the information from Christy Hall's former attorney.

She texted Liam to meet her at the sheriff's. He lived with Caitlin and Zach in downtown Stillwater, only a few minutes from the sheriff's station. Despite the early hour, both he and Miller were waiting for her in his office.

Nikki took a donut from the box on Liam's lap and sat down. "Thanks for meeting me here. And for the donut."

He and Miller sat in silence as she told them what Kelsey had said.

"Logan's mother picked up on that, too," she reminded Miller after she'd finished.

"She did," he agreed. "Let's say this is all true. Is there any indication that Taylor somehow knew? Did he run away?"

"I don't think he'd leave his sisters in that situation if he did," Nikki said.

"Is it possible he could have confronted Jared?" Liam asked.

"Taylor is close to Jared, right? The guy's his hero. Finding out the truth would shatter him."

"And if he confronted Jared, who knows how he would have reacted?" Nikki said. "I asked hospital security to go through all of their footage from the day, every entrance, in search of Taylor. They hope to get back to me today."

"But Jared was at the hospital," Miller said. "We confirmed his shift started in the morning. He stayed because they were short-staffed in the ER." He looked at Nikki.

"The charge nurse did confirm it before I left," Nikki agreed. "She seemed a little miffed that I would dare question Doctor Hall, but he told her that I needed to know so we could cross him off the list."

Miller drummed his fingers on his cluttered desk. "It's not implausible. The guy hurting himself to frame her is pretty extreme, but it's happened before. Problem is, there's no evidence, right? And Christy herself admitted to the domestic violence."

"That's what I was thinking," Liam said. "We know she lied about when she came home, too."

"In front of Jared," Nikki reminded him. "Maybe she didn't want him to know she'd driven around searching for Taylor."

"Or she didn't want Jared to know she'd had an issue with Taylor, and she overreacted," Miller said. "She could have panicked."

"And done what?" Now that she'd spoken to Kelsey, a lot of things began to add up. "She seems so meek. If she is a battered woman and she's allowed her son to think Jared is the good guy, is she really going to snap?" She looked at Miller. "Any luck on finding the car Taylor got into at Culver's on CCTV?"

"Adrian only saw the make and model," Miller reminded her. "Chevy Malibu is one of the most popular cars on the market. He said it was a dark-ish color. We watched the CCTV at the nearest intersection and saw two at a light that we've confirmed weren't the car that picked Taylor up. But two of the same model cars at the intersection doesn't bode well for us finding him that way."

"No one saw him after that," Liam said. "For all we know, this isn't related to the abuse allegations at all. He could have met someone online and got into trouble."

"They only have Instagram, according to Jared," Miller said. "Taylor didn't post much. We can't track his phone because it's an older model and shut off."

"School computers, friends' computers," Liam answered. "The library. It's pretty easy for kids to get around those kind of rules."

Nikki thought back to Logan's twitch when she asked about additional social media for Taylor. "I'll talk to Logan again. I felt like he knew a little more."

"What about Taylor's siblings?" Liam asked.

"I don't know," she admitted. "If that's the rule in the house and he didn't follow it, would he trust them not to rat him out? Even if they get along, siblings fight and use stuff like that against each other all the time. But if Logan can't tell me, we'll look at talking to them." She gestured to Miller.

"I never noticed any signs of controlling issues other than how Jared spoke to Christy," Miller said. "No locks on the cabinets or refrigerator. In every domestic case I've seen that involves complete control, stuff in the house is restricted."

"Christy restricts it." Nikki remembered something Neena had said. "She doesn't let them get snacks out of the cupboard, they have to drink water or milk." Her heartbeat accelerated the way it always did when her instincts were spot on. "He controls her completely, and she controls them. That way, he's the good guy. It's a lot easier not to get caught for abuse when the children don't realize you're behind it." Nikki looked at her vibrating phone. Matt Kline had already called twice this morning. "I have to take this."

She stepped into the hall. "Hi, Matt, sorry I haven't called back."

"I know you're busy." Excitement colored his deep voice. "But we just found birth certificates."

TWENTY-THREE

Nikki met Matt in the lobby, her eyes drawn to the entrance. "Snow's starting early, I see."

"Sleet mixed in," Matt said. "Which means I'll probably be busy today." He handed Nikki a large manila envelope wrapped in clingwrap. "The police finished their search and said I could go back into the house and start working, so we decided to start on the room next to the kitchen. It's pretty empty, including the closet, just dirty. Luke was sweeping the closet and basically knocked out the side wall at the bottom. Vacuum barely touched the wood, too. Anyway, this envelope was hidden inside. I'm the only one who touched it. There are four birth certificates, but I didn't take them out, so I don't know any more than that."

Nikki wanted to hug Matt for being so careful. As a firefighter for Stillwater, his prints were on file and would be easy to dismiss. "I'll let you know what we figure out when I can."

"I saw you guys were looking for a missing kid," Matt said. "Obviously this isn't priority, but I wanted to get them to you to protect the evidence."

She thanked Matt again for his quick thinking and then

headed back into the secured area to rejoin Miller and Liam. She fished a pair of latex gloves out of her bag and carefully took off the clingwrap.

"They were hidden behind a side wall in the closet." Nikki explained how Luke had discovered the envelope. "Matt protected the evidence. He didn't take the birth certificates out." She carefully removed the yellowed documents and laid them out on the table. All four had been issued in Ohio.

Nikki tapped a gloved finger on the nearest document. "Bianca Carrero, born 1973 in Cleveland, Ohio."

"This must be Ms. Smith's real name," Miller said.

"Most likely," Nikki said.

She took out the next birth certificate. "Rebecca Lincoln. She would have been eighteen that summer." The next certificate was Jason's, who was three and a half years younger. His last name was also listed as Lincoln. "We might actually have a surname."

"I've gone through the online Ohio public records," Liam said. "There's a marriage license for Bianca Carrero and Shane Lincoln dated May 30th, 1995."

"Rebecca was born two years later," Nikki said. "Is there any kind of divorce record for Bianca and Shane?"

Liam's grim expression made her hopes sink. "Yeah, Shane Lincoln died in a car accident in 2005. I'm trying to see if Bianca remarried, but it's like finding a needle in a haystack without more information. At least a date."

"What about the last certificate?"

"Bailey Carrero." Nikki thought of "Bailey" written on the whiteboard in Taylor Hall's locker. "Bianca Carrero is listed as mother, and there's no father. This certificate says it's a copy."

"Nothing that explains why Taylor Hall had Bailey's name and the date the family disappeared?"

"Unfortunately, no."

Nikki opened her laptop and typed in "Bianca Carrero,"

expecting to see dozens of options. Her heart hammered inside her chest. "There's a missing persons page."

"What?" Miller asked. "How did the Hendrickson attorney not discover it?"

"She didn't have the right name," Nikki reminded him.

The page appeared to be run by Elena Carrero, an older cousin of Bianca's. "According to this page, Bianca and her three children went into hiding the summer of 2015 and were never heard from again. Elena has been searching for them since then."

"So she did remarry," Miller said. "Or at least have another relationship that resulted in Bailey. If he is the abusive one, that could be why the birth certificate is a copy. Bianca may have changed his name so that he'd have her last name instead of his father's."

Nikki skimmed through the photos Elena had shared. Bianca had been a beautiful, dark-haired Latina, and all three children appeared to favor her. Nikki understood Stephanie Bancroft's jealousy. Both Bianca and Rebecca were stunning. Nikki kept scrolling until she reached the page's earlier posts.

"Listen to this." Nikki had found the first entry from late 2015. "Bianca endured abuse from her boyfriend until he moved on to her daughter, Rebecca. That's when she decided to run."

"She give the boyfriend's name?" Liam asked.

"Redacted." Nikki liked Elena's style. "Literally, it says "redacted" instead of a name."

Miller glanced at his vibrating phone. "It's Chen." He answered the call. "Hey, Lieutenant, what's up?"

"Comm center got a 9-1-1 call from one of Christy Hall's neighbors. She found her lying in the yard, blood everywhere, and called the police. They are headed there now."

TWENTY-FOUR

Nikki rode with Miller, with Liam in his own car. "The caller didn't give any indication about the condition of the rest of the family?"

Miller shook his head, gripping the wheel. "You think she'd kill them all and then herself?"

"I don't know," Nikki admitted. "I don't think her and Jared's relationship is everything they make it out to be, but Christy might have snapped."

"Or Jared confronted her about Taylor."

"Why would he do that?" Nikki asked. "We think Taylor left on his own."

"Right, but circumstantial evidence says that might be due to his bad relationship with his mother."

Nikki's fingernails dug into her armrest as Miller turned sharply onto the Halls' road. Emergency lights lit up the cul-de-sac, but Nikki didn't see an ambulance. Hopefully that meant Christy was still alive and had been rushed to the hospital. Every window in the house blazed with light. Nikki prayed the kids were okay.

She nearly jumped out of Miller's SUV before he stopped

behind the Stillwater police car she recognized as Chen's. The lieutenant emerged from the house as she and Miller jogged up the sidewalk.

"Just her," Chen said. "No one else in the house."

"Thank God." Nikki's relief disappeared. "Is Christy alive?"

Chen nodded. "The neighbor heard what sounded like fire-crackers and then screeching tires. He found Christy and called the police. She's hanging on." Chen shined his light on the snow toward the garage. "Blood trail comes out the garage door, past the Chevy Suburban in the garage, into the snow. She'd fallen face down." He shivered and looked up at the sky. "Frigid temps might have saved her life."

"The Suburban's in the garage?" Nikki felt hot inside her coat despite the cold air freezing her face. "What about the Chevy Tahoe?"

Chen shook his head. "Looks like a big fight in the house. Furniture overturned, glass, dresser drawers open and half empty. Looks like they left in a hurry."

Nikki, Miller and Liam donned booties before entering the house. Her gaze landed on the massive flatscreen television on the wall. A heavy glass vase lay in pieces on the floor below, the television screen shattered. Chen led them to the kitchen, where the family laptop had been busted into more pieces than Nikki could count. Liam slipped on gloves and knelt over the destroyed computer. "Motherboard's busted in three pieces. We aren't getting anything off that thing."

"Jared's phone goes straight to voicemail," Miller said. "We can get GPS from the carrier—"

"It's here." Nikki pointed to the broken iPhone on the floor near the table. "If he's behind this, we don't have any way of tracking him."

Chen's eyes darkened. "I think it's safe to say he is. Come upstairs."

Nikki followed him, dread nearly choking her. She couldn't stop thinking about what Kelsey had told her. Her heart fell to her stomach when Chen stopped in front of Amelia's door. Her porcelain figurines had been broken with books strewn all over the floor.

Nikki didn't see any sign of blood in the room. "He shot Christy and took the kids. Why? Did he do something to Taylor?" They hadn't turned up a single thing to make them think that Jared would abuse the kids, but maybe they'd missed something.

Nikki's phone rang, and she almost ignored the unknown number but decided against it. "Agent Hunt."

"Um, hi. This is Caleb. I'm a friend of Christy Hall's."

Nikki snapped her fingers to get the others' attention. "I'm putting you on speaker. The sheriff and my partner, Agent Wilson, are here with me. What can you tell me about Christy's relationship with Jared Hall?"

"He finally did it, didn't he?" Caleb's voice shook. "We told her he'd never change. He moved her thousands of miles from her friends, who were family."

"Christy's been shot," Nikki said. "We don't know her condition. Jared and the kids are missing."

"Of course they are." Caleb's voice shook. "He's insane. Like the kind of guy you see on *American Monster* or something. Do you know he hurt himself right in front of Christy? That's how she ended up having to go to anger management. No one believed her. You know she never drank or anything like that before he came into her life. She worked a lot, but she was sober."

"Do you have any contact information for Jared's former employer? Or have any idea where he might have taken them?"

"No," Caleb said. "Jared claimed he came from the same kind of background as Christy. Foster care, all that. He liked to brag that he climbed out of poverty on his own, while simultaneously mentioning that Christy had needed him to do the same. He said this within the first month they started dating. Next thing we know, they're engaged and he's adopting the kids. I begged her not to marry him. Begged her not to go back to him or let him move her out of state."

Caleb didn't know anything else about Jared, and it sounded like that had been by design. "He was a foster kid like her, in Cincinnati. I wanted to confirm that, but I had no idea how—or if I even could."

"Not without permission," Nikki assured him. "Or a warrant. The kids all loved him, though, right?"

"That was the worst part. Taylor thought the sun rose and set on the bastard."

Nikki promised to keep him updated, and Caleb said he would talk to their circle of friends to see what else they could find out about Jared, but it didn't sound like they knew any more than he did.

"Christy's attorney was right." She looked at the others. "He could be anywhere."

Chen had disappeared to take a call while they were talking to Caleb. He returned, excitement on his face. "One of our drones spotted the Tahoe parked on the trailhead near Lake McKusick."

TWENTY-FIVE

Lake McKusick was only about a five-minute drive from the Halls' home, so Nikki jumped in Miller's big Suburban while Liam stayed with Chen and worked the scene.

Miller turned on his emergency lights as they sped down the highway, sleet and snow pelting them. Thankfully it wasn't so cold that the highway department hadn't been able to put down road salt to combat the ice.

Nikki checked her phone. "Liam just texted. APBs for Jared and the kids, as well as BOLOs have gone out to all law enforcement in Minnesota and Wisconsin. State police are in the process of setting up road checks on the major highways, and Wisconsin State Troopers are going to be checking every vehicle coming into the state."

Courtney's number flashed on the screen. Nikki knew she'd been working late the last couple of days, trying to get through the evidence collected from the Hendricksons' while Blanchard and the forensic anthropologist worked on the skeletal remains.

"Hey, Court." Nikki cradled the phone against her shoulder. "We're headed into a wooded area so I might lose you. This Hall case is getting more and more confusing."

"It won't take long," Courtney said. "I finished analyzing the DNA from the remains in both the trunk and skeleton in the closet. Mitochondrial DNA confirms they're mother and son."

"What?" Nikki said. "But the woman in the hit-and-run from that day had given birth…"

"I know," Courtney said. "I ran the samples against that Jane Doe. Mitochondrial DNA means the hit-and-run victim is the daughter, not the mother."

"He got Rebecca pregnant," Nikki said after she ended the call. "Remember, the Facebook page said that Bianca left after she found out he'd moved on to her daughter. If Rebecca gave birth, then she has a kid out there. Bailey. Where the hell is he?"

"Trailhead's up here on the right," Miller said. "Maybe you should have had Courtney come work the scene."

"There isn't going to be a scene," Nikki said defiantly. "We're going to save those kids."

Since the vehicle had been spotted by the drone pilot, she and Miller were the first to arrive. Miller turned on the SUV's brights as they crept closer to the black Tahoe. He flashed them several times. Nikki didn't see any movement or shadows inside the vehicle, but they couldn't take any chances.

"Your CSIs are coming out, right?" Nikki asked Miller. "I can have Courtney send Arim."

He nodded, checking his Kevlar. Nikki had put on her bulletproof vest before they'd left the Halls' house, and between the heat in the vehicle and the restriction of the vest, it felt like a hot flash. "They're about ten minutes out."

Nikki checked that her SIG Sauer was loaded and grabbed another clip, sticking it into her tall boot. She and Miller exited the vehicle, both using the door as a shield. Miller aimed his long rifle at the Tahoe and shouted for Jared to get out of the vehicle. Seconds went by, the night silent save for the sleet hitting the vehicle.

She kept her pistol pointed at the Tahoe, shifting behind the open door to get a better look at the side of the big SUV. "There's half an inch of sleet on the doors. This thing's been sitting for a while. Likely right after he peeled out. Cover me."

Gun secure in her hand, Nikki dropped to a crouch and approached the Tahoe, trying not to slip on the frozen ground. She shined her big flashlight inside the rear-side window, her heart pounding, fear of what she was about to see choking her.

"Empty." She looked out at the dark lake. This time of year, most of Minnesota's lakes had several inches of ice on them. Hard to get rid of a body, but not impossible. Nikki knew that from prior cases.

Miller flanked the Tahoe's left side, pointing his light at the ground. Despite the sleet that had been coming down for the last hour or so, they could still see footprints leading away from the Tahoe. They stopped about ten feet from the vehicle. "Tire tracks," he said. "Smaller tread than the Tahoe and Suburban."

"He must have had a smaller vehicle here, waiting." Nikki checked the passenger door. It opened easily. She shined her light inside the expensive vehicle. It was clean as a whistle, with no sign of a struggle of any kind. "I think two different sets of prints in the snow on this side, probably Caden and Amelia's. One of them probably carried Penny." Nikki hoped Jared had taken warm clothes for the kids.

She and Miller checked the rest of the Tahoe but didn't find anything useful.

"There's my crime scene guys." Miller pointed at the head-lights coming down the main road.

Nikki's phone rang. "Chen," she said to Miller. "We're at the Tahoe. Looks like he had another car…"

Chen spoke rapidly, the words as bizarre as anything she'd heard tonight.

"We'll meet you at the sheriff's station in fifteen minutes.

The house is still being processed." She ended the call and looked at Miller.

"What?" he asked. "Did they find one of the kids after all?"

"Taylor Hall just came home."

TWENTY-SIX

Chen had already brought Taylor Hall into a conference room by the time Nikki arrived with Miller and Liam. The woman sitting next to him looked familiar.

"Where are my mom and siblings?" Taylor demanded. Nikki checked Taylor's shoes before she sat down across from him. "I'm here to tell you everything. But you have to tell me about Mom and the others."

"Your mother's in surgery, fighting for her life," Nikki said. "We believe your siblings are with Jared."

His face turned white. The woman next to him grabbed his hand, muttering something in Spanish. Nikki remembered his mother bragging on how easily Taylor had picked it up after Jared had offered to teach it to him.

"You're Elena Carrero." Nikki recognized her from the Facebook page. "What are you doing with Taylor?" Nikki knew the answer as soon as she asked the question. It should have been obvious from the start. "Jared is the boyfriend your sister ran from, isn't he?"

Elena nodded. "I think it's best if you hear the story from Taylor. He found me."

Nikki waited, her eyes on Taylor.

"A couple of days after Thanksgiving, Mom asked me to go to the garage to get Christmas stuff out of storage. I couldn't find the box that has garlands, so I started checking the ones sitting under Jared's workbench. I found an envelope of pictures and stuff taped underneath the bench. This photo was inside."

He slid a photo of a dark-haired woman. "She looks like Caden." Taylor blinked back tears. "I started looking at the other photos, and they were of the same girl, a few years older maybe. They look like stills from a video. One is a school photo, the last three she is on the bed…" Nikki let Taylor take a breath. He didn't need to finish his sentence. It was clear he'd worked out that Jared had been abusing Caden's mother.

"Rebecca," Elena said. "It's Rebecca in the photos."

Nikki took the envelope of printed stills, sickness rolling through her at the sight of the fear on Rebecca's young face. In the last enlarged photo, Nikki could make out Jared's distorted form in the mirror, standing in front of the bed, leering at Rebecca.

"Did you tell anyone what you found?" Miller asked.

Taylor shook his head. "I spent the next month trying to figure out what I should do. Jared's my dad… I didn't think he could do something like that." Anger flashed in his eyes. "The last night of winter break, my sister told me she felt like someone was in the room, watching, even when they weren't. She hadn't found a camera, but I knew then he was going to do the same thing to my sister. I used the school computers to run an image search of the school photo, and the missing persons page for Bianca and her family was the first result. So I contacted Elena and arranged for her to pick me up."

"Near Culver's," Nikki confirmed. "Why didn't you go to the police?"

Taylor flushed. "I started thinking about the last few years differently. Little things that he said and did, and how Mom changed." He looked down at the table. "I told the police I saw her hit Jared, but I didn't. She kept telling the police he'd done it to himself to make her look bad. They acted like she was crazy. I should have believed her."

"It's not your fault," Elena said. "Jared is a master manipulator. He's got a gift that makes people trust him so much it's easy for him to gaslight any situation."

Nikki picked up the school photo of Rebecca and studied her features. "How old was she here?" she asked Elena.

"Thirteen, I think. The same age Bailey is now."

Nikki's head shot up, her eyes locking with Elena. "Caden?"

"Yes," she answered.

Nikki's mind raced. She grabbed the envelope still in clingwrap out of her bag. Liam tossed her a pair of latex gloves. Nikki carefully removed all four birth certificates, placing them in front of Elena.

She closed her eyes and covered her mouth with her right hand, whispering the Lord's Prayer. "Where did you find these?"

"Your cousin worked for a man named Karl Hendrickson that summer. The third weekend in August, Karl went on a fishing trip. He was gone all weekend. When he came home, Bianca and the kids were gone. No note left. No sign of foul play, but he and his grandson only did a cursory walk-through of the apartment that's attached to the house. All her personal items were gone, along with a couple of family antiques she might have taken to pawn."

Nikki chose her words carefully so she didn't give Elena false hope. "Karl was devastated and had his grandson board up the apartment. The home has sat empty since he went into a nursing home and subsequently passed a few years ago. It sold in November and the new owner started remodeling this week. He started with the back apartment."

Fear shined in Elena's eyes. "What did he find?"

"Remains inside the closet. Karl and his grandson noticed the beds had been standing up against the closet door after the family disappeared, which is how they'd had them when Bianca and her kids moved in. They assumed she left things the way she found them."

"I want to know exactly what happened to them." Elena's chin trembled.

"We don't know cause of death because of the amount of time that's passed." Nikki avoided the word "decomposition" for Elena's sake. "But the medical examiner confirmed an adult female and a male between twelve and twenty-five. We learned a few hours ago the remains were matched to a Jane Doe from that same weekend. She died in a hit-and-run."

Elena brushed the tears off her cheeks. "I knew they were gone. It's been too long. He must have found them. They had a plan for Rebecca to run and get help."

"That's why Caden has nightmares." Taylor had been crying as well. "He's had them for years. He's running in the dark and people are screaming. Then it all goes quiet. It's the same nightmare every time."

"Bailey—I mean Caden—was his own flesh and blood," Elena said. "Bianca endured the abuse and hid it from the children. Rebecca initially said she didn't know who the father was, but she eventually told her mother. Bianca had no idea Jared was molesting Rebecca. She said it started in seventh grade, not long after the school picture was taken."

Nikki glanced at Liam and knew he was thinking the same thing: that's why Jared had kept that specific photo. It was a souvenir of sorts.

"Now he's done the same thing to my family," Taylor said. "We have to find my sisters and brother."

"The entire tri-state area has Jared's photo, along with your siblings'," Miller said. "The Minnesota and Wisconsin State Troopers are doing traffic stops. Jared abandoned the Tahoe. His Chevy Suburban was still in the driveway. Do you know of any other vehicles he owns?"

Taylor shook his head. "His phone has GPS."

"He destroyed his phone and left it," Liam said. "You and Jared are close—"

"It's not my fault," Taylor sobbed. "He was so nice, and he made it seem like Mom was the one ruining our lives. I was so mean to her!"

Nikki leaned over the table to grab his hands. "Look at me." She waited until Taylor made eye contact. "None of this is your fault. You're still a kid. He manipulated you because he's done this before. And frankly, without you, he would have continued doing it. I'm not sure your mom would have been able to confront Jared without your actions. And for you to track down Elena... it's impressive. We wouldn't have been able to find out what happened to Elena's family without you."

Liam pushed a box of tissues toward Taylor. "Did Jared ever mention any kind of place he liked to go to get away, relax?"

Taylor shook his head. "He said work relaxed him."

"What about a cabin?" Miller asked. "Maybe your family never visited, but it was discussed?"

"Mom hates the woods," Taylor said. "We talked about Florida for spring break."

Elena had been quiet, her eyes on the birth certificates. "Bianca owns a cabin in the north woods. Shane Lincoln owned it, but after he died in the car wreck, the property went to Bianca. She kept it secret from Jared. That's where she stayed when she first ran with the kids, until she found work. I don't think she sold it."

"Where's it at?" Nikki asked.

"I don't know other than somewhere in the north woods.

She wouldn't give me any other information. She was afraid
Jared would come after me."

"Got it." Liam looked up from his laptop. "The property is
in Pine County and is still owned by Bianca Lincoln."

TWENTY-SEVEN

Miller raced out of the room to call the Pine County sheriff. Elena and Taylor watched him, eyes wide with shock.

"I'll make sure we've got all our tactical gear." Liam hurried after the sheriff.

"What are you going to do?" Taylor asked.

"I'm going to get your siblings from that monster," Nikki said. "We'll work with the Pine County sheriff, so things go as smoothly as possible. In the meantime, do you want to go to the hospital to be with your mom or wait here?"

"I should be with her," Taylor said. "Even if she..." His voice caught.

Elena wrapped her arms around him. "I'll go with you if that's all right with them."

"It's fine." Nikki could tell the two had bonded. If Christy did pass, she didn't want Taylor to be alone at the hospital. "We'll have a deputy escort you."

"Just got off the phone with the Pine County sheriff," Miller said when he returned. "The cabin's located on the Snake River, near Chengwatana Forest. He's headed there now with a deputy to confirm someone's there, but it's over an hour's drive for us." He looked at Nikki. "I can drive."

Miller's chief deputy took Elena and Taylor to the hospital, while Nikki and the others loaded their tactical equipment into the Suburban.

"Sheriff just texted." Miller slammed the back hatch closed. "You need a four-wheel drive to get to the cabin in the winter. It's at the end of a long gravel drive. Dark sedan parked about fifty feet off the road and looks like they walked up to the cabin. They ran the license plate. It's a Hertz rental car."

Nikki let Liam have the front passenger seat and climbed into the back. "He didn't check it out before," Nikki said. "Or he would have rented a four-wheel drive." Jared's mistake told her he was starting to lose control. That could work in their favor or cause things to end very badly for the Hall family.

"At least Pine County is a straight shot up Interstate-35," Liam said.

Nikki pulled up the location on Apple Maps. "Definitely not easy to access but looks like it has an amazing view of the Snake River." The words hung in the air between the three of them. Proximity to the river in these situations was never good.

"Ice is pretty thick on it," Liam offered. "DNR reported just last week."

"He won't hurt Penny," Nikki guessed. "Amelia is his target right now, so he'll fight for her until he can't escape. Caden is the wild card."

"Caden's his kid, though," Miller said.

"And proof of his previous crimes, plus he's bigger and stronger than Amelia and could fight back," Nikki said. "He adores Christy. If Caden knows his dad shot her, he isn't going to keep quiet."

The late hour meant less traffic, but the snow and sleet forced them to drive slower than the speed limit most of the time.

"The Pine County sheriff isn't going in, right?" If Miller had been the one keeping watch, she would have trusted him to make the decision to move in only if he thought he needed to before they arrived. But Nikki didn't know anything about Pine County. She didn't care about bruising egos. Those kids weren't going to die tonight.

TWENTY-EIGHT

Once they turned onto the narrow, dark road that led to the cabin, Nikki and Liam wriggled into their Kevlar vests. Miller was in uniform, his bulletproof vest always on. "There's the rental car. Where is the sheriff?" Worry crept through her. The sheriff should have been right here, waiting for them.

Liam pointed to the tire tracks in the snow, leading up the road to the cabin. "Those are fresh. What the hell is the sheriff up to?"

Nikki's heart sank to her knees as they drew closer. The entire area had been lit up by crime scene lights, illuminating the cabin. Three Pine County cruisers blocked access to the cabin.

"I told them not to send more than one car." Miller braked and Nikki yanked the door open, her boots sinking into several inches of snow. She wrestled her badge out of her pocket and marched up to the group of three men positioned behind the trees, sizing up alternative routes to the cabin.

"Who's the sheriff?" Nikki demanded, kicking ice chunks out of her way.

A portly man with graying temples and dark eyes stepped forward. "I am. Sheriff Landry."

"We asked you to stay down the road and secure the scene," she snapped. "Jared had no idea we knew about this cabin. You just screwed us out of any chance at surprise."

"This is my jurisdiction, Agent Hunt."

The way he said her name sent a chill down Nikki's spine. His thick, dark eyebrows and hard jaw were familiar. "How do I know you?"

"Sheriff Hardin was my uncle." Landry hitched his pants. Nikki remembered Hardin well; he was the man who botched her parents' murder case. "You destroyed his reputation. The hell if I'll let you come in here and swoop in on the biggest case this county has seen—"

Nikki stepped so close to the short sheriff she stepped on his boot. "Your uncle put an innocent man away for a long time, and I don't give a damn about your agenda. You are not in charge, I am, and if any of these kids are harmed, I will make it my life's mission to remove you from law enforcement. Do you understand me?"

Landry snickered and turned away. "Gas 'em out."

The two deputies followed the order and jogged closer to the cabin.

"Stop," Nikki shouted. "There are three kids in there; one is three years old."

Her words fell on deaf ears. The heavy tear gas canisters crashed through the cabin windows, followed by screams.

Nikki looked at Liam and Miller. "His only escape route is the other side of the property. You two stay here and make sure these idiots don't cause more problems."

She made sure the SIG was loaded and jogged down the hill out of sight of the cabin. She stayed behind the tree line, creeping up on the north side of the cabin. From this angle, she could see the lights burning in the cabin, the tear gas pouring out of the windows. Nikki dropped to all fours and crawled through the snow and ice, taking cover behind a fir tree not far from the house.

Thanks to the ridiculous floodlights, she could see Miller and Liam in Landry's face. His deputies hovered nearby, apparently unable to make decisions on their own.

The sound of splintering wood pulled her attention back to the cabin just in time for Nikki to see a dark figure rush outside, barreling into the trees.

"Daddy, no. I want Melia." Penny's terror sent Nikki into action. She raced into the dark woods, following Jared's footsteps.

Be calm. Be quiet. He knows Pine County is here. He doesn't know you're on his tail.

She slowed, blinking against the onslaught of falling snow. His tracks were easy to follow, and the trees provided excellent cover.

Nikki had studied the map on the drive over. The cabin wasn't actually in the forest, but located on the road leading into it, not far from the forest entrance. Jared was running straight east, into the heart of the forest. She called Liam, keeping a safe distance between her and Jared, who appeared to have run out into the snow without boots, carrying Penny. He slogged through, his head whipping from side to side occasionally, spooked at every sound.

"Listen," she whispered. "Jared's moving straight east through the forest, right to the Minnesota/Wisconsin border."

"I'll let the troopers know. Amelia and Caden are okay, just trying to recover from the tear gas. We can't find Penny."

"He has her," Nikki whispered. "I'm going to let him know I just want her, that he can keep running."

"You think that's a good idea?" Liam asked. "He probably expects troopers."

"Maybe, but he's rattled." She could tell Jared was getting

tired, he didn't have a coat on, and the wind and snow had to be screwing with his sense of direction, especially in his panicked state.

"I'll let the troopers know and I'll find you in the woods," Liam said. "Try not to reveal yourself until you have backup."

"Then hurry."

Nikki was fairly certain they were in a swampy, low-lying area, making this some of the most dense terrain they'd encountered. She could see Jared struggling with Penny. The little girl's fists pummeled his head as she screamed for her mother. He suddenly shifted southeast and disappeared.

The river.

TWENTY-NINE

Nikki burst through the snow, trying not to let her imagination run wild. The river ran east as well, but it was frozen solid. Jared had no escape route.

She nearly missed the embankment, half sliding down the sharp decline. Jared had reached a dock, still struggling with Penny. He pointed his phone light toward the water. She couldn't see the hole, but she could see the ice auger lying on the dock.

"Stop." Nikki shouted as she moved forward, her SIG pointed straight at Jared. He was at least two hundred yards away, visibility was bad, but Penny was too close to the water for Nikki to risk.

"Just let Penny go, Jared," Nikki said. "Let her come to me. You can run and take your chances."

"Christy did this to me." Jared had the little girl pinned in his arms. "You don't understand how crazy she is, Agent Hunt. I've put up with her verbal and physical abuse for so long, but I won't do it anymore. And I won't let Penny grow up that way."

Nikki moved toward the dock, pointing the bright light on the SIG into his face. He looked sweaty and exhausted, sleet collecting in his eyebrows. "I know about Bianca. And Rebecca and Jason. Their aunt says hello."

Jared's pleading expression disappeared. He transformed into another person, a menacing scowl on his face. "Who?"

"Taylor found her. He's with Christy right now. She's still alive, by the way."

"She shot herself—"

"Shut up," Nikki said. "I know everything. I know you hurt yourself and framed her. We found Bianca's and Jason's remains in the closet."

A muscle in his jaw worked, the cords in his neck taut with rage. "You want to know how we identified them? It wasn't Elena. It was Bianca. She hid birth certificates in a closet in the main house. You missed them when you took all of their things from the Hendrickson home that weekend. She beat you, Jared. You tried so hard to erase her from existence, but she won."

"Please, Daddy," Penny begged. "You're hurting me."

"Let her go and run," Nikki suggested. "It will take a while for Pine County to mobilize and chase you."

"You're just going to let me go?"

The last time she'd done this, early in her career, she'd let a serial killer go free. Had Liam contacted the state troopers? Had she bought enough time for them to get set up? She glanced at the black sky, searching for the telltale flash of the drone the state troopers would likely use to spot Jared.

"If it means saving Penny, yes." Nikki kept her light trained on his face. Sweat ran down his face despite the cold. She wasn't sure how much farther he'd have to walk to get out of the woods, but from the looks of him, he'd be lucky to make it out without succumbing to hypothermia.

"Why Christy?" Nikki asked, hoping to buy the state troopers more time.

He smirked. "She was perfect for me."

"What does that mean?" Nikki asked.

"A lot of baggage and guilt. I could smell her vulnerability a mile away. It was easy. All it took was the promise of my supporting them and her not having to work."

"Being a stay-at-home mom is a lot of work."

"Not if she did it right." He scowled. "Keep the house clean. Keep the kids clean. Follow the rules. That's it."

"Plus soundproofing in the bedroom?" She thought of what Kelsey Richard, Christy's attorney, had told her. "That's how you've gotten away with it for so long, right? You didn't beat the kids or give them a reason to distrust you."

"Takes a special kind of person." Jared grinned. "I'm that person."

"Special isn't the right word."

"Daddy, let me down, now." Penny's sharp little voice shook. Her foot connected with Jared's crotch. It probably wasn't intentional, but he flinched enough for her to wriggle out of his arms. She crashed to the dock and curled into a ball, crying.

Sweat froze on Nikki's forehead. She was pretty certain the hole Jared had cut in the ice was in front of the dock, and Penny was dangerously close to it. Jared could kick her into the water before Nikki could reach her.

"Penny, I'll take you to your mom and Taylor," Nikki said.

Penny stopped crying, sucking in gulps of air. Her entire body shook from cold. "Taylor?"

"He came home, sweetheart," Nikki said. "He's waiting for you."

"Taylor's okay?" Jared looked genuinely relieved. "Where did he go?"

"He's a smart kid," Nikki said. "Thinks like an investigator."

"What are you talking about?" Jared demanded.

"He found Rebecca's school photo. And the others," Nikki said. "The ones you kept from there. He noticed your reflection in one of them. The night before going back to school after the break, Amelia told him she thought there was a camera in her wall. He found the page Elena had set up for Bianca and her children."

She wished Taylor were here to see the shock on Jared's face. He likely hadn't thought a teenager would be his demise.

Jared's chest heaved. "How did you find me? No one knows about this place."

"Elena did. This is where Bianca first stayed when she escaped you. The cabin's still in Bianca's name."

"No." Jared shivered in the freezing cold. "She told me it was in my name. Even showed me the document."

"Like I said, Bianca beat you." Nikki struggled to hide her smile, knowing it would set Jared off. "But you can still win this one. Go now, get a head start. Let Penny go back to her mother."

"Good idea." Liam's voice came from behind Nikki. "I've got a scope and made harder shots than this, Jared."

Nikki almost smiled. A few years ago, Liam had made an incredible shot to save Nikki from one of the worst killers she'd encountered. "He hit the guy on the other side of the St. Croix. He won't miss you this close."

Penny glanced up at her father, who watched as though he were in a trance. Nikki kept talking before Penny could realize the danger her father was in. "Penny, don't you want to see Taylor?"

Penny inched forward. Nikki held her breath, waiting for Jared to reach for Penny and the gunfire that would follow if he did. But Jared let Penny crawl to Nikki. She stowed her weapon and pulled off her coat, wrapping it around the freezing child.

"Now you're going to arrest me," Jared said.

Liam crept out of the trees, his rifle still pointed at Jared. Nikki glanced at her partner, who nodded. State troopers were ready.

"A deal's a deal." She hefted Penny in her arms. "But you better go now."

Jared watched as she backed up to Liam, holding Penny against her. Stunned, he watched as they moved toward the trees, giving him a clear path to run.

Given his exhausted state, he'd be lucky to reach the other side of the forest.

"Is Taylor really okay?" Penny asked.

"Go on," Liam said. "I've got eyes on him."

Nikki squeezed the little girl and turned to walk back to the cabin through the dark woods. "Sure is. I talked to him myself."

"No!" Jared's terrified voice cut through the air, followed by a splash. Nikki spun in the snow, nearly falling. Caden stood at the edge of the dock, staring motionless down into the dark, frozen river.

THIRTY

Liam raced to the dock and Nikki followed. She handed Penny to Caden, who stood motionless watching Liam shine his light into the water. Nikki flung herself down on the dock next to Liam. His flashlight made the exposed water look like thick, black ink. "Do you see him?"

"No," Liam said. "But the currents are fast."

Nikki had fallen into the frozen water once, pushed by the serial killer Frost. The thin ice near the shore had given Caitlin enough time to pull Nikki out, but she could still remember the water pressure in her lungs, sinking deeper into the lake...

Liam nudged her. "Don't look into the water if it bothers you. He's gone."

Nikki looked at the surrounding ice, but several inches of snow covered the lake. "That's a big hole."

Liam glanced back at the two siblings. "Big enough for him."

"Did he push him?" Nikki whispered.

Before Liam could answer, one of the Pine County deputies shouted for Caden as he pushed through the deep snow. He half slid down the riverbank and hurried to join them at the edge of the dock.

"How did someone fall in? The river's frozen. Who was it?"

"Jared." Nikki pointed to the ice auger lying in the snow. "It was here when I followed him. He'd cut the hole ahead of time, and it's good sized."

The deputy's bright pink cheeks paled. "Jesus. What happened?"

"Jared panicked when he saw Caden and slipped," Liam said. "You'll need a dive team."

They all knew the rushing currents of the St. Croix would win the battle.

The grim-faced deputy nodded, still trying to catch his breath. "Agents, for what it's worth, I tried to talk the sheriff out of it. But he really doesn't like Agent Hunt."

"It's not my fault his uncle was corrupt and retired in disgrace."

The deputy shined his light onto the frozen water. "You guys take care of the kids," the deputy said. "I'll call the dive team."

Nikki and Liam gingerly stood, careful not to step too close to the edge. Caden had retreated to the end of the dock, clutching his little sister, Nikki's coat still wrapped around her.

Someone had given Caden a Pine County trooper's jacket, but he was still shivering and pale. Penny grabbed his cheeks to make him look at her. "Where is Melia?"

"She's with Sheriff Miller," Caden said. "I made sure she was safe before I came for you."

Sheriff Landry arrived with more deputies and directed them to search the shore. He marched through the thick snow towards them.

"Dive team's on the way," he huffed, his face bright red from the exertion. He glared at Nikki. "You're coming back to help, right?"

"It's your jurisdiction, Sheriff," Nikki said.

"It's your case," he snapped back. "Isn't that what you said?"

Nikki pointed to Caden and Penny. "They were my case. Recovery is on you."

"I already told the deputy what happened. Get your brief from him." Liam turned his back on the sheriff and handed Nikki the long rifle, ignoring the complaints coming from Landry.

Liam shimmied out of his coat. "I knew this coat having two layers would come in handy someday." He unzipped the warmer coat from the interior. "Put it on and don't argue."

"No problem." Nikki zipped it to her chin and approached the two siblings.

"So that's it? You show up and someone falls into the water, and you leave?" Landry demanded. "I thought you were supposed to be the great Nikki Hunt."

"Sheriff, you created this situation," Nikki said. "You know damn well a review is going to show that you acted with malice in order to avenge your uncle you think I wronged. It won't look good on your record, and it will follow you to any other job, I promise."

She could tell by his purple face that he understood her meaning. While Landry sputtered, she and Liam joined the siblings at the edge of the dock.

Caden still looked shell-shocked. Nikki couldn't imagine what he'd been through. The next several months, if not years, would likely be rough for Caden. She would make sure the family had counseling options, and she hoped that Christy would take advantage of the programs offered for victims.

"Did Penny tell you?" Nikki asked.

"Tell me what?"

She smiled at Caden. "Taylor came home. He's at the hospital with your mom."

"Is she..."

"The last I heard, in surgery." Nikki squeezed his shoulder. "You guys go first. We'll follow."

Caden nodded, his eyes on Liam. "Agent Wilson, am I in trouble?"

Liam didn't answer right away, working to control his emotions. "Your dad slipped right before you reached him. Not your fault."

He didn't look at Nikki, but she didn't need to see his eyes to know the truth didn't matter. Jared was gone.

THIRTY-ONE

Christy survived surgery and was in recovery. The bullet had caused a lot of internal damage, but lying in the freezing cold and snow had slowed the bleeding enough that doctors had managed to save her life. The kids had been all but silent during the ride back to Stillwater, with the exception of Penny asking her sister questions about every little thing. Lacey had been the same way at that age. She still talked all the time and asked a lot of questions. Rory said that meant she was smart. Her teachers mostly agreed, but Lacey had a knack for asking tough questions about the world and making her teachers give her some kind of answer.

Since the sheriff's station was on the way to the hospital, they stopped so Miller and Liam could go in and start working on the report. Nikki loaded the kids into the big Jeep and headed to Lakeview Hospital.

She glanced in the back seat at Amelia, who'd been mostly silent save for whispering to Penny.

"I'm sorry this happened to you," Nikki said. "And I want you to know that without Taylor, we wouldn't have found the cabin."

"I knew he'd figure it out." Amelia finally spoke, her soft voice barely audible. "I wanted to tell you, Agent Hunt. I tried when I showed you the shoes. But Taylor said we couldn't trust anyone. 'Don't tell anyone until I come back.'" She hesitated for a few moments. "He said to undress in the bathroom, behind the shower curtain, in case he had cameras in there."

"You didn't tell me," Caden said from the front passenger seat. "You didn't tell me he killed my real mom."

"I didn't know the whole story," Amelia said. "Taylor said to wait until he came home."

Nikki glanced at Caden. "Christy loves you as her own, Caden. Finding out Jared lied about what happened to your mother isn't going to change that. She's raised you. Don't forget that."

"She loves my dad more, and he's gone." Caden's voice cracked.

"Let's not talk about that moment." Nikki didn't want Caden confessing to pushing his father into the water. The more she knew, the harder it would be to forget. "I think it's one of those things you should work through in therapy. You know, they have to keep your privacy, no matter what? The only exception is if you're in danger."

"I dreamed about it all the time when I was little. Dad kept telling me it was a nightmare."

"You were Penny's age," Nikki reminded him. "Your mind was protecting you."

"What happened to them?" Caden asked.

"Can you tell me what happened at the house before Jared took you guys first?" Nikki wasn't sure how much Caden actually knew about his past.

"It's my fault," Amelia said. "Mom heard me crying, and I told her about the camera. She lost it. She kept saying how stupid she was, thinking if she took it, Jared would leave me alone. She never told me what 'it' was, but I knew what she meant. That's why he soundproofed their room."

"Your mom confronted Jared?"

"She told me and Caden to take Penny into my room and lock the door," Amelia said. "And not to open it for Jared." Her voice cracked. "I've heard them arguing, but he was beating her and saying all of these awful things. I knew there was a pistol in their closet, because I'd found it one day when I was looking for something to borrow from Mom. I take archery at middle school. I have good aim." She started sobbing.

Nikki had a sinking suspicion she knew what Amelia was about to say.

"I shot at him, I swear," Amelia burst out.

"He grabbed Mom and used her as a shield," Caden said. "It's not your fault."

That likely explained why the bullet had missed enough vital organs that Christy had survived. "No, it isn't your fault," Nikki agreed. "Jared did this. He played on your mom's vulnerability and did terrible things."

Nikki parked in Lakeview's emergency lot, close to the door. Miller had called ahead to the hospital and arranged for them to be escorted to the ICU. A hospital volunteer greeted them, curiosity burning in her eyes. She led them through a maze of hallways to the elevator to the ICU. They rode up in silence, tension hanging between them.

The volunteer used her card to unlock the ICU doors. "The charge desk is straight ahead. They'll take you to the patient."

"Taylor!" Penny's shrill voice echoed in the hall. She ran to her older brother, who scooped her up and hugged her tight. Amelia followed, throwing her arms around her brother and crying. "It's my fault. I was trying to hit him. He pulled her into the way—"

Taylor pulled his sister close. "It's okay. Mom didn't hit him with the bottle. I didn't see it." Tears streamed down his face. "I just said I did to protect Jared, like an idiot."

Caden hung back, hands in his pockets, until Taylor grabbed his arm. The three siblings huddled close, whispering. Caden started to sob, and Taylor grabbed him by his shoulders and turned Caden to face him. "Do not cry for him. Ever. There's someone I want you to meet."

"She's going to take me away from you," Caden said. "I just know it."

"Mom legally adopted you when we were little," Taylor reminded him. "Elena can't just take you, and she's not like that."

Nikki seized her chance. "Where is Elena? I'd like to fill her in before Caden meets her."

"She's in the waiting area, down the hall," Taylor said.

Nikki left the siblings in their huddle and walked down to find Elena. She sat in the dimly lit room, staring out of the window. "Jared's dead."

Elena whipped her head around and stared at Nikki. "How?"

"He fell in the ice hole he'd cut ahead of time. We can only imagine his plan." She glanced behind her. "I wanted to talk to you before you met Caden. He's pretty shell-shocked right now and worried about where he'll end up, especially with Jared presumed dead. Christy is his legal parent."

"Poor child," Elena said. "I truly have no interest in custody. I never wanted kids. I'm not sure I'd be very good for a teenager. I'd just like to get to know him." Elena looked back out the window for a few moments, gathering courage. "I would also like to help take care of them while Christy is recovering. My apartment has two extra bedrooms, and Taylor said he would be okay with it."

Nikki had been worried about having to place the kids somewhere until Christy could come home. They had the

DNA to prove Elena was Caden's blood relative. If Taylor vouched for Elena and Christy agreed, they could circumvent CPS.

"I think that's a good idea, but it's up to Christy," Nikki said. "Caden doesn't know that Bianca wasn't his mother. He doesn't know about Rebecca."

Elena nodded. "I've been worrying about this. I don't think we should say anything until Christy is well enough to understand the truth. She's his mother and knows him best. I don't want to pile onto his suffering."

"I agree," Nikki said. "I wish I could say something comforting about your family. I'm so sorry they were Jared's victims." His rage about Bianca's revenge flashed through her mind. "He knew that Bianca hid the birth certificates. He knew she is the one who helped get him in the end, and he was mad as hell."

Elena smiled through her tears. "She did, didn't she?"

Nikki turned to leave.

"Agent, this isn't the best timing, but Rebecca wore her father's wedding ring on a chain around her neck. Do you think it might still be with her possessions?"

Memories of the last week flew through Nikki's mind like cards shuffling, finally settling on Spencer Bancroft sitting next to Matt at the Hendrickson property, the ring shining on his chest.

"I'm not sure," Nikki said. "I'll see what I can find out."

THIRTY-TWO

Nikki wasn't surprised to see Stephanie Bancroft sitting with Rodney Atwood in the interview room. She was surprised that it had taken Stephanie two weeks to crawl out of her hole. "My client is willing to confess, for a plea deal."

"Wow." Nikki looked across the table at the pock-faced redhead. "What made you suddenly decide to admit your guilt, Rodney?" Especially when they still didn't have any damn evidence to convict him. Nikki had been considering pulling out every possible mostly legal trick in order to entice a confession, and now Atwood was sitting at the sheriff's station, practically gift-wrapped.

"I thought it was time we let Scott rest in peace," Stephanie said. "I called Rodney and we talked. I told him I would fight for him to get the best deal, but that he couldn't keep running from this."

"How generous of you," Miller quipped.

"I thought so." Stephanie looked at Rodney. "He's prepared to tell you everything in exchange for manslaughter."

Nikki laughed. "That's not going to happen, and we can't

make those deals. The DA might agree to a lesser murder charge, but not without knowing the actual story."

Stephanie nodded at Rodney. He talked for forty-four minutes, explaining how he'd gotten sick and tired of his stepson disobeying his orders and defying him. The kid was lazy, never listened, his mother babied him too much. "I told him he wasn't going nowhere that weekend because he was going to help me in my garage. His mom calls me from work that night and tells me little precious is going to spend the night at his friend's, he's been there all evening." Rodney's eyes looked like blue ice. "I called him from my burner phone and told him I was picking his ass up. I also told him to say nothing to his mom or his friend, just that he had to come home."

"You have a burner phone?" Nikki asked.

"My wife paid the bills, so she saw the phone records. I had a couple of girlfriends on the side."

Nikki was tired of hearing his whining voice. "Scott left and met you?"

"A block down the road, and then three houses over. I was pretty sure it was a dead spot for cameras." He wiped the spittle out of the corner of his mouth. "He gets in the truck and starts yelling at me, like I did something wrong. I told him to shut up. I warned him. He kept talking."

"What did you do?" Miller demanded.

"I warned him first," Atwood said. "Told him I was going to knock him out with the wrench." He shrugged. "I guess I hit him too hard."

"He was breathing when he went into the water," Miller said through clenched teeth.

"Don't worry, there wasn't anything left up here, if you know what I mean." Atwood pointed to his own head. "Swollen to the size of a melon. He was barely breathing, too."

Nikki almost vomited in disgust.

Miller kept talking. "I'm not asking the DA for shit," he said. "Because you planned this."

"My client did no such thing."

"He basically just told us." Miller pointed to the camera in the corner. "Want me to play the part about parking out of sight from any cameras back to you, Stephanie?"

"No." Stephanie stood up and looked down her nose at Rodney Atwood. "I'm sorry, I'm no longer able to represent you." She looked at Nikki and mouthed "you're welcome."

Fuming, Nikki followed her out of the room and grabbed Stephanie's skinny arm. "Jared said you were the one who tipped him off," Nikki lied, confident she was right. "Somehow, you found Bianca's driver's license or other form of identity and let Jared know where she and her children were so that he could kill them."

Stephanie opened her mouth to retort but Nikki held up her hand. "Don't speak. And don't worry. I'm not going to charge you. I don't have anything but his word, and Jared is dead. I just wanted to make sure you spend every day of your life knowing that I know exactly who you are. I'll know it every time I see your face in court. So will the sheriff and Agent Wilson. You're no longer invincible, Stephanie."

Nikki left the woman standing in the hallway, shell-shocked. She wished arresting Stephanie was an option, but they didn't have the physical evidence, only Brandon Kelly's word against hers that she knew about Ms. Smith being in the will. Stephanie would chew them up and spit them out in court. At least she'd been taken down a peg. She knew her bad deeds were on Nikki's radar.

Her phone vibrated with a text message. Her heart skipped a beat as she realized it was from Chen. Her finger trembled as she unlocked her phone to read the message, praying that Eli and his family had a happy ending.

Eli safe, suspect in custody.

EPILOGUE

THREE WEEKS LATER

Nikki knocked on the door of Matt Kline's Stillwater home. He'd moved into the old Hendrickson house with Luke to start the renovations. Matt suggested Christy and her kids take his old place while they looked for a new home in the area.

Elena opened the door wearing an apron covered with flowers. Penny squeezed between Elena and the doorframe.

"Hi, Agent Hunt. We're making cookies for Mom."

Elena ushered Nikki into the house. Christy was sitting in the living room, her feet propped up in the reclining chair.

"How are you feeling?" Nikki asked.

"Tired, but better," she said. "The kids are at school. They'll be sad they missed you."

"I know," Nikki said. "I've got to testify on another case this afternoon or I would have come later." She glanced in the kitchen where Elena had retreated with Penny to finish her cookies. "How's it going with her?"

"It's the strangest thing," Christy said. "I just feel like I've known her forever. I'm so lucky it worked out this way, selfish as it sounds."

"It's not selfish," Nikki said. "You two have a bond most

can't imagine. You are seeing the therapist together, right? Obviously, you all need individual as well, but I think family therapy will help because there's a lot to sort out."

"Penny saw Caden push Jared in." Christy's whisper sent a shock wave through Nikki. "Or she thinks he might have, because he was running to the dock and then Jared fell. I told her that Agent Wilson saw it differently but…"

"He said Jared slipped in the official report." Nikki hadn't spoken with Liam about it since he filed the report. She told Garcia her back had been turned, but Agent Wilson had his weapon aimed at Jared in case he tried to stop them from going into the woods. If Garcia suspected anything, he wasn't questioning it. "It was dark and Penny was traumatized. Her eyes played tricks on her."

She could tell Christy didn't believe her. "Thank you, Agent Hunt. And thank Agent Wilson."

"Just doing our jobs," Nikki answered.

"Caden said he heard you talking to Jared, that you were willing to let him go and possibly get in trouble for doing so, in order to save Penny."

If Caden had been watching, that meant he'd been waiting for the right moment. Nikki couldn't believe how at peace she was with Jared's demise. Years of seeing victimized women and children had robbed any empathy she had for someone like him.

Penny ran into the room with a chocolate chip cookie on a napkin. "It's hot and gooey." She giggled.

"Thank you." Nikki devoured the cookie while Penny brought one to her mom. She and Elena joined them in the living room. Penny went to her dolls and started telling them about the cookies she'd just made.

"Elena, before I leave, I have something for you." She reached into her bag. "I found Rebecca's necklace. Since she's been a Jane Doe, everything was still in evidence."

"Found" wasn't the right word. She'd waited for Spencer

Bancroft to finish his shift at the fire station. He hadn't seemed surprised to see her.

* * *

"I trust Matt brought you up to speed on everything."

Spencer leaned against his truck and nodded. "I had no idea Ms. Smith was running from something like that. I shouldn't have listened to Grandpa and my mom. I should have gone to the police when he realized they were gone. It just didn't feel right."

"Rebecca Lincoln was the victim of a hit-and-run while she was rushing for help to save her family."

Spencer nodded, averting his eyes.

"What happened to that souped-up Nissan GT-R?" Nikki asked him. "The one you drove when you guys snuck out to the concert?"

"Why are you asking me about that car?" Spencer laughed. "I ran the hell out of it, that's what. Junked it years ago."

Nikki had already done her homework. It had taken some digging, but she'd discovered the car's title had been changed to a salvage title six days after the hit-and-run that killed Rebecca— Jane Doe at the time. "Six days later, to be exact."

Spencer stared at her, frozen. She didn't want to hear his comeback story. Nikki already knew he'd gone to a rehab center for alcohol and depression the next week and had come back a more reserved, less reckless version of Spencer. He'd been a model citizen since then, including saving a woman and child from an apartment fire that could have taken his life.

"Agent Hunt," Spencer started. "I wanted... my mom... I didn't know about the others."

Nikki held up her hand. "I'm going to stop you right there. I believe you. And the statute of limitations has passed."

Tears welled in Spencer's eyes. "It was an accident. The rain... I relive that night every day of my life."

"Sometimes the best punishment is having to go on and walk away." Nikki pointed to the chain on his neck. *"But Elena would like her niece's things back."*

"I can't believe it was still in evidence." Elena held the necklace and ring close to her chest. "This means more than I can say."

"I'm glad I was able to return it." Nikki checked her watch. "I'd better head out. This particular judge is brutal if you're late."

Elena walked her to the door. "I spoke to Doctor Blanchard about the remains. It's too cold for a service now, but I know Bianca wanted to be buried in a Catholic cemetery. I'm planning on having a service in the spring. I'd love for you and Agent Wilson to attend."

"We'd be honored," Nikki answered. "I'll stay in touch, stop in and check on you guys."

"Thank you again for giving me my family back," Elena said. "Part of me wishes we knew exactly what happened, but it doesn't matter. I know where they are now, and that's all I've wanted for years."

Nikki said goodbye and headed out to her Jeep. What happened to Bianca and her kids had been awful, but she was grateful to be part of Christy and her children's new beginnings.

A LETTER FROM STACY

I want to say a huge thank you for choosing to read *Little Child Gone*. If you did enjoy it, and want to keep up to date with all my latest releases, just sign up at the following link. Your email address will never be shared and you can unsubscribe at any time.

www.bookouture.com/stacy-green

The idea for this book took root while I was writing *Stolen Mothers*, the previous book in this series. Depending on my mood, I'll have true crime shows on in the background when I write, and I lost count of how many cases were simply about men not getting their way with the women they thought they owned. The sheer number of women killed for this reason alone is just staggering. More than one case showed men hurting themselves in order to frame their estranged wives or girlfriends, and the police almost always sided with the men, because of their stature and ability to manipulate.

I knew I had to write about it, and the idea for this book began. I know I have male readers, and this certainly isn't an attack on men. The majority aren't abusive or controlling, especially younger generations, but it's an issue that's much more prevalent than we realize. It's amazing how easy it is to isolate a woman from her family and friends, regardless of social status.

Midway through the writing, a Facebook friend posted in a group about an abusive experience and how she was struggling to get away because she had no one nearby to help her. We were able to encourage and guide her and she was one of the fortunate ones, but women truly need to learn from the past and be wary. If a violent ex or even a verbally abuse ex wants to meet with you in private, refuse. If no one can go with you, meet in a very public place. Do not get into his vehicle. Do not trust him once you've walked out that door. And don't think there aren't organizations out there that can help. There are programs run by the states and local areas—even in rural counties. Many states have rural initiatives for abused women.

The National Abuse Hotline is 800-799-7233, and they can guide you to state resources.

Thank you to Hennepin County Medical Examiner Dr. Andrew Baker for his invaluable guidance on the state of the remains in the Hendrickson house.

Stillwater Police Chief Brian Mueller has been an enormous help in this series, helping me through procedural stuff as well as providing various resources.

John Kelly is my Washington County guru, helping me with terrain and natural resources to make sure scenes are set in the best areas.

The Hendrickson home is based on my grandma and grandpa Green's home in Greenwood, Indiana. Grandpa Green and his father built it, and though the house is gone now, I still see it exactly as it was when they were still here. Thanks to my cousin Betty Sluder for helping me make sure I had the details correct—and for believing the truth when everyone else was lying. You have no idea how much that helped me get through some very dark times.

I apologize for the longer gap between *Stolen Mothers* and *Little Child Gone*. I wrote this during a tumultuous summer, with my daughter graduating high school, us moving to Colorado from Iowa and then her eventually starting college. A back injury took swimming from her, and she ended up getting a spinal fusion, so we've had to navigate that the last several months, but things are settled now and she is feeling good, so I'm excited to be working on book eleven, with the goal of a late 2025 release date.

Thank you to my editor, Jennifer Hunt, for her endless patience and support, along with everyone at Bookouture, including the authors. I am so lucky to be with a publisher and group of people that wants everyone to succeed instead of jealousy and pettiness. Lisa Regan, thanks for putting up with my drive-by messages, and thanks to my social media assistant Tessa Russ. Her group takes care of the soul-sucking social media so I can write, and they do an amazing job!

Thanks to Rob and Grace for their support and faith in me. To my extended Minnesota family, John, Kristine, Jan and Tim: it means the world to me to have you and know that I've got people in my corner beyond Rob and Grace.

And to the most important people, my readers, thank you for sticking with me despite publishing delays. I would be working a nine-to-five job and likely be a miserable person without you guys, and I promise to keep writing Nikki books as long as you keep reading!

I hope you loved *Little Child Gone* and if you did, I would be very grateful if you could write a review. I'd love to hear what you think, and it makes such a difference helping new readers to discover one of my books for the first time.

Thanks,

Stacy

KEEP IN TOUCH WITH STACY

www.stacygreenauthor.com

 facebook.com/StacyGreenAuthor
instagram.com/authorstacygreenwhisenand

PUBLISHING TEAM

Turning a manuscript into a book requires the efforts of many people. The publishing team at Bookouture would like to acknowledge everyone who contributed to this publication.

Audio
Alba Proko
Sinead O'Connor
Melissa Tran

Commercial
Lauren Morrissette
Hannah Richmond
Imogen Allport

Cover design
Blacksheep

Data and analysis
Mark Alder
Mohamed Bussuri

Editorial
Jennifer Hunt
Charlotte Hegley